NUN
IN THE
CLOSET

A MYSTERY BY
JOANNA
MICHAELS

NEW VICTORIA PUBLISHERS

Published by New Victoria Publishers Inc., a feminist, literary, and cultural organization, PO Box 27, Norwich, VT. 05055-0027.

09689

Acknowledgements:
My love and my thanks to Ann Gargano and Eugenia Kozlowski of the Ulster County Probation Department, Dr. Fran Arje, Ellen Fiorillo, Dr. Elise Fulmer, Pat Kerwick, Barbara Neveu, R.J.S., Peg Stevens. and especially to Pat Kerick who believed in me before I believed in myself.
I gratefully acknowledge the support and assistance of ReBecca Béguin, Claudia Lamperti, Vicki P. McConnell, and Madelaine Larsen.

Cover Painting and Design by Ginger Brown

First Printing. Printed and bound in the U.S.A. on recycled paper
1 2 3 4 5 1997 1996 1995 1994

Library of Congress Cataloging-in-Publication Data

Michaels, Joanna, 1954-
       Nun in the closet : a mystery / by Joanna Michaels.
          p. cm.
       ISBN 0-934678-43-X ; $9.95
       1. Probation officers--New York (State)- -Albany- -Fiction.
     2. Women detectives-- New York (State) - -Albany - -Fiction. 4. Albany
  3. Lesbian - -New York (State) - - Albany Fiction. 4. Albany (N.Y.) -
  -Fiction.   I. Ttitle.
PS3563. I2718N86   1994   94-2197
813' .54--dc 20   CIP

In memory of "Helena."

ONE

The seven year itch had hit me. All that time avoiding my hormones and romantic relationships as much as possible, the permanence of my job settling over me... Maybe that's why I handled the Hollis case the way I did.

My name is Callie Sinclair. I'm a probation officer in Albany, New York, with a private office on the third floor of the county building overlooking the hustle and bustle of State Street.

Jokingly, I tell my friends that I'm the human resource department's answer to affirmative action. Besides being a woman, I'm a lesbian ex-Catholic, over forty, ten years sober and whose mother's maiden name was Rodriguez—the perfect example to prove Albany County doesn't discriminate against gender, sexual orientation, religion, age, handicap, or national origin.

I've worked for the county for seven years, the longest I've ever been in one job. I never intended to stay so long. I planned to go to law school after earning my master's degree in criminal justice, but then a job became available in probation and I decided law school could wait a year or two. I never went back. Maybe I got too lazy, or too comfortable, or maybe being a lawyer wasn't really what I wanted after all. Or maybe recovering from alcoholism and the kind of habits and relationships that went along with it was a big enough job. For whatever reason, here I sit with the seven year itch.

I'd just gotten back from lunch and was standing near my desk, untying the laces on my Reeboks, when Sid Kasselbaum dropped

1

by my office. He's my boss—tall and thin, with grey running through his beard. Sid's a nice guy, slow to anger, and very tolerant—even when pushed to the limit.

"Hey Callie," he said, "how are you?" His smile displayed the space between his two front teeth, wider than Arnold Schwarzenegger's.

"Just great, Sid. You?"

"Good. Listen, I've been meaning to tell you what a good job you did handling the Murchison case."

"Thanks." I slipped my socks off and stuffed them into my Reeboks.

"The department can always count on you." He looked at my feet. "Out running again, eh?"

"Thirty minutes of aerobic walking four times a week."

"Good weather for it," he said, looking out my office window at the trees in new leaf and patting his stomach with his free hand. "Maybe I should try that to keep in shape."

"You could quit smoking," I said, grinning. "That'd be an excellent start."

"Wouldn't want to get fat," he said. "By the way, you look really nice today. I like that dress. Is it new?"

I grunted. "No, it's not." I was wearing a kelly-green shirt-dress, and the only reason I had it on was I had court that morning. The department makes its employees play dress up on court days. Actually the exact rule, according to our Personnel Policies and Practices Manual, goes like this: Probation Department employees are expected to maintain a professional appearance at all times. Women will wear dresses or suit jackets and skirts, and men will wear ties with sports jackets or suits.

"You look terrific in green, Callie. Goes great with your red hair." Sid plucked his beard with his fingers. "You're the best probation officer I've got. Having you here means a lot to me."

I smiled. "Okay, Sid, what is it you want?"

He held a hand up, feigning innocence. "What makes you think I want something?"

"It's the only time you compliment me."

"Come on, Callie, that isn't true."

"Are you telling me you don't want anything?"

2

He smiled. "Well, I have this file, but honest, Callie, that's not why I praised you. I think you're the best, you know that."

"Can it, Sid. Just give me the file."

He held it up. "Her name is Anne Hollis. Jerry inherited the case from Schoharie County, but since he's in the hospital..." He looked sheepish. "Do you mind?"

I grabbed the file and tossed it on top of my IN box. "I'll get to it soon as I can."

"Callie?"

"Yes, Sid?"

"She's in the waiting room."

I stared at him. "You're kidding."

Sid smiled. "This is an easy one, Callie. Vehicular manslaughter, cut and dried. Do a PSI and send her on her way."

I groaned. "You're gonna owe me for this one."

He backed up toward the door. "Thanks, Callie."

I opened the file for a quick scan of the initial police investigation. Then I tossed my Reeboks in the bottom drawer of my filing cabinet, slipped my shoes on, and walked down the hall to the waiting room. I scanned the room and was about to call out the name, Anne Hollis, when my voice caught in my throat.

It was as if she were the only woman in the room, seated along the west wall reading a paperback. Casually elegant, she wore a black and white houndstooth jacket, black slacks, and a white silk blouse. Her blonde hair was worn short, like mine.

She glanced up as I entered the room and slid her reading glasses to the tip of her nose. I flushed as our eyes met, hers blue with pale, feathery lashes. Something about Anne Hollis made me feel lightheaded, the way her lips parted when she looked at me, the way she studied me as I crossed the room to the front desk. I asked our receptionist, Marylou, for a blank Pre-Sentence Investigation form.

"Which case is yours?" Marylou asked, indicating the probationers.

"Uh, Anne Hollis," I managed, glancing across the room, her gaze meeting mine once again with a steadiness and a question.

"Thanks," I said, turning back to Marylou, and taking the form I crossed the room as the woman slowly closed her book, marking the place by folding over a corner of the page. Clearing my throat, I extended my hand, "Ms. Hollis?"

"Yes, I'm Anne Hollis." Her voice reminded me of Godiva chocolates. She stood up, and we shook hands. Her grasp was strong, her skin smooth and warm. My knees threatened to buckle. Steady now, Sinclair, I scolded myself, no more infatuations with gorgeous strangers, a bad old habit, remember? And yet something about Anne Hollis was different—oh, but didn't I always tell myself that?

"I'm Officer Callie Sinclair. I've been assigned your case."

Her face registered surprise. "I was expecting to meet with Jerry Rappaport." Was she disappointed?

"Your case was reassigned," I said firmly. "Please follow me."

As I led her down the hall, I noticed she stood a tad shorter than my five eight. Reaching my office, I stepped aside to let her enter first. The smell of her perfume, a light musky fragrance, sent shivers of delight through my body. Oh sweet Goddess, I murmured to myself as I moved around behind my desk and sat down heavily while indicating for her to take a chair on the opposite side. Even so, she seemed close because I could see that tiny crows' feet were beginning to show at the corners of her eyes. I wondered what it would feel like to reach out and trace them with the tips of my fingers... Once again I cleared my throat.

"I only had a moment to review your file," I said, apologetically. "You're currently out on bail awaiting sentencing?"

"That's correct," she said, her voice tense.

Businesslike and feeling back to my normal professional self, I glanced through her file, reading aloud. "At your arraignment you pleaded not guilty to vehicular manslaughter."

She frowned, speaking clearly, "Yes, because I'm not guilty."

"Then your attorney plea bargained down to a lesser charge, reckless endangerment..."

"My attorney advised me to do so in order to avoid a trial."

"Yes, it's done all the time." I looked at the police report and continued reading aloud. "Let's see, you were the one driving the vehicle...and your passenger, Mary Elizabeth Powell, was killed."

"Yes." Her voice was almost a whisper.

"So, your lawyer advised you to enter a plea of guilty in order to keep you from serving a prison term of three to five years. Good advice. You'll probably end up with five years probation."

Anne Hollis clenched her fists in her lap. "I can't begin to tell you how frustrating this is. It seems as if no one, including my attorney, is willing to believe what really happened. They all act as if I'm making it up, but I'm not." She leaned forward confidentially. "This was no accident. Beth was murdered."

I'm used to hearing wild, even ridiculous stories from defendants, comes with the territory, so I don't get rattled when someone cries foul. And yet I found myself leaning forward too. "I get paid to listen, Ms. Hollis. Why don't you just tell me what happened."

"Somebody rammed my Jeep over the guard rails." She placed her hands on my desk. Her fingers were long and her nails short and well shaped. No polish. "The police don't believe me," she said, shaking her head. "No one believes me."

"The police told you they don't believe you?"

"They asked me if I had any witnesses to corroborate my side of the story. The only witness I had was Beth, and she's...she was..." Anne Hollis' eyes filled with tears. She paused and swallowed before continuing her story. "They told me a truck driver witnessed the accident. He called the police and reported something about me driving like a lunatic."

I shuffled through the police report, but I didn't find mention of the eye witness.

"I thought a person was innocent until proven guilty." Her voice rose angrily, "But you people have it backwards!"

I tried to be impassive. "I understand how you feel...there are times I get just as frustrated sitting on this side of the desk...."

"I'm more than frustrated," she said, those blue eyes flashing. "I'm angry and frightened. I've been unjustly convicted of manslaughter. I now have a police record, and, as you say, I'm probably going to be sentenced to five years of probation. All for something I didn't do!" Anne Hollis turned away, obviously trying to regain her composure.

I spoke as gently as I could. "The purpose of your visit here today is for me to begin a pre-sentence investigation for the judge. He'll be taking my report into consideration at the time of sentencing." I glanced at my desk calendar. "Which will be in about three weeks. Do you think you can answer some questions?"

"Yes, of course," she replied, her eyes focusing on something outside the window behind my desk. I studied her face a moment, the high cheekbones, the firm jaw line, the full, sensuous mouth. Her gaze returned to me, and I looked away, fumbling in my desk for a legal pad to make notes. I referred to the police report and confirmed her full name and address.

"Do you live alone?" I asked.

"Yes," she replied. "Except for my two cats." She smiled, revealing the type of even teeth you get only from having worn braces.

I smiled back. "I like cats," I said. "Marital status?"

"Single."

An irritating inner voice of mine cheered, Yes! I squelched it immediately. "Children?"

She shook her head.

"Age?"

"Forty-one."

"Brothers or sisters?"

"No."

"Parents still alive?"

"Mother in Florida."

"Really? Where? My favorite aunt lives on the west coast, in Sarasota."

"Mom lives in Venice."

I smiled. "They're practically neighbors." I glanced back in the file, mentally chiding myself for trying to make small talk during a PSI. "Let's see, you don't have any priors...."

"Excuse me?"

"Prior arrests."

Her cheeks colored. "No."

"Okay, Ms. Hollis. Now I'd like you to...."

"Can you call me Anne?"

"Oh. Uh, sure. Anne." What was the matter with me, I wondered. Since when do I get so tongue-tied with a defendant? "I'd like to hear your version of what happened."

"Beth and I were driving..."

I referred to the police report. "That's Mary Elizabeth Powell?"

"Yes. She and I were driving from Albany to Cobleskill where I

6

have a second home. The time was early Saturday morning, around three a.m. We were driving on I-88."

"Why were you on the road so late? Or so early?"

"We left right after the bar closed."

I must have looked surprised.

She added hastily."I own the bar, Hooper's."

I felt something flutter in my chest and figured it was my heart missing a beat. Hooper's is one of two lesbian bars in Albany, and then my eye caught the name in the report: Hooper's—plain as day. Danger alarms went off inside me, but I ignored them. "Go on," I said, returning to my note-taking. I could feel my cheeks color.

"So we left the bar and were headed to my place when all of a sudden a car pulls up in back of us—"

I interrupted. "Had you been drinking at the bar?"

"Two glasses of wine, maybe three. I was off-duty. I don't drink when I'm working."

"Of course not," I said, thumbing through the report. "Your blood alcohol level was point zero five. You were charged with a D.W.A.I., driving while alcohol impaired..."

"I was not intoxicated."

"Well, not legally."

"Not in any way," she said, offended.

"What about Beth?"

"She doesn't...didn't drink."

"Go ahead. A car pulled up in back of you...."

"Yes. We were in the slow lane, driving sixty, when this guy starts tailgating me."

"You clearly saw that the other driver was a man?"

"I'm not sure, I thought so at the time. I couldn't understand why he didn't just pass me. He blew his horn a couple of times. I even moved into the fast lane so he could pass on that side. But he moved in behind me. I moved back. He moved back." She stopped and shuddered.

"Then what happened?"

"I was really frightened by then. Have you ever driven I-88 in the middle of the night?"

"No."

"There's almost no traffic, really no place to pull off the road.

When he came up behind us we were already past the town of Central Bridge. The road is a two-lane highway traveling west with a guard rail on the right. The left side of the road rides along the bottom of a mountain, the top of which is a two-lane highway traveling east. You can't pull off and you can't make a U-turn. We were stuck heading west with a maniac on our tail."

"Did Beth recognize him?"

She shook her head. "At one point Beth turned around to see if she could get a look at him, but it was impossible. We couldn't see behind his headlights."

"You mentioned before that his car rammed yours?"

"Yes. When I realized he wouldn't get off our tail I tried slowing down. That's when he rammed my bumper. I think he was trying to get me to increase my speed, and I did a little, but I was afraid of going too fast."

"How fast were you traveling?"

"I think my top speed was sixty-five. That's when he pulled into the fast lane, came up next to me in my blind spot, and hit my left rear bumper. In my confusion, and because of trying to see him in my side mirror, I lost control. Next thing I knew, we hit the guard rail and flipped over." Anne closed her eyes and swallowed. Her hand shook as she pushed it through her hair. "The car just kept rolling and rolling, five or six times."

"You were thrown from the vehicle?"

"Yes. Generally I wear my seatbelt, but I guess I forgot to put it back on when I stopped earlier to put on my sweater."

"When and where did you stop to do that?"

"Almost as soon as we got onto I-88 just beyond the Thruway toll booth."

"Do you remember any other cars being around the toll booth at the time?"

Anne frowned. "No, I don't think so."

"Were you hurt when the car flipped over?"

"A few bruises. I was very lucky."

"Okay, once your Jeep went over the guard rail, and you recovered from the wreck, did you see the vehicle that pushed you?"

"I was dazed, of course…when my car stopped rolling I made my way down to the bottom of the hill searching for Beth. When I reached the Jeep I looked back up toward the highway. I didn't see a car, but I thought I saw someone standing at the guard rail. My main concern was getting to Beth. I turned back to the Jeep which was resting on its right side, the passenger side. I climbed onto the car's body and kneeled behind the driver's door. I lifted the door and the inside lights came on. When I looked into the front seat I saw Beth. Her neck must've snapped when she was thrown against the windshield." Anne covered her eyes with her hands as if to block out the memory. She took several deep breaths, struggling for control. "I must have passed out then. The next thing I remember was riding in the ambulance."

I wanted to offer comfort where there really could be none. "I'm sorry you had to go through that, Anne."

"What I went through is nothing compared with what Beth went through."

I waited a moment for her to recover. "Can you tell me what you remember about the vehicle that hit you?"

She concentrated. "It was an older car, and big. Like a Bonneville or Impala. What we used to think of as a tank. I'm only guessing at a dark color."

"I don't suppose you saw the license plate?"

"No." She paused, making eye contact with me. "I know this looks bad for me, but he came out of nowhere, and the whole incident was all over in less than two minutes. I wish you could believe me. But why should you? No one else does."

I laid my pen down and smiled. "I do believe what you've told me, Anne."

Her face brightened and she smiled back.

"But I'm not the one you have to convince," I added quickly, not wanting to get her hopes up. "That's the judge."

Her smile disappeared. "Then it's hopeless."

"Not necessarily," I said. "It's not going to be easy. You're asking the court to believe that drinking isn't what caused the accident; that someone followed you onto I-88 for the express purpose of getting you to increase your speed to the point that one side swipe would toss your four-wheel drive vehicle over the rails. Who would do that? With what motive?"

"You mean why would someone have wanted to kill Beth?"

"Or you."

"Me?" She looked shocked, and hesitated. "There's considerably more to this than I've told you. Is our conversation privileged information—as with a priest or an attorney?"

I shook my head. "Any information you share with me may be shared with the court. I can't guarantee confidentiality, but if you have information that may help your case, I strongly urge you to tell me."

She sighed. "This is difficult because...the information includes intimate details about Beth. I feel uncomfortable revealing those things. Do you understand?"

"Of course. Still, that may be necessary to help sort all this out."

Anne paused, then nodded. "Beth told me that she'd been followed recently."

"By whom?" Now we were getting somewhere. She had my full, professional attention.

"She didn't know. It was always after dark. She said she didn't recognize the car, and she never got a good look at the driver."

"This happened more than once?"

"Beth only mentioned it once, but I got the impression it happened repeatedly."

"Had she called the police?"

"I know she didn't. I don't think she felt in any danger."

"Why do you say that?"

Anne shrugged. "I'm not certain, but I think Beth suspected the person might be one of the women she lives...lived with." Anne took a deep breath. "Here's where things start to get complicated. Beth lived in a convent residence. Six nuns live as roommates, two to a room, while the Mother Superior has her own room."

"Beth Powell was a nun?" I was unable to mask the astonishment in my voice.

Anne nodded. "Yes. Sister Mary Elizabeth. Isn't that in the report?"

"Probably, I didn't get that far." A new thought occurred to me. "What was Sister Mary Elizabeth doing in Hooper's Bar?"

Anne hesitated. "This is the part of Beth's life I have a problem revealing." She took a deep breath. "Hooper's is a lesbian bar. And Beth was a lesbian." Her cheeks colored slightly. "And in case you're wondering, so am I." Her eyes challenged me as I fought to preserve self-control.

I wanted to blurt out the truth about myself, but I caught myself. Professionally, I couldn't do that; she'd have to guess. Instead I said, "Please continue."

Anne maintained eye contact with me. "Apparently Beth kept her sexual orientation in the closet for years until she fell in love with one of the other nuns, Sister Jackie."

"Another 'particular friendship'...much frowned upon, much practiced."

Anne was surprised by my comment—heartened even. "Beth was planning to leave the convent. She told me Jackie couldn't handle the guilt, and they were both miserable."

"Did Beth suspect Jackie was following her?"

"Yes, but she didn't confront her."

"How did you meet Beth?"

"She walked into Hooper's one afternoon. She ordered a diet soda, and we got to talking. She told me she heard about Hooper's through her job as an alcoholism counselor at a place called Foxmoor. She said a couple of her clients mentioned drinking at Hooper's. She didn't tell me right away that she was a nun. I think she came by three or four times before she finally got around to telling me. And when she did, the scene was quite emotional, like a dam breaking. The poor kid, I felt sorry for her. She was trying to come out of the closet, and she needed a friend."

"What kind of person was she, Anne?"

Anne considered the question. "Controlled," she finally said. "Beth liked her corners squared, a place for everything and everything in its place. And that included her feelings. Rather than feel them, she'd put them in a box and label them—except where Jackie was concerned." Anne shook her head. "Beth has done more crying over her...."

I leaned back in my chair and stared at the blank wall behind Anne. Then I looked at her and shook my head. "I honestly don't know what to do at this point."

"What would you do if this were a normal case?"

I smiled at her choice of words. "Normally, I would go out and talk to employers, family members, anyone who could give me information helpful for the PSI. Then I'd put it all together with my recommendations to the judge."

"So what's stopping you?" Anne's eyes held the same irresistible challenge from earlier in our meeting.

"An allegation of murder—I'm a probation officer, not a police officer. My job is to investigate a case so a judge can make a fair sentencing decision. I'm here to help keep offenders out of prison."

"That's exactly what I'm asking you to do. Help the judge to make a fair decision."

Already I could hear Kasselbaum warning me not to play detective...and where was the time anyway, my caseload had peaked and then some, maybe if I gave up sleeping....

"Callie, if you don't investigate this, no one else will." She leaned with her hands on my desk. "Please."

Those pleading, blue eyes seemed worth losing sleep over, and the thought of bringing Anne justice made my heart beat faster. I picked up my pen without further hesitation. "Give me the name of the convent."

TWO

What a beautiful June day, the clouds in smears and patches as if an artist cleaned her brush against the sky. I dialed the number Anne gave me for The Sisters of St. James, hoping Sister Laura would grant an interview that afternoon so I'd get out of my stuffy office. I felt vaguely uncomfortable. I don't have fond memories of my years in Catholic school; the scars remain in my psyche. All during sixth grade Sister Mary Martinez would call me out into the hallway and slap me across the face because I had been bad. I never cried and I never told my parents, but more than thirty years later the rage was still palpable. I used to hold an image of Sister Mary in my mind while I beat a bataka against a pillow, venting my pain. Only then did I cry, my fury finally abated.

Someone answered politely, "Sisters of St. James. This is Sister Laura."

"My name is Officer Callie Sinclair," I said, "with the Albany County Probation Department. I'm conducting a pre-sentence investigation of the automobile accident in which Sister Mary Elizabeth Powell died."

The Mother Superior's voice grew deep, almost raspy. "Oh, yes, such a misfortune. She was one of our most promising novitiates. I admit we aren't over the shock yet. But how can I help you?"

"I wonder if I might drive out to speak with you in person?"

"I do have another appointment, but at two o'clock I can see you for half an hour."

"That will be fine." I hung up, surprised and relieved by her responsiveness.

My black Civic was parked in a lot four blocks from the office in a reserved parking space. It took me five years to get that space and I pay dearly for it each month. Before then I rode the bus to work. The bus stop was two blocks from my apartment at one end, and practically at my office door at the other. The only way I could rationalize taking my car to work was to move further away from the bus stop. So two years ago I opted for the tax shelter of home ownership and bought a newly constructed one-bedroom townhouse in the Pine Bush section of Albany. The stucco walls are painted white, and the cathedral ceiling and oversized windows keep the place looking bright and airy. I have a private fenced yard, and lots of pine trees, but I sometimes miss living downtown where all the action is.

The Sisters of St. James owned a white stone house on Manning Boulevard that most people in Albany would give their eye teeth for. The house, set back from the street like its neighbors, had large pillars that gave it an imposing look, but the open windows and brick walkway were inviting.

I parked in the driveway and stepped onto the large open front porch complete with rocking chairs and two large pots of red geraniums. I guess it pays to belong to a Catholic religious order when it comes to nice real estate.

I was about to ring the bell when the door opened and a tall handsome woman greeted me. She was dressed simply, a white tailored blouse, navy blue skirt and loafers. "I'm Sister Laura Bennett," she said. "Come in." She smiled stiffly, her manner no-nonsense.

"Officer Sinclair," I said, flipping my badge. "Thank you for seeing me today."

She led me across highly polished floors through a formal entrance, past a large dining room, and into a bright sitting room. "Please make yourself comfortable," she said.

I complied, perching on one of the chairs facing the sofa.

She sat opposite me. "You mentioned you were in charge of investigating Anne Hollis."

"I'm investigating events which took place around the accident. I'd like to get as many questions answered as possible within the next couple of days."

She leaned forward, as if I'd piqued her curiosity. "I was told that what happened was caused by drunk driving, and that Anne Hollis has been convicted of manslaughter. Have I been misinformed?"

"Ms. Hollis had plead guilty to reckless endangerment. My investigation will affect her sentencing, and is routine, Sister. Now, I need you to give me more information about Sister Mary Elizabeth—where she worked, how long she's been in the order, names of her nearest relatives...."

"Sister Mary Elizabeth showed exemplary dedication in her years with us," she said intensely. "Isn't it Miss Hollis you should be investigating?"

I flashed a patient smile. "In order for me to evaluate the circumstances surrounding this death, I need to know as much about the passenger as the driver."

Undaunted, she said, "I still don't understand why you need information about Sister Mary Elizabeth."

Clearly, she was annoyed, and the feeling was mutual. "Whether or not you understand is irrelevant. I need to conduct an investigation. If, for whatever reason, you're unwilling to provide me with the information I'm requesting I can obtain a court ord—"

She put up a hand to stop me. "Please, don't misunderstand, Ms. Sinclair. I'm really not trying to make things difficult for you. It's just that...we're not over the shock of losing Sister Mary Elizabeth. I'm afraid I'm still very shaken. Of course I'll do whatever I can to help you." She rubbed her forehead as if wondering where to begin. "For the last three years, the Sister worked with outpatients at Foxmoor Alcoholism Treatment Services."

I lifted my brows. "I thought yours was a teaching order."

"Primarily, but with my permission a member of the community may choose another vocation. Before Vatican II there were teaching Orders, nursing Orders, cloistered Orders and so on. After Vatican II some teaching Orders became combination Orders. Ours was one of them. Nowadays, Sisters may choose almost any occupation, even that of accountant."

"Really! Is there really a C.P.A. in your community?"

"No, we have three teachers, two alcoholism counselors and

Sister Roseanne, our chief cook and bottle-washer."

"I see. Getting back to Sister Mary Elizabeth—did she seem happy with her vocation?"

Sister Laura closed her eyes for just a moment before replying. "She took First Vows five years ago, so she was Junior Professed, scheduled to take Final Vows next year. She told me often how much she looked forward to that event." Then, maybe as a way to get rid of me, Sister Laura said helpfully, "If you'll wait a moment I can get you the name and address of her sister."

I studied Sister Laura as she walked deliberately to a corner desk and began leafing through a rolodex. She was younger than I expected, maybe late forties, with a few silver strands running through her brown hair. She had combed her short hair over her ears, probably in a vain attempt to hide their slight protrusion.

I speculated as to what it was about Sister Laura that pushed my buttons, and realized her aggressiveness reminded me of one of my former lovers, Dixie. It was the way she walked, the way her fingers rifled through the file. Too much like Dixie who pursued me for eight months until in frustration, she kicked a hole in the bottom of my door because I wouldn't go out with her again. Her kicking in the door just proved my point about her.

Maybe Dixie had missed her calling. She should have been a mother superior. I studied Sister Laura out of the corner of my eye as I waited, my notebook and pen ready. She stood very straight and was on the thin side, but looked strong. Her manner made her seem taller than she was. I figured she was around five nine—

"Here it is," Sister said, walking back towards the sofa. "Claudia Powell. She lives in Cohoes on Simmons Avenue."

I took down the number and asked, "How did Sister Mary Elizabeth come to be traveling with Anne Hollis in the middle of the night?"

"I understand they had met through Sister Beth's work. Perhaps Sister Beth was counseling Miss Hollis."

That was bullshit if I ever heard it, but I kept my opinions to myself. Instead I asked, "Was Sister Mary Elizabeth expected home that evening?"

"No, she wasn't. I understood she was to spend the night with Claudia."

"I see." I laid my pen down. "Would it be possible for me to see Sister Mary Elizabeth's room?"

"Of course you may see her room, but why is that necessary?"

"Well, sometimes it helps."

"I don't see how it could in this case."

God, I thought, this woman is a pain in the ass. "Perhaps it would be easier if I explained why my department is so interested in Sister Mary Elizabeth."

"I'd appreciate that," she said.

"Anne Hollis has stated that her Jeep was forced off the road by another vehicle." Mother Superior's brow furrowed. "She also stated that Sister Mary Elizabeth mentioned to her that she had been followed recently when driving her car."

"Followed?!" Sister Laura's hands went to her mouth. "By whom?"

"That's what I'm trying to find out."

"But that's absurd! Surely Miss Hollis made that up."

"I don't think so, Sister," I said in a firm, professional voice.

Sister Laura stood and walked to the windows, parting the white curtains and peering out. Her back was to me. "Sister Mary Elizabeth never mentioned being followed. Why would she be?" She turned and said, "Do you think her being followed had something to do with her death?"

"I don't know what to think, Sister. I'm merely telling you what was told to me with the hope that you may be able to validate it."

"I'm sorry, but I can't."

"Perhaps Sister Mary Elizabeth mentioned these episodes to one of the other sisters in the community?"

"You're free to question any or all of them."

"What about her roommate?"

"Sister Jackie." She nodded. "If Mary Elizabeth had been followed, surely she would have told Jackie. They were very close."

Did I detect a pinch of resentment in her voice? "Can you tell me where I might reach her?"

"She also works at Foxmoor, will be there until nine tonight. You might try seeing her there."

"Thank you." I slipped my pen into my briefcase. "Now about Sister Mary Elizabeth's bedroom...."

17

"Certainly. It's on the second floor."

I stood and said, "I appreciate it, Sister."

She led me upstairs, through a narrow hallway which smelled faintly of furniture polish. All of the doors along the hallway were closed. Beth and Jackie's room was at the far end, on the right. Sister Laura opened the door and stood aside for me to enter.

The room was large, with tall, skinny windows, and a high ceiling. Twin beds faced us from the far wall. Separating the two beds was a nightstand, over which hung a crucifix.

"Which bed belonged to Sister Mary Elizabeth?" I asked, my voice almost a whisper.

"The one on the right, with the teddy bear."

I walked over to the bed and ran my hand over the white chenille bedspread. The small brown teddy bear was propped against the pillow, a blue patch fashioned over one of its eyes. I reached for it and lifted the patch. One button eye was missing.

Beth kept a small bookcase near her bed. I knelt down and read some of the book titles. Most of them dealt with drug abuse or alcoholism. I recognized A.A.'s Big Book and several volumes on Adult Children of Alcoholics. There was a book on shame, and another dealing with the subject of incest survival. If I expected to find any lesbian novels, I was most certainly disappointed.

Sister Laura stood in the doorway. "There's not much here to see."

"You're right, Sister." I agreed. The bleakness of the room struck me. I would have expected nuns in the nineties to be a bit more with it, but the nightstand held nothing but a reading lamp and a small statue of The Virgin Mary, and her dresser was bare on top except for a framed photograph of a baby.

"That's her niece, Terri," Sister Laura sighed. "We've been expecting her family to reclaim her belongings. I suppose it's time we packed them away. I should mention something to Sister Jackie."

I scanned the rest of the room—pale pink walls, white ceiling and woodwork, white curtains, and pink scatter rugs alongside the beds. A pair of skis was propped in a corner near the closet.

Jackie's dresser displayed several family photographs, but not much else. I walked over to Jackie's nightstand where a small stack of books lay adjacent to the lamp, a hymnal, a book of prayers. Neither of the women seemed into decorating, but maybe that was part of the convent requirements. Aside from the teddy bear with its eyepatch, the room struck me as impersonal. Any two nuns could have lived in it.

As I reached for the knob on the drawer of Sister Beth's nightstand, Laura's voice was shrill behind me. "That's enough now. You've seen enough."

I withdrew my hand and spun around. Was it the harshness of her tone or the look of hostility on her face that caused the hairs to rise on the back of my neck? I would have liked to poke around a bit, say under the pillow or under the bed, but her presence was overbearing. Annoyed, I brushed past her, preceding her down the carpeted staircase.

When I reached the bottom step I turned to her and said, "One more thing, Sister. The car that Sister Mary Elizabeth drove. Does it belong to the convent?"

Her voice returned to the normal, smooth Mother Superior tone she had used throughout our interview. "No, it's hers—which is very irregular, you see. Her sister, Claudia, gave it to her as a gift."

"May I see it?" I asked, walking toward the front door.

Sister Laura frowned. "What possible clue could her car provide? She didn't drive it the night of the accident, and the police haven't asked to see it."

"I'm just trying to cover all the bases."

She looked at her watch and sighed. Probably to make me feel guilty. It didn't work. "It's the dark blue Ford parked in the garage."

"Do you have the keys, Sister?"

"The garage isn't locked."

"No, I meant the car keys."

"You're not planning to drive it, are you?"

I smiled. "Just sit in it."

"Give me a moment to find them," she said in a tone of long-suffering as the front doorbell rang. The door's window was curtained, but I was able to see a man wearing a white collar standing on the porch.

Sister Laura strode to the door and opened it, all smiles. "Father Brannigan," she gushed. "You're right on time."

He nodded to her, then turned to me and smiled, a questioning look on his shiny face.

"Father, I'd like you to meet Officer Sinclair from the Albany County Department of Probation. Ms. Sinclair, this is Monsignor Michael Brannigan of St. Martha's Parish.

Ah, her boss. I stuck out my hand. "Pleased to meet you, Father."

"I'm very pleased to meet you," he said, grasping my hand between both of his. His hands felt very smooth. And why shouldn't they? You don't get calluses doling out penances.

"Officer Sinclair is here to investigate the case surrounding our dear Sister Mary Elizabeth," she said, too sanctimoniously for my liking.

"Such a sad circumstance," he murmured, bowing his head.

Father Brannigan was still standing in the doorway so Sister Laura moved out of the way and said, "Father, please come in." She smiled and her silly grin was still on her face when she turned to look at me. I don't think I concealed my smirk very well. I detest women who act so stupid around men, even if they are priests. I guess I expected Sister Laura to be assertive with everyone, regardless of gender or position. Her subservience pissed me off even more.

"The car keys, Sister," I said.

"Of course." She opened the closet and removed a set of keys from one of the hooks.

I had a sneaking suspicion she would have liked to walk me out to the car so she could watch me search the vehicle. I snatched the keys from her hand and said, "I'll bring them right back," then hustled my butt out the front door.

Having seen Beth's immaculate room, the condition of her car surprised me; its exterior looked like the inside of a vacuum cleaner bag. I was tempted to print 'WASH ME' on its trunk. I unlocked the door and sat in the front seat. The red dashboard was covered with a thick film of dust. It appeared as if Beth had driven the car, windows rolled down, on a very dusty road. I rummaged through the glove compartment, finding nothing unusual, then glanced under the seats and beneath the floor mats. Except for the dust, the car was as neat as her room. I sat for a moment thinking, what am I looking for? I didn't know, but figured I'd recognize it if I saw it. I leaned my elbow on the steering wheel, chin in my hand. Damn, I thought. That's when I noticed the word printed in the dust on the dashboard: ACE.

I returned to the house and rang the doorbell.

"Did you find what you were looking for?" she asked.

"I don't know, Sister," I said. "Can you tell me how Sister Beth's car got so dirty?"

"No."

"Does the word or the name Ace mean anything to you, Sister?"

"No, it doesn't."

I placed the key in Sister Laura's palm and walked away.

Foxmoor is located on Route 155 in the Pine Bush, not far from my townhouse. It's an area that still remains somewhat undeveloped, primarily because it's the breeding ground of the Karner Blue Butterfly, a dying species that environmentalists are trying to protect. I temper my guilt about living in the Karner Blues' natural habitat by feeding the birds and planting trees to replace the ones removed by the construction company.

The folks who owned Foxmoor must be tempering their guilt as well. Their building was very modern and airy, with skylights all over the place. Trees remained close to the building, and several had been planted inside, beneath the skylight in the reception area. A number of people were sitting around the plantings in this part as I entered the room, maybe waiting for a group counseling session to begin.

I walked up to the receptionist's window. Two women and a man stood behind the glass talking. I asked if Sister Jacqueline was available.

"Hey, Jackie," the man called. "There's someone here to see you."

A young woman with brown curly hair poked her head around the corner. She looked at the man who called her. He nodded toward me. Jackie walked to the window. "Hi, I'm Sister Jackie. Are you here to see me?"

I showed her my badge. "I'm Officer Sinclair," I said. "I'm investigating the accident in which Sister Mary Elizabeth lost her life."

Sister Jackie's face blanched, and she turned her head away to look at the wall clock. It was three-forty-five. "I was just about to take my dinner break," she said. "I was going to eat at a picnic table out back."

"May I sit with you for a few minutes?"

She thought for a moment, then said, "I guess that'll be okay. I'll meet you there in five minutes."

I walked out the front door and around to the back of the building where several picnic tables stood empty. I sat down at the one nearest the building and watched flies buzzing around a trash can until Sister Jackie came out of the back door. She was carrying a brown bag and a bottle of diet Pepsi.

"I only get a half hour," she announced.

"This shouldn't take very long. As I said, I'm the investigator for Anne Hollis' case, and want to talk to you about Sister Mary Elizabeth."

"What do you need to know?" She busied herself opening the brown bag and removing its contents—an egg salad sandwich in a baggy, a nectarine, and a yellow paper napkin. The only jewelry she wore was a gold tone Timex with a brown leather strap, and the thin gold wedding band symbolizing her marriage to Jesus on one of the fingers of her small hands. She wore khaki shorts, sandals, and a pink T-shirt. In spite of her medium-length curly hair and freckles that made her seem rather young and cute, I guessed her age to be about thirty. She had the longest eyelashes I'd ever seen on a woman. I noticed the hair on her arms was very long and fine. It made me want to peek to see whether or not nuns were allowed to shave their legs, but we were at opposite sides of the table and it would have been rude of me. "You two were roommates at the convent residence, correct?"

She nodded, fumbled with the egg salad sandwich, brought it halfway to her mouth, then changed her mind and placed it back on the table. Her lips stretched into a smile, but her eyes were wary.

I continued, "I understand Sister Mary Elizabeth was contemplating leaving the convent. Did she talk to you about that?"

She held onto the smile as if for false comfort. "She hadn't made a decision yet."

"But she was thinking about it—do you know why?"

Sister Jackie unscrewed the cap on her Pepsi bottle and took a swig. "Beth wasn't sure she still fit in with the community."

Jackie had the look of someone shut down emotionally. I wondered if I should have waited a bit before questioning her. After all, Beth's funeral had only been three days ago. Then I thought of Anne Hollis facing the judge in three weeks and pressed on. "Why did she no longer fit in?"

Instead of answering me, she asked, "What do Beth's feelings about the convent have to do with the accident?"

"There may be evidence that determines this was no accident." Her eyes widened, but she made no protest. I continued, "Apparently another car bumped Ms. Hollis' Jeep so that it went off the highway."

"Why would anyone do such a thing?"

"That's what I'm trying to find out. Now, are you willing to help by providing me with some insight into Beth?"

"What do you want to know?"

"Well, for starters, you said she wasn't sure she still fit in with the community. In what way? Was she having a hard time with the routine of being a nun?"

Jackie shook her head. "Beth loved the community, and she especially loved all the ritual stuff. When she was a novitiate she really got into prayers, the silences, kissing the floor—"

"Excuse me, did you say, 'kissing the floor?'"

"Yes. I particularly remember her speaking about 'the modesty of the eyes.' As a novitiate, Beth was supposed to walk with her eyes lowered, not look at anything or anyone without having a reason. One day she checked the time on a clock when she wasn't supposed to and so she reported herself. She had to kneel in front of the entire community, kiss the floor, say an Act of Contrition, and ask the sisters for forgiveness."

"Beth enjoyed that?" I asked dubiously.

"Yes." She smiled. "She really did. You act surprised."

"I am surprised. And what about the Mother Superior? Did she demand this sort of self-punishment? Did she administer it?"

"She'd witness it and encourage self-reporting for infractions. It pleased her to have you take punishment voluntarily. Beth wasn't unusual. Others would do things on purpose in order to confess. It was like a cleansing—that's what Mother Superior would call it." Jackie picked up her sandwich and took a bite.

"I've heard of horror stories about convent life but I didn't think stuff like that was still going on nowadays, after Vatican II and all."

"Strict discipline which can seem harsh still exists with novitiates. It's all part of the training. If you aren't put through rigors, you'll still be part of the world." She became thoughtful for a moment, then waved her hand dismissively. "I was never part of the pre-Vatican II era. I'm sure there are still some Orders that flog themselves on Good Friday."

"You speak of it so lightly, Sister."

"Please call me Jackie." Her smile was engaging.

"Okay, Jackie, but you were a novitiate once. You went through the rough training, right?"

"True, but if you compare it with being a Marine Corps recruit, for instance, you realize that basic training will one day be over and in the end you'll have a good life because of the rigor."

"And is that what you have now? The good life?"

"My life suits me."

"But community life no longer suited Beth." I swatted a fly from my knee. "Can we get back to that, Jackie? I'd like you to tell me about your relationship with Beth."

She picked up the sandwich again and was bringing it toward her mouth when I reached over and touched her wrist.

"Please don't," I said. "I'd like you to answer my question."

Her eyes stared at me blankly, but I could almost see the turmoil behind them. She put the sandwich down. "Beth and I have been friends for three years, ever since she took her vows." Jackie placed her hands in her lap and began scrutinizing them.

I looked at her pointedly. "Particular friends?"

Her cheeks colored. She nodded.

"Is that why she was thinking of leaving the convent?"

"Yes."

"And how did that make you feel?" Damn, I thought, I sound just like my old therapist.

Red blotches appeared on Sister Jackie's face around her eyes and nose. I was certain she was going to cry.

"I didn't want her to leave, begged her not to. I loved Beth...."

She lowered her head, dabbing at her eyes with the yellow napkin. When her gaze returned to me all I saw was her defiance. "The subject of Beth's leaving never even came up until she started hanging around Anne Hollis. She's the one who put those ideas in Beth's head!"

"What ideas do you mean?"

"About coming out of the closet, living free, not being ashamed of who we are...."

"Sounds pretty positive to me," I said.

"Maybe for other people, but in our case we'd have to give up God and our lives in the religious community to live in the gay community."

"Wouldn't staying mean you'd have to deny your sexuality?"

Her temper flared. "We took a vow of chastity!"

"I'm aware of that, Sister."

"Then you can understand why I couldn't approve of her relationship with Anne Hollis!"

"Weren't they platonic friends?"

"So they claimed. I'm not so sure." She turned away, squinted her eyes.

Was I sensing jealousy there? I put my hands up and smiled. "I'm sorry, Sister—uh, Jackie. My intent was not to debate with you. I'm really interested more in finding out what happened the night of the accident. Did Beth ever confide to you that someone was following her?"

She looked surprised. "Someone really was following Beth?"

"I can't prove it, but that's what she told Anne."

"I just thought Beth had an overactive imagination. Why would anyone follow her?"

"Who knew about your relationship with Beth, your particular friendship?"

Jackie's cheeks colored again. "I don't think anyone did."

"You never told anyone?"

"Never!"

"Was Sister Laura aware of it?"

A curious expression crossed Jackie's face, one I couldn't interpret. "No."

"Can you think of any reason why someone would want to harm Beth?"

She shook her head, tears spilling from her eyes. "But I knew something like this would happen."

"What do you mean?"

"Beth's getting mixed up with Anne Hollis, hanging out in a lesbian bar!" She spat out the words. "Have you read the statistics on violence against gays and lesbians?" Her eyes burned with fury. "One in five gay men and one in ten lesbians are victims of violence."

I showed my surprise.

"And did you know that a middle class white family's least preferred neighbors are no longer Blacks, Hispanics, or Jews? No—they least want gays next door."

I nodded. I had read the recent Albany Times Union article, too. "What has that got to do with this accident?"

Jackie stuffed her lunch back into the brown bag, then flung it at a trash barrel. "Somebody couldn't handle a nun coming out of the closet." She stood up. "I have to get back."

"Just two more questions, Sister. Does the name Ace, or the word ace mean anything to you?"

"Should it?"

I didn't reply, just stared at her until she finally said, "No, it doesn't. Now, what's your final question?"

"Do you happen to know where Sister Mary Elizabeth was driving to get her car so dirty?"

"No."

And that seemed to mark the end of what I found to be a frustrating interview because she revealed so little about her relationship with Beth. Jackie's words, 'So they claimed,' bothered me. Obviously, she doubted a simple friendship. Was she jealous or had she rejected Beth's sexual advances, denied her own feelings? Talk about being in the closet. I hated to admit it, but the thought of Anne being lovers with Beth, with anyone, ignited a spark of jealousy within me. Forcing the feeling aside, I allowed the thought some room. I was supposed to be considering Jackie's emotions. Was Jackie so jealous over such a possible affair between Beth and Anne that she would try and run them both off the road? I knew I would have to explore the idea further, that I would have to bother Jackie again before long. Meanwhile I thought I'd let her get used to the idea of my investigating.

I stood up from the picnic table and nodded to her. "I won't keep you any longer today, but if there is anything else you can think of, here's my number." I put my card on the table in front of her but didn't wait to see if she would pick it up.

I stopped at a pay phone to call my office, tell them I wouldn't be back that day. Marylou answered the phone. "Callie, Anne Hollis stopped by with a package for you. She left it here at the reception desk."

"A package? What kind of package?" Why would Anne leave a package for me?

"A small box, tied with string. D'ya want me to open it?"

"No, don't. What did she say when she left it?"

"She said, 'Please give this to Callie Sinclair.' That's all."

"I mean, what did she say about the package, Marylou? Did she tell you what was in it?"

"No, but she wrote a note. It's taped to the package. D'ya want me to read it to you?"

"No! I'll be there in a few minutes." I was too curious to wait until morning, so I drove all the way downtown to fetch it, then sat double-parked in front of my office building, reading Anne's note.

Callie,

It wasn't until after I left your office that I remembered Beth's overnight bag was still at Hooper's. This package contains Beth's diary which I found in the bag. I doubt it will provide any clues for your investigation, but surely it will give you some insight into Beth.

Anne

Beth's diary! So she did have at least one most personal possession! My fingers fumbled with the string as I tore the brown paper from the package as if it were a gaily wrapped birthday present. The small leather-bound book fell into my lap. So far the sisters were revealing more by their attitudes than any details about Beth. What would her diary reveal? I could hardly wait, and yet...well, I had my own personal revelations to make that had nothing to do with the Hollis case, and which I had been thinking about much longer.

The A.A. meeting I was going to started at seven-thirty. I walked in, helped myself to a cup of tea and a couple of chocolate chip cookies, and took a seat near the front of the room. A guy named Reggie opened the meeting by reading the preamble. Someone else read the twelve steps. Then Reggie said, "Celebrating her tenth anniversary with us is tonight's speaker...Callie."

The applause as I walked up to the podium was not for me, but for my ten years of sobriety.

Public speaking makes me nervous, so I took a deep breath and said, "Hi, my name is Callie and I'm an alcoholic.

"My theory is that I was born an alcoholic, but back in the forties not much was known about the disease, particularly how alcoholism affects fetuses. My mother was an active alcoholic and from what I've been told, a daily drunk. When my father left for work in the mornings, Mom left for the bars. Sometimes she'd make it home before he did, sometimes not. Usually, I was alone most of the day or after school. My needs weren't being met physically or emotionally, and as a result I grew up not only with abandonment issues but unresolved anger.

"And I swore I wouldn't become an alcoholic. The first time I drank wine I hated the taste, but I drank it anyway because I loved the way it made me feel—free, uninhibited, as if I could do anything I wanted to do and not be responsible. The first time I got drunk was with some friends in high school. Nothing significant happened. I drank until I got drunk, threw up, then fell asleep. It was the pattern it started that was significant. I began to drink very quickly. I was drinking Seven and Sevens. Once I was handed a rum and coke, hated it, but drank it anyway. Then chased it with a six ounce glass of straight whiskey. I remember kneeling at a toilet bowl, puking my guts up, then later coming to on the end of someone's bed. Two people were in the bed having sex, and every so often they'd kick me to see if I was still alive. Even two days later the whites of my eyes were yellow. And I felt so sick I thought I was going to die. When friends asked me what was wrong with me I sincerely replied, 'I had an allergic reaction to some rum that I drank.'"

Several people in the meeting chuckled at that remark. So did I. The laughter reminded me of my first A.A. meeting where a guy talked about totalling his car and ending up in jail charged with a hit and run. Everyone laughed at his story except me. I thought they were either cruel or demented to find humor in such a tragedy, but today I understand that sometimes we need to laugh to keep from crying.

"After that episode I curtailed my drinking somewhat, allowing myself to get drunk to the point of throwing up, but not to the point of passing out. I thought I was a success because I wasn't the daily drunk my mother had been. I drank only on weekends and never alone. Hell, I thought my life was manageable. I went to work every day, paid my bills on time, and was never picked up for driving under the influence.

"My life's unmanageability became clear when I realized I couldn't live alone, and worse, couldn't be without a romantic relationship. I needed to have a roommate, preferably a lover. I needed to have someone tell me I was worthy, someone to be there at night when the lights went out because I had become afraid of things that go bump in the night. I was so afraid of being alone I was willing to be in relationships that were unhealthy. When one relationship became too hard for me to handle, I'd find someone who was willing to rescue me and take care of me or control me. I began to recognize that if I became attracted to someone I didn't know, I probably wanted someone to get a grip on me one way or another. My emotional problems and my alcoholism fed off one another. My life continued to be unmanageable until I put down the bottle. What brought me to acceptance was a conversation I had with a friend of mine ten years ago. I said that every time I drank, I threw up, and said I wished I could stop. She suggested I try A.A. I laughed and said, 'I'm not an alcoholic. I don't want to stop drinking, I just want to stop throwing up.'

"She said, 'What would you do if you threw up whenever you drank a glass of milk?' The answer was that simple. So here I am, ten years later, celebrating my return to sanity. Today, because I stopped drinking, I have learned to take care of myself, to live on my own and to keep out of unhealthy relationships until I could trust myself. I'm still working on that though, and my anger. I wish I could say I've resolved all the issues, but I haven't. This program talks about progress, not perfection. I'm comfortable with where I am today, living clean and sober one day at a time."

I was left with one thought after describing all my relationships in such terms—why the hell was I attracted to Anne Hollis, an owner of a bar and someone whose life was obviously a mess at the moment? Being a Probation Officer was one thing. I knew I was probably doing the job so I would be taking care of others, and so learning to cope myself. But this case went beyond that, and it was exactly what I didn't need. And somehow, I wasn't saying no, in fact I was taking it on, actually wanting to take a look at a dead nun's diary because some pretty face gave it to me. How could I possibly know what I was getting in to? Anne may as well have been handing me a rum and coke.

THREE

Although Sister Mary Elizabeth's diary dated back to 1984 when she was a postulant, there were long periods of time when no personal entries were made. Instead I found meditations, prayers from various saints, things she must have copied down as thoughts for the day.

I skipped through the pages until I came to her own record. Beth's writing was very cramped, which made reading the diary difficult. I skimmed through several months of the first year's entries, trying to get a feel for her:

April 20, 1984: Today was my first anniversary in the convent. I received cards from the novices and the Mistress of Postulants, Sister Jennifer. I also received a very special card from Sister Agnes. It was special because there was a picture of The Virgin Mother on the outside of the card, and inside was a sweet note from Sister Agnes, telling me how happy she is that I am her friend. After dinner, Sister Agnes and I walked on the grounds. It was a beautiful cloudless evening. The stars were all visible in the heavenly skies. It felt so good to be with Agnes. I always feel good when I am with her. We walked for more than an hour before we finally went inside.

Hm, what did we have here? So Beth had friends in the convent other than Jackie. Well, well. I read on:

April 30, 1984: I saw Sister Agnes every day this week. We talked about our families, our lives and how much we care for one another. I love being with her because she makes me happy.

May 15, 1984: Today was very difficult because I didn't get a chance to talk with Agnes, although I saw her many times. I wish I was already a novice so we could be together more.

July 16, 1984: Last night after everyone had gone to bed I met Agnes downstairs and we talked for more than an hour. She told me then how much she cared for me.

July 17, 1984: Tonight at dinner I reported myself for breaking silence with Agnes last night. For penitence I was given extra prayers to say, but Sister Agnes was made to crawl beneath the table and kiss the shoes of all the nuns. Agnes received the harsher penitence for not reporting herself.

July 18, 1984: Sister Jennifer took me aside and told me it was wrong of me to break silence to talk with Agnes, and that I should remember the rule of travelling in threes. Then she said, 'Because of your nature you will have to be more careful around particular friendships.' She warned me that from now on I must speak to Agnes only during the proper times. I don't know what she means or if I'll be able to do that. I pray to God for help.

Somehow I had a feeling that prayer wasn't going to be answered.

September 10, 1984: I have not been happy ever since Agnes and I were chastised. We seldom see each other alone. I feel her drifting away from me. Tuesday, I skipped evening prayers on purpose, hoping the attention of my punishment (three days of silence!) would draw Agnes back to me, but my effort was in vain.

In vain! The diary had me hooked now.

October 9, 1984: I spent some time today with Agnes. What a lovely talk we had! It felt so good to be with her again. I only wish we could be together more often.

January 16, 1985: Agnes presented me with the cutest teddy bear today, in honor of my nineteenth birthday! She also gave me a beautiful card with a picture of lovely spring flowers. The message inside said that I remind her of a flower: pure and graceful. She told me she misses me, and she squeezed my hand when I told her I love her. Feeling her hand on mine made butterflies flutter in my breast.

So, the teddy was not a remnant of childhood but a love-token! She had had something of great personal value in her room after all.

August 10, 1985: I saw Agnes talking with Sister Catherine again. Why is it that she and Catherine are able to spend so much time together?

I seem to be the only one to notice their friendship. I wish seeing them so happy didn't make me feel so jealous. I watched them together during supper, always sitting near each other. It makes me want to fling a spoonful of mashed potatoes across the table. I know these feelings are wrong, but I don't know how to report myself, so tonight I will spend an extra half-hour on my knees in penitence.

November 2, 1985: Yesterday Agnes and Catherine left the novitiate. Some of the other sisters said Agnes and Catherine have a 'particular friendship.' When I heard them say that I ran to my room and fell on my knees in prayer. I prayed very hard for both of them. I also prayed for myself, and for understanding of my feelings. I miss Agnes so much. I don't know how I am going to go on without her. I think if Agnes had asked me to leave with her I would have done it. I hurt so much, I feel as if I am being crucified.

I know that in my own past experience, I would have gone for a good stiff drink in such a situation. But she wanted martyrdom.

March 12, 1986: After all the rigor, I think I am much stronger, more capable. My life is so much fuller now that I have taken First Vows. I feel I'm really at peace for the first time since I entered the convent. I feel ready to accept whatever God decides is best for me.

The novitiate back on track. From this point, Beth focused on her religious life within the community. No particular sisters were mentioned with any consistency until 1987 when Jackie's name began popping up in a manner similar to the earlier entries about Sister Agnes. Toward the end of 1990, however, their relationship took on a different tone:

September 9, 1990: Last night Sister Jackie came into my bed again, but instead of just holding me, she kissed me on the mouth. I'd never been kissed like that before, but I liked the way it felt. This time she stayed in my bed almost the entire night. I hardly slept a wink, wanting her to kiss me again and again. The next day Jackie prayed the rosary. She said I should, too.

Uh oh.

November 16, 1990: Jackie finally allowed me to touch her. We had been in my bed, just holding each other, when I cupped her breast in my hand. When she didn't push me away, I slipped my hand under her nightshirt to stroke her. I have no words to explain the beauty of kissing her breast.

December 4, 1990: I have never been so happy, and yet my feelings are so confused. I love Jackie more than I can say. When I think of her or look at her, I am so filled up inside that there is hardly any room left. Tonight, after dinner, Jackie warned me not to look at her the way I do. She says the others will notice, especially Sister Laura, and we might be separated. I couldn't bear for that to happen. And so we both spent extra time in the chapel, separately. I prayed the rosary three times, but I am not sure that what I prayed for is God's will.

April 6, 1991: I don't understand what is happening. I try talking with Jackie about my feelings, but she doesn't want to hear me. When I told her that I love her, she put her hands over her ears and begged me to be quiet. She said she feels ashamed because we each took a vow of chastity and are now going against our vows. I am so confused. Jackie is the one who came into my bed, but now that she thinks we will be caught, she wants to stop. I don't think I can stop, but I will pray to God for help.

April 8, 1991: All I can think about anymore is Jackie, and the feelings I have for her. I am so afraid to say what I am feeling, or even to write the word, but I am beginning to believe I am a lesbian. Somehow I must find out the truth.

April 9, 1991: Jackie ignored me all afternoon at work. Instead of eating dinner with me she went to Garcia's with some of the other counselors. She told me again that I am being too obvious. 'Obvious about what?' I said, more confused than ever. ' Our friendship,' She said. Sometimes I'm tempted to report my feelings to Sister Laura, but Jackie warned me not to. She said Sister Laura would transfer one of us to a different community, or we may both be removed from the Order. I know I don't want to be separated from Jackie, but I have to do something. I can't go on this way.

April 10, 1991: I don't know what came over me tonight, but as soon as my shift was over I drove to Hooper's Bar. Thank God the place was nearly empty because I made such a fool of myself. I wanted to walk in and pretend I belonged there, just to see how that felt. Two women sitting together at the opposite end of the bar were holding hands and laughing. All I could think about was Jackie, and I began to cry. The bartender, a woman named Anne, offered me comfort. We talked for a very long time.

I barely caught my breath as the first mention of Anne jolted me. I knew perfectly well that my curiosity was now other than professional. I read on:

...in fact, I got home so late that Sister Laura grilled me. I lied. I told her I was with Claudia, but I don't think she believed me. She chastised me,

and warned me that if it happens again I will need to have a talk with Father Brannigan. When I told Jackie where I had gone, she became angry and warned me never to do that again. All these warnings! Sometimes I wish I could report myself and take the consequences, but I know the penitence would be harsher than kissing Sister Laura's shoes.

April 23, 1991: Thank you, God, for the gift of Anne Hollis. I think she is the most wonderful woman in the world. She's not just a bartender, she listens to me talk about my feelings without judging me like Jackie does. I tell her how confused I am about my sexuality. She tells me 'just take things a day at a time,' which makes me laugh because that's what I tell my alcoholic clients. Meanwhile, I've been spending every chance I get with Anne, even visiting her cottage in Cobleskill. Of course I don't tell Sister Laura where I'm going. I tell her I'm with Claudia.

May 10, 1991: Glory be! The confusion has lifted. I feel certain that I am a lesbian. I wish Jackie could understand, but I haven't much hope of that. She seems more angry now, and is acting very jealous of Anne. But she need not concern herself because no matter what I have shared with Anne, I will always, always love Jackie.

May 19, 1991: I told Jackie I am leaving. She begged me to reconsider. She said we could still have our special friendship if I would be willing to be discreet. I wanted to shake her, but instead I took her face in my hands and said, 'Look at me Jackie. Look into my eyes and see the love I have for you.'

Her eyes were filled with tears. 'I love you, too,' she said. We held each other for a long time, then I said, 'Please come away with me and let me love you forever.' She shook herself free and said she would never leave God, not even for me. Her denial of what we shared infuriated me.

May 21, 1991: I have been praying fervently but nothing works. My situation with Jackie has not improved and Sister Laura has become very strict with me. Yesterday she told me I may not visit Claudia, but must spend the evening polishing the staircase. I think she suspects something, but surely not that I am spending time with Anne Hollis. Even so, I am on edge waiting for the other shoe to drop.

May 25, 1991: I don't think I can stand the suspense much longer. Sister Laura hasn't confronted me about my time away from the convent, but I feel it will be any day now. I am even more tempted now to report myself to put an end to my misery.

May 27, 1991: I could no longer stand the agony. Last night I knocked on Sister Laura's bedroom door and asked for a meeting. I had planned to disclose everything, my feelings for Jackie, my new self awareness, and my friendship and visits with Anne. Laura invited me in, but she was in one of her strange moods. I can't put my finger on it, but sometimes when I am in her presence I feel as though I am with a stranger, not my Mother Superior. She greeted me with a casual familiarity, yet there was something in her eyes. If I didn't know better I would describe it as loathing. Instead of reporting myself, I asked permission to sleep overnight at Claudia's tomorrow. I was surprised when Sister Laura consented.

Beth's final entry was dated two weeks before the accident:

May 29, 1991: I was followed again tonight. I wish I knew who is doing this. Maybe then I would understand why. It began happening after I began my friendship with Anne, which makes me think it might be Jackie. Tonight I thought the driver was a man, but I'm still not sure. If only I could see the license plate, or recognize the make of car.

Damn, I thought. Damn, damn, damn. I closed Beth's diary and pulled the sheet over my head.

The next morning I placed a call to Investigator William Hughes of the New York State Police. I wanted to know more about the eye-witness to the accident. Officer Hughes told me what he knew. "All we have is a report from the dispatcher who took the call."

I was surprised. "No actual statement from the witness?"

"None."

"Would you read the dispatcher's statement to me?"

"Here goes: A man called in at four twenty-three a.m. and said, 'There's been an accident on I-88 between Central Bridge and Cobleskill. A car flipped over the guard rails.' I told him to hold on a minute, I'd connect him to a police officer. He said he couldn't hold, he was in a hurry. 'Just tell the police where the accident occurred. I think the driver's drunk. She was all over the road.' The man disconnected, and I radioed for a black and white to report to the scene."

"That's it?"

"That's it."

"I wonder how the caller knew the driver was a woman?"

Investigator Hughes chuckled. "Guess it was obvious from the way she was driving."

I couldn't keep the edge out of my voice. "I assume you're aware of Ms. Hollis' statement that another vehicle pushed her Jeep over the rails?"

"That's what she says, but there's no corroboration. On the other hand, we have a witness who says Hollis was all over the road."

"Some witness," I said, annoyed.

"And there's the matter of her blood alcohol level being point zero five."

"That's only a D.W.A.I., and maybe she wouldn't have been charged with that if there hadn't been a death."

"Probably not, but there was a death. Hey, you hear Hollis is a dyke?"

Now Hughes had me grinding my teeth. "What's that got to do with the accident?"

"Maybe they were having a lover's spat and she lost control of the car."

"Investigator, is it possible that your prejudice against lesbians is shutting your mind to the possibility that Hollis is telling the truth?"

"Don't get your back up, Sinclair. For your information, my sister's a dyke, for chrissake. It's just that we got nothin' to go on here."

"Well, I believe her," I said.

His sigh was audible. "Find something we can use and give me a call."

"You can be sure I will, Investigator. In the meantime will you send me a copy of the dispatcher's statement?"

"Will do." We hung up.

I dialed Anne Hollis' home number and her machine picked up on the fourth ring. Hearing the sound of her voice was so unnerving I almost hung up without leaving a message. I was about to try her at Hooper's, but decided instead to stop by during my lunch hour. I called Claudia Powell, Beth's sister, in Cohoes, a twenty minute drive in good traffic. We arranged to meet at her apartment.

At the turn of the century, Cohoes was a booming mill town divided into three areas; The French population settled on "the Hill," the Italians on "the Island," and everyone else in what is called "the City." Claudia Powell lived in a two-family white house on "the Hill."

The plastic strip beneath the bottom doorbell had the name

DESNOYER scratched in pencil. The one beneath the top bell read BOURGOISES/POWELL. I pushed the button and waited. A baby shrieked somewhere in the distance. I watched a carpenter ant scurry across the grey porch, rushing towards the far end where a baby carriage was parked. I rang the bell again.

Claudia Powell was breathless when she opened the door. "Officer Sinclair? I'm Claudia, c'mon up. That's my kid screaming in case you're wondering."

I followed her upstairs into a living room littered with baby toys. The apartment was typical of Cohoes with a medium-sized parlor, formal dining room/family room, an eat-in kitchen, and a bathroom off to the side. Off the parlor were tiny bedrooms. Closets were almost non-existent.

"Sorry for the mess," she said, leading me into the kitchen. The baby screamed from her play pen in the middle room. Claudia picked her up, reducing the shrieks to a whimper.

"What's her name?" I asked politely even though I recognized Beth's niece.

"Teresa, after my mother. We call her Terri. Here," she said, pulling a kitchen chair out.

I sat down. "She's beautiful."

"Thanks. Can I get you a cup of coffee?"

"No, I'm fine, thank you. As I explained on the phone, I'm investigating the accident involving your sister and Anne Hollis. I'd like to ask you some questions about Beth."

Before I'd even begun, Claudia's face mottled and her eyes filled. "Jeez," she muttered. "I didn't think I would do this. Can you hand me one of those tissues?" She wiped her eyes and blew her nose. "I don't know how I'm gonna get over this. Beth was absolutely the sweetest kid. Kid! She was twenty-five, but she was my baby sister, you know." She sniffed and wiped some more.

I offered to come back another day. She shook her head. "I'll be okay. What do you need to know?"

"Did Beth discuss her feelings about the church with you?"

"Yes. To a point. I never wanted Beth to be a nun, and I let her know that, but it was something she wanted all her life. She talked about it ever since she was a little kid. You know what happens when you go to Catholic School? They try to recruit you. Those nuns are as good as the goddamn Marines. It was like you had three choices. You could be a nun or a school teacher or a secretary. I was a secretary for an insurance company, and I hated it, but at least I didn't end up trapped in the convent. Beth didn't like me to talk that way, but sometimes I couldn't help myself. Hey, do you mind holding Terri for a minute? I've got to get a clean diaper."

"I'd love it." As I placed my pen on the table, Terri's pudgy baby hands reached out to me. She came willingly into my arms, giggling. Scents of baby powder and wet diaper assailed my nostrils, but I didn't mind. "Hi, sweetie pie," I cooed. The ticking of my biological clock was almost audible.

"Here, I'll take her back," Claudia said. "Mommy wants to change you. That's a good baby." Claudia laid the baby on the table and stripped her wet diaper off. Terri laughed. "So where was I? Oh, yeah. Beth going into the convent. For the most part, she was happy. Until lately, anyway. If you want my opinion, she was getting ready to split."

"What makes you say that?"

"A few times during the past month she's called and asked me to cover for her with Sister Laura. You know, for her whereabouts on weekends and one or two evenings."

"Did she say why?"

"Beth was very private. She never offered any explanation. And I didn't ask."

"Did Sister Laura actually check up on her?"

"Only once. One morning she called and said Beth had not come home the night before, asked if she was with me."

"Was she?"

"No, but I said she was because Beth had called me the day before and told me Sister Laura had given her permission to spend the night away. I understand there was a big deal over that one, Beth insisting she had Laura's permission, and Laura denying she had ever spoken with Beth."

"Did it bother you to lie for her?"

"Nah, as I said, I would have loved for Beth to get out of there. I'm sure lying bothered Beth a lot. She was always so honest. It must have been something important to her because even as a kid she always confessed, even if it meant getting a spanking."

"Did Beth ever come right out and tell you she was going to leave the convent?"

"Not in so many words, but she talked about being less and less able to take her final vows. She said she felt confused about things, but she didn't say what those things were."

"Do you have any idea where she may have been spending her time?" I wanted to step lightly in finding out how much Claudia knew or guessed about Beth's changing lifestyle.

"Not until the accident. That Friday was one of the nights she'd told them at the convent house that she would be here. Instead I guess she was spending time with this Anne Hollis."

"So you don't know Ms. Hollis?"

"We never met. I heard she was in jail during the funeral. I also heard she claims they were pushed off the road by another car, but the police don't believe her. Paul told me. The baby's father. One of the guys he works with has a brother in the police department. They say she had been drinking. He also said Hollis owns a gay bar. Do you know if that's true?"

"It's a women's bar," I said, "called Hooper's."

"I wonder if that's why Beth had been acting different lately, you know?"

"What do you mean?"

Claudia turned her eyes away from mine. "I wouldn't have been shocked if Beth was coming out. She's always been a tomboy, preferred playing with boys as a kid. Then when she got older, she wasn't interested in dating them. I don't ever remember her having crushes on guys, but I guess I chalked it up to her decision to be a nun."

"Did Beth ever talk to you about any of the other sisters?"

"Not in any detail," she said, closing the snaps on Terri's shorts. "As I said, she was pretty private. She talked about Sister Jackie, and I don't think she liked Sister Laura much. Most of the other nuns are quite a bit older." Her mind seemed to drift away for a moment. "Ouch," she grunted, as the baby pumped her legs into her mother's chest. "This kid packs a hell of a kick." She rubbed her left breast. Then she leveled a look on me. "Do you believe what Anne Hollis says is true? Do you think someone did ram their car on purpose?"

"I don't know, Claudia. I'm trying to find a reason...a motive. Did Beth tell you she'd been followed?"

Claudia's face registered shock. "No, she never said a word. Who followed her?"

"I don't know that either. Can you think of anyone who'd want to hurt Beth?"

"No way," she said. "Like I said, Beth was the sweetest thing. She was always doing nice things. She volunteered at a local animal shelter, and every so often she'd take dogs to visit elderly folks at a nursing home. When one of the nuns had open heart surgery, Beth visited her every day until she was released from the hospital. Let me show you her picture." She ran into the next room to fetch an eight by ten glossy in a cheap goldtone frame. "It's old, her high school senior picture. Looked like a nun even then, didn't she?"

Beth had the look all right. If she had been a public school kid, people would have said she looked like a P.E. major, but in Catholic school, she looked like a surefire nun candidate.

"She looks so serious, with her Mona Lisa smile," I remarked.

"Yeah, well, that was Beth all right." Claudia sighed and took the photograph back.

"Sister Laura told me Beth had her own car, one that you gave to her."

"Can you believe the Order doesn't allow a nun to own a car? You either share the one owned by the convent, or if you work for the diocese, you get to use one of theirs. So me and Paul talked about it, and we gave Beth my old car when I bought a new one. We didn't actually put it in her name. We kept it in mine because of the insurance. I think it pissed Sister Laura off."

"I think you're right about that. Does the word or name Ace mean anything to you?"

"Ace?" She shook her head. "No, should it?"

"I don't know. Someone printed the letters A-C-E on the car's dashboard."

"Jeez, I'll give it some thought. If I come up with something, I'll let you know."

"Thanks." I flipped my pad closed and said, "One last thing, Claudia. Does anyone benefit financially from Beth's death?"

"You mean insurance?"

"Any way at all."

"All she had was a small policy from when we were kids. But the total amount is only fifteen hundred dollars. As far as money goes, she didn't have any yet because Rose Vanderslice is still alive. Lately, though, I hear Rose isn't doing very well."

The name was news to me. "Who's Rose Vanderslice?"

"One of Loudonville's grandest matrons. Her granddaughter, I forget her name, was a patient at Foxmoor, one of Beth's alcoholic clients. A teenager. She tried to commit suicide one night, but Beth and Jackie saved her life. I don't know all the details, but grandma Rose was very grateful. She's awarded Beth and Jackie a million dollars upon her death."

A million dollars? I almost exclaimed. A million dollars could make for a million motives! Calm down, I told myself, then said flatly, "But you say she's not doing well, this grateful grandmother?"

"Just hanging on, I guess. I read in the paper that she's at St. Peter's."

"Do you happen to know the details of the will?"

"Both girls get half a million, unless one of them dies before Rose. Then the half million goes to the surviving nun."

"So as far as you know, Jackie became eligible for the entire million when Beth died?" I said with emphasis.

"That's right." She stroked her chin. "But shit, there's no way Jackie would've done anything to Beth. No way."

"How can you be so sure?"

Claudia looked incredulous. "Jackie was her best friend! Jeez."

Well, maybe Claudia could say 'Jeez', but I knew for a fact, then and there, that I was going to have another little chat with Jackie, and that this time she was going to have a lot less to hide from me— jealousy and a million bucks for starters.

FOUR

A BMW was pulling out of a parking space in front of Hooper's so I grabbed the spot, then sat in my car a few minutes getting up the nerve to go in. I didn't know whether it was because I'd have to face Anne again, or whether it was the fact that I actually had to walk into a bar. Screw it, I thought, and pushed through the front door.

The first thing that hit me was the overwhelming smell of stale beer and whiskey. It's a wonder I didn't get sick just on the smell alone. I've heard of smokers who after quitting become intolerant of cigarette smoke. Well, even though I hadn't been in a bar in ten years, I didn't want to breathe. Fighting back my repulsion I adjusted my vision to the dim interior.

The second was the sight of Anne Hollis behind the bar. She was wearing a yellow and white rugby shirt tucked into white jeans, gold hoop earrings, and a gold bracelet.

When Anne saw me her eyes did one of those quick up and down scans, beginning with the head, then down to the feet and back up again. If a man did that, I'd be pissed, but I was never offended when a woman looked at me that way. And having Anne's eyes undress me made me forget the smell of alcohol.

She smiled. "I like your shirt. Blue is one of my favorite colors."

I smiled back. "Thanks, but you wouldn't want to get too close to me. Claudia Powell's baby, Terri, threw up on me and I probably smell like sour milk."

"I'll get you some cold water for that." She turned away to the sink.

I slid onto a stool and laid my sunglasses on the bar. Anne handed me a glass of cold water and a cloth napkin, then slid a paper coaster in front of me. "What'll you have to drink?" she asked.

"Diet Coke, please." I wet the napkin and began rubbing at my shoulder, trying to see the stain which was past my line of vision.

"Pepsi okay?" She filled a glass with ice.

"Great. I don't suppose you have caffeine-free?"

"Sorry." She hesitated at the taps. "Want 7-Up instead?"

"No. I'll take the Pepsi."

Anne placed the glass in front of me and walked around to my side of the bar. "Here," she said, "you'd better let me do that." She took the damp napkin from my hand, then slipped her other hand beneath the collar of my shirt in order to hold the material away from my shoulder. The touch of her fingers on my skin entranced me. She leaned towards me, her face almost against my neck. "Mmmmm. Can't smell Terri anymore, just you." I blushed at her seduction, then stiffened, but she had already backed away.

I mumbled my thanks, and forced myself to look around the room. The bar was to the left of the entrance, with tables and chairs surrounding a tiny dance floor in the center of the room. A jukebox and an old upright piano shared an alcove.

Two elderly men sat at the opposite end of the bar drinking beers. I nodded toward them and said, "I thought this was a women's bar."

"It is," she replied, straight-faced. "That's what lesbians look like when they get old." Then she laughed. A wonderful sound from deep in her throat. "Those guys are locals. I don't get much gay trade during the day. So, did you get the package I dropped off yesterday?"

"Yes, I skimmed through most of Beth's diary last night. Thanks for bringing it by." I used my most professional voice, not wanting her to know how eager I was to talk about it.

She nodded. "Can you tell me how your meeting with her sister went?"

I took a sip of my Pepsi. "So far I haven't heard anything I can't share with you," I said. "Did Beth tell you she was about to inherit half a million dollars?"

"You're kidding? Who from?" Anne's astonishment seemed to be genuine.

"A woman named Rose Vanderslice. According to Claudia, Beth and Jackie saved her granddaughter's life, so she willed each of them a half million. The interesting part is that because Beth died before Rose did, Jackie gets the full million."

Anne stared at me. "That means Jackie had a motive."

"Two motives actually."

"Two? What's the other?"

I sounded lighter than I felt. "Beth made an entry in her diary— 'No matter what I have shared with Anne I will always love Jackie.' She also mentioned how Jackie was jealous of you. I'm wondering just how jealous."

Anne frowned. "What are you suggesting?"

I took a deep breath. "Maybe that you and Beth were having an affair, Jackie found out about it, became very jealous, and using some car or other from who knows where, pushed you both off the highway."

"Yes, but why would a nun who wants to remain a nun and who stands to inherit a half million dollars herself kill her best friend and lover for the other half? I don't get it."

I shook my head. "I don't see Jackie as a killer. Something's missing, Anne."

"Excuse me a minute," she said moving to the other end of the bar. "You fellas ready for a refill on those beers?" One of them said something to her that I couldn't hear. Anne laughed and said, "She's comin' on in a few minutes." She poured their beers, then poured a glass of white wine which she placed on a coaster next to my Pepsi.

I looked at the glass horrified, even as the smell assaulted my nose. Surely, she wasn't going to drink on the job. As a bartender she had to know it was against the law, besides she had said she didn't drink while she worked.

She took the money from the men, rang it up on the register, then returned to my side of the bar and slid onto a stool next to mine, fingered the wine glass, saying, "Don't worry, I'm off in a few minutes." Then, without looking at me, she said, "Look, I did sleep with her once, Callie."

Her words smarted, and I was really pissed at myself for feeling the old familiar sting of jealousy again. That wasn't why I was here. I didn't meet her eyes when I asked, "Do you know if Beth shared that information with Jackie?"

"She said she would."

So, if she had, Jackie was hiding at least one thing when I talked to her.

"Jackie told me that Beth and you claimed to be only friends." My tone was too accusing.

"Look, Callie," Anne said angrily, "I'm not going to make excuses for myself. It was an honest mistake—we settled it. She wanted things to work out with Jackie."

We sat in silence for a while, Anne rotating her glass of wine, me pretending to look through my notes.

She spoke first. "Have you talked to anyone else?"

"Only Laura Bennett, the Mother Superior—and Jackie. Oh, and I took a look at Beth's car. Maybe you can tell me where she might have driven. The car's interior is full of road dust."

"Hmmmm. She used the car to go out to my place in Cobleskill a couple of nights before the accident. Wednesday, I think. I wasn't with her; I'm usually only out there on weekends. Sometimes Beth liked to be completely alone, so I let her use my place. There's a dirt road out by the reservoir where Beth would go to sit by the water. I'll bet that's where she went. Do you think her going there is important?"

"Possibly." Having Anne so close to me was intoxicating. I wanted to trace my finger along the side of her cheek. Instead I said, "Anne, does the name Ace sound familiar to you?"

"I don't think so. Why?"

"I found the word written in the dust on Beth's dashboard. I'm not even sure the letters are meant to be a name." I drew the letters on the shiny surface of the bar with the tip of my finger: ACE. "The word could be a clue, or nothing at all."

"Callie, do you think the information about the million dollars is enough to convince the police to investigate this?"

"That's doubtful, Anne. Rose Vanderslice is still alive, so technically there is no million dollar inheritance. I'll try to talk with her next, see what I can find out."

The door opened and a tall gaunt woman strode in wearing black jeans and a western shirt with a scarf tied around her neck. Her sand-colored hair was crewcut short. We both took one look at each other, but she spoke first, whooped was more like it, "C.J., you old sonofabitch, how the hell are ya?"

I stood and caught Tink in a bear hug. "I'm fine, buddy, how are you?"

Anne stared at us, raising her eyebrows. "You know each other?"

Tink's grin was wide. "Know each other? Hell yes! C.J. and me go way back to the Hudson Arms, don't we C.J.?"

Anne looked shocked. "C.J.?"

"For Callie Jean," I whispered, embarrassed by the attention Tink's arrival focused on me.

Tink turned to Anne, chuckling. "Say, boss, is C.J. the 'hot probation officer' you were talkin' about last night?"

I know I should have cringed but I was used to Tink not knowing to spare one's sensitivity.

It was Anne who flushed hotly! "Don't you have work to do, Tink? Your buddies at the end of the bar have been asking for you."

Tink looked down the bar. "'Course they are. I told'em I'd buy 'em both a beer if the Yanks won last night and don'tcha know they did? Shit. Say, C.J., it's good seeing you again."

"Same here, Tink. See you later." Tink walked down to where the guys were sitting, leaving me and Anne by ourselves.

Anne leaned her back against the bar, hands folded across her stomach, elbows on the bar. I perched on the stool next to her and grinned. "So..."

Anne blushed. "Tink has a big mouth."

"Some things never change."

"I'm not sure the word I used was 'hot.' I think what I said was that I thought you were very attractive."

I laughed, embarrassed, and searched my mind for the right words to say, but none came.

"Well," Anne said. "Now that that's out of the way, where were we?"

"I don't remember."

"I think you were saying something about Rose Vanderslice."

Anne was gazing directly into my eyes, flustering the hell out of me.

"Oh, God," I murmured, beginning to stammer, "Anne, I, uh…."

"Yes?" She leaned closer, obviously amused by my discomfort.

"I'm trying to say two things. First, that I'm very attracted to you, and second, that there are definite department rules against probation officers becoming personally involved with defendants or probationers."

"What does that mean, Callie? That we can't be friends?"

I shook my head. "Not yet. Not until we get your case discharged."

Anne backed away. "Don't worry," she said, her smile intact. "I won't compromise our professional relationship by coming on to you."

I sighed. "The problem is that part of me wants to be compromised."

"Ah, but what does the other part want?"

I hesitated, overwhelmed by frustration. "To be ethical," I said. "But at the moment that's the very smallest part of me."

We were both quiet for a few moments, then Anne spoke. "So where do we go from here?"

"The first thing we have to do is prove your innocence," I said, glancing at my watch. "I'd better run over to St. Pete's. Try to see Rose Vanderslice. I may also want to see Jackie again. How about if I catch up with you later? Maybe we can have dinner together if you don't mind getting together rather late."

Anne sighed. "In this business I do everything late."

Traffic on New Scotland Avenue was stop and go, but I didn't care. I was too busy trying to shake thoughts of Anne Hollis out of my head. I needed to concentrate on the Hollis file, not the Hollis body. I stared at the car in front of me. The driver was a bumper sticker freak into contradictions, one reading: IF YOU DON'T LIKE MY DRIVING, DIAL 1-800-EAT SHIT, while the other read, YOU HAVE A FRIEND IN JESUS. I looked at his license plate, BEN 231.

"Holy Shit," I said aloud. "ACE. That's the solution!" I looked around for a pay phone and spied a drug store half a block up. I parked illegally and ran in, hastily dialing my office to speak with Marylou. When she came on the line I asked her to access NYSPIN, the New York State Police Information Network, and to generate a list of all vehicles registered in New York State beginning with the prefix ACE. She promised to have the list ready for me first thing in the morning.

I found that Rose Vanderslice had a private room. Her bed was empty when I arrived, so I sat in one of the visitor's chairs and waited. The room looked more like a motel room than a hospital room. Instead of paint, the walls were papered, and the drapes matched the bedspread. Several magazines were scattered on a table, and the television, volume low, was tuned to a daytime soap. I picked up a magazine and read an article on 'how to enjoy the warmth, charm and comfort of country living no matter where you live' until Rose Vanderslice entered the room in a wheelchair pushed by a nurse. She was hooked to an I.V. which rode alongside on wheels.

She surprised me. I expected wrinkles, drool, and pallor, but what I got was cold hard steel. "Who are you?" she bellowed.

I stood up, fishing for my badge. "I'm Officer Callie Sinclair," I said, "with the Department of Probation."

"Let me see that." She grabbed my I.D. "Where're my glasses." She glared at the nurse. "Angela, you know I can't read without my glasses." The nurse handed her the glasses, but instead of putting them on she used them like a magnifying glass, holding the glass above my photo. "That's you alright. Good picture. Does the Department of Probation hire professional photographers to take these pictures?"

"No ma'am," I said, returning the identification to my bag.

"You should see the picture on my driver's license," she said, narrowing her eyes. "I look like a cross between Lauren Bacall and Humphrey Bogart." She laughed, revealing very large white teeth. "So, what's a probation officer want with me?"

"I'd like to ask you some questions about your relationship with sisters Mary Elizabeth Powell and Jacqueline Prescott."

Her face softened, but not her voice. "They told me Sister Mary Elizabeth died a couple of weeks ago. I was sorry to hear that." She turned to her nurse. "I don't need to get right back into bed. Why don't you go smoke a couple of those vulgar cigarettes of yours so this young woman and I can have some privacy." The nurse hesitated. "Go on, I'm not going to croak while you're gone, but if I do

I'm sure this young woman can handle things." She looked at me. "Can't you?"

I smiled at the nurse. "I'll call if she needs you."

The nurse left, wearing a long suffering look, and Mrs. Vanderslice turned to me. "Being in a hospital today is the pits. They're so short staffed I've had to hire my own nurses 'round the clock. Good thing I'm dying. The world's changed too much the wrong way. So, what do you want to know?"

"I was told you willed Sister Mary Elizabeth and Sister Jackie each five hundred thousand dollars."

"Who told you that?"

"I'm sorry, Mrs. Vanderslice, but I can't reveal…"

She waved her arm at me. "Doesn't matter. Nothing is private anymore. What else?"

I cleared my throat. "And that if one of them should pre-decease you the other will inherit the entire million."

"That's right. And did this informant also tell you that if they both pre-decease me, the money goes to their order, the Sisters of St. James Retirement Fund?"

That was a surprise. "No, ma'am."

"Of course that's not likely to happen. The doctors told me I've only got three months left, but what do they know? They're all idiots, and Sister Jackie's in the pink, isn't she?"

"Yes, she is."

"Good. I wonder what she'll do with all that money. Do you think she'll stay in the convent? So many young women are leaving today. Can't blame them. Are you Catholic?"

"I was raised Catholic, yes."

"What's that supposed to mean?" she thundered. "That you've stopped going to church?"

"I'm more comfortable in a different church today," I replied, steeling myself for a lecture.

Instead she cackled. "I go to the Spiritualist church, myself, over on Whitehall, but don't tell Bishop Hubbard or I might not get my last rites."

I smiled. "Mrs. Vanderslice, just so I'm certain I have this correct, if both Jackie and Beth pre-decease you the entire million goes to the convent?"

"To the sisters' retirement fund," she corrected. "Young lady, why are you asking me these questions? What business is my will of the probation department?"

"I'm sorry. I should have explained my interest sooner. There's some evidence that Sister Mary Elizabeth's death may not have been an accident. I'm looking for a motive."

"Sounds like you're thinking money is the motive."

"Money often is."

"Well, I'll bet a lot of folks would say you're barking up the wrong tree by looking in a convent for a murder motive, right?"

I smiled. "Some would, yes."

"Well, I disagree with them. Where money is concerned, you'll find evil in the most unlikely places."

Her response surprised me. "Mrs. Vanderslice, do you think Sister Jackie is capable of murder?"

"Absolutely not! Where'd you get such a preposterous idea?"

"You just said..."

"What I said was to look in the convent. The convent! Not at Sister Jackie!" Mrs. Vanderslice leaned forward and continued in a conspiratorial whisper. "Everybody thinks the Catholic church is the richest business in the world, and I quite agree. So where's all the money go? Hah! Ask the priests! The old nuns who have no money get placed wherever the church can find some spot. No way to support themselves as they choose when they retire. They could make good use of a million dollars."

I stood up. "I appreciate your talking with me," I said.

"You're welcome," she said. "And now that I've solved your case for you, will you fetch that nurse back here for me?"

I telephoned Foxmoor from the hospital's lobby, and asked Jackie if I could talk with her. She met me at the door, and led me to her office, a small room with barely enough space for a desk and two chairs. The desk was pushed against the left wall. Anyone entering the room would get a side view of Jackie. Her visitor would also be seated on the side. I figured this would give Jackie an opportunity to swivel her chair so that she'd be knee to knee with her client, which is both cozy and non-threatening, provided the client isn't claustrophobic.

I glanced around the room. A framed poster of the Albany skyline hung over the desk. No photographs, no plants, no little tacky knicky-knackies. Her office was very much like her bedroom.

"Have a seat," she said, pulling her swivel chair away from the desk. She sat down and faced me, crossing her left ankle over her right knee. It was not an action I would have expected from her—more like her to cross her feet at the ankles. Such a butch gesture seemed out of place, as if she were putting on a bold front. And I couldn't help seeing her legs—they were shaved.

"I just came from St. Peter's," I said. "I was visiting Rose Vanderslice." I watched her face for a reaction, and was not surprised when I didn't get one. "I was confirming the information I received that you are soon to become a millionaire." Still nothing. "Why didn't you tell me about the money when we met yesterday?"

"What money?"

"Can it, Jackie, I'm not playing games with you today."

She glowered. "I didn't think that inheritance was any of your business."

"There's a strong possibility that your best friend was murdered, and it's my job to find out why. That means I'm searching for a motive, and a half million dollars sounds like a good one."

Her eyes widened. "You can't think I murdered Beth!"

"I need to explore every possibility."

"I can't believe this, " she said. "And you think money was my motive?"

I shrugged my shoulders; she shook her head. If I did believe the half million dollars was a good enough motive for homicide, then who else but Jackie would have murdered Beth? And if Jackie wasn't the murderer, but money was the motive, then Jackie was very likely in danger too.

Interrupting my awful realization, she blurted, "I don't have a car!"

"For half a million, one can always find an accomplice." I pressed.

"I'm going to be a nun—" For a minute it seemed like she was about to swear. "Look, the money wasn't going to be for our personal use. We discussed it. It had nothing to do with us, it would have gone to charity!"

Hm. Should I believe Rose Vanderslice's theory then, that a

bunch of old nuns, desperate for a retirement fund, would knock off Beth in the hopes that the money for charity would channel through them—only to stop with them on the way? Nah.

"Money is one motive, Jackie, there could be others. I'd like to talk about your relationship with Beth—"

"We've already been through all that," she almost wailed. "I have nothing more to add." She had pulled her legs up under herself in the chair, huddled.

"I have Beth's diary."

"So?" The wary expression on her face belied her casual tone.

"In her diary Beth talks about her feelings for you and also for Anne Hollis. She maintained that you were jealous of Anne."

Jackie sputtered, "I was angry, not jealous. Anne Hollis took advantage of Beth's innocence by sleeping with her."

"How's that?"

"Beth expressed certain feelings for me that I couldn't return in the same way. We had taken a vow of chastity and she was having trouble. As you know, she was uncertain about her sexuality, and I believe that if Anne Hollis hadn't seduced her into her bed, into her way of life, Beth would have come around to her first vocation and recaptured the serenity of convent life."

"You're saying that Beth's desire to leave the convent was a result of her relationship with Anne Hollis?"

"Yes. After Beth met Anne, she changed, she became more demanding. She asked me to leave with her."

"But you refused."

"This is my calling! I had hoped to convince her to remain...."

"With you. Discreetly."

"Yes." her voice was barely audible. She began to weep. I was speechless. I'm uncomfortable in a nurturing role, so I didn't offer my shoulder, nor did I pat hers. I simply waited.

Jackie's sobs were becoming wracking, and I was worried she was going to throw up in that small office. That's what happens to me if I let myself cry too hard. I took a deep breath and stood up. Moving behind her chair I placed my hands on her shoulders and rubbed, speaking as gently as I could. "Jackie, try to get control. Crying is good, but I'm afraid you're going to make yourself sick."

"You think I killed Beth," she sobbed.

"No, I don't think that," I said, leaning close to her ear. "I don't think you had anything to do with what happened to Beth, but I'm going to need more information from you."

She was slowing down to what I call hiccup sobs. "I don't (sob) know anything (sob) else (sob)."

I moved away from her and sat down, keeping one hand on her arm. I squeezed gently and said, "I need to know who else besides the convent would benefit from your death."

"My death?" She pulled her arm away.

"Let's say Mrs. Vanderslice died yesterday and you've inherited one million dollars. Who would get the million if you died and you had no chance to give it to charity?"

"Oh." She shrugged. "My mother would. She's the only family I have."

"You wouldn't leave any to the convent sisters?"

She frowned. "I guess so. I suppose I'd have to have my will changed."

"You have a will?"

"Yes." She smiled and blew her nose. "Once a nun has taken her Final Vows she's required to have a will if she owns any property. One of my clients at Foxmoor is an attorney and told me I should have one now, even though I'm not due to take Final Vows for another two years. She did the will for me for free. I don't own very much, a few thousand dollars in a savings account which my grandmother left me, rosary beads made of real rubies, also from my grandmother, a fourteen carat gold crucifix, and a pair of skis."

"What does your will say?"

"That everything goes to my mother except the crucifix, which I left to Beth." Fresh tears came to her eyes and she dabbed at them with a tissue.

"Your mother is your only living relative?"

"Yes."

"What about a father?"

"He died several years ago. My mother remarried, but I'm not really close to my stepfather."

"Brothers or sisters?" She shook her head. I pulled my notebook out of my bag. "Does your mother live in the area?"

"Guilderland. Why are you writing that down?"

"I write everything down, Jackie. What are their names?"

She frowned. "Pam and Harry Loomis. You're not going to bother my mother with this, are you? She'd be upset, and she doesn't know anything, really."

"I'll try not to bother her, but I can't promise." I reached out to Jackie and took her hand. "Do you have anyone you can talk to about all this? Somebody who can help you work through your grief?"

She shook her head. "I'm okay. I don't need anyone."

I took one of my cards out of my wallet and wrote a phone number on the back. "This is the number of a good friend of mine. She's a therapist, and a former nun. If things get too rough for you, give her a call."

FIVE

I got home at five-thirty, called the Quintessence restaurant to make dinner reservations for eight, then phoned Anne at Hooper's to ask if she would meet me there. I didn't want to pick Anne up in my car and be in the awkward position of dropping her off late at night, as if we were on a date. I rationalized that if I didn't think of our having dinner together as a date, it wasn't a date, and my conscience would be clear.

I changed into shorts and a boxy T-shirt, slipped an Anne Murray tape into my Walkman, and did a few stretches before embarking on a thirty minute walk through the development. When I returned, I took a long hot shower and thumbed through my closet for something to wear for dinner with Anne Hollis.

Wanting to look casual, I tucked a kelly-green shirt into a pair of khaki chinos, and slipped my feet into tan woven huaraches.

When I walked into Quintessence, Anne was standing in the tiny reception area. She wore a skin-tight black jumpsuit tucked into black leather boots, a turquoise and silver belt accentuating her waist. She turned to me and smiled, her lips shimmering crimson, her eyes challenging. Having left the top three buttons undone, it didn't take much imagination to know she wasn't wearing a bra and that if she moved in just the right way I would have a clear view of her cleavage. Instantly, I was absorbed in a fantasy involving Anne in a black camisole and garter belt, pulling black stockings over creamy thighs.

Right. I could also remember Jackie saying that Anne had seduced an innocent Beth. Or else this was Anne's idea of casual, businesslike attire.

The hostess seated us at a back table, complete with cut flowers and candlelight. Blowing the candle out would have been gauche so I left it alone, hoping to ignore the glow of the candle's light against Anne's skin, the way the flame sparkled in her eyes.

The waiter took our order: a glass of Chablis for Anne, a diet Coke for me, and the house special, chicken terriyaki.

"I'm glad you chose Quintessence, Callie. I love their food."

"I do, too," I said with a deep breath. "I like everything about the place, except their taste in music."

"You're not a fan of jazz?"

"Not the improvisational stuff," I said, grimacing. "For me, jazz is akin to scraping chalk on a blackboard."

She laughed. "What kind of music do you like?"

"Will you respect me in the morning if I tell you I love country and western?"

"Of course," she said, quizzically. "What's wrong with that?"

"Used to be, if you said you liked country music some people would get a smug look on their faces."

"No." She laughed again.

"Yes. Country music is simple, so, supposedly, the people who listen to it are also unsophisticated." I shrugged a shoulder. "I like the rhythm of country music, and I especially like Reba, Juice, and k.d.. And what about you? Tell me you're into jazz and chamber music."

"My taste in music is pretty diverse. At home I listen to classical or rhythm and blues, but most of the music I'm exposed to comes from the juke box at Hooper's."

"Rock?"

"Rock and roll, Callie. There's a difference. The juke box is filled with oldies, just as many ballads as up tunes. Patsy Cline, Brenda Lee. You can actually slow dance at Hooper's."

"You're kidding? No Saturday night D.J.?"

Anne shook her head. "Only once a month to attract the younger set. But that's very expensive. I get some live music on occasion— more like a coffee house atmosphere then. But ends don't always meet. I suppose if I were the only women's bar in town, I'd be fine, but I'm not. It's a constant experiment to make a go of it. Like any small business, I guess. I invested all I had to get it going, and it takes a constant reinvestment. I guess I wanted it to be an old-fashioned bar with a regular clientele."

I nodded in agreement remembering my bar days. "Pool table, jukebox with music you can dance to?"

"Exactly. But you have to keep up with the scene, with what younger women want."

Pouring house dressing over my salad, I said, "You seem to be doing okay though, Anne—a house out in Cobleskill. Countryside is beautiful out there."

Anne's eyes sparkled. "Have you ever driven from Cobleskill to Albany in the morning, Callie? When the early morning sun shines on those hills, the trees, fields...well, it's like a Grandma Moses print. I'm lucky to have the house, but I can afford it only because I don't have a mortgage."

I raised my eyebrows. "Nice."

"Yes, well nothing comes without its price. The house belonged to my ex-husband, a camp then, really. I did some work on it. I was married many years ago, very young, very foolishly, to a man who was abusive."

"You got the house in a divorce settlement?"

She shook her head. "Bobby was killed in Viet Nam. I inherited it and enough money to fix it up. I cherish the house but during the winter months it's a struggle to pay additional utility bills, and the taxes take a big chunk out of my monthly income."

I picked at my salad and thought about Anne's financial difficulties. Maybe Beth's inheritance would have kept Hooper's in the black, but as far as I knew Beth hadn't willed any to Anne. Seemed to me, Anne would have benefitted from Beth alive, as a generous friend—or lover. "How old were you when you got married, Anne?"

"Eighteen. We hardly knew each other and had very little time together before he was shipped out...Sometimes I feel guilty."

"Why? You said he was abusive."

"Yes, and if he had remained in the States I would have left him. I was in the process of filing for a divorce when he was killed. I inherited his house, insurance, everything."

"So at eighteen you were married...When did you come out as a lesbian?"

"I knew by the time I was fourteen—one of the dykelings at summer camp brought me out." Anne smiled ruefully. "I wish I could have accepted myself, but I struggled so much with my sexuality. When I think back on it, marrying Bobby was how I became very clear as to who I was, what I was."

The waiter brought our chicken, and I realized I was starved. I hadn't eaten lunch. Anne ordered another wine. "Wouldn't you like one or are you still on company time?"

"Another diet Coke would do just fine," I said, not wanting to talk about my alcoholism. After ten years of sobriety I still feel shame telling people outside the program that I'm an alcoholic. Most people see the stereotype: a bum on a street corner, guzzling booze from a bottle hidden in a brown paper bag. I didn't want Anne to see me that way, so I changed the subject back to her. I asked, "What did you do before you bought Hooper's?"

"Wrote promotion literature for a direct sales company for five years. After the first six months I hated every second of it, so I began saving my money to go into business for myself. When I had enough for a down payment, twelve months of operating expenses and six months of personal expenses, I quit my job. That was four years ago."

"How do you like operating a bar?" I had been asking so many questions, Anne hardly had a chance to eat. My chicken was half finished while Anne barely had more than a mouthful.

"The setting is comfortable. You see, my grandparents had a neighborhood bar and grill in New York City. After my grandfather had a stroke, my Dad ran it. I was raised in two rooms back of my grandfather's tavern, wheeled my doll carriage around the pool table. My grandmother used to sit at the table nearest the pot belly stove and watch Hopalong Cassidy on the black and white TV. A tavern feels like home to me, Callie. Dad taught me to tend bar to earn money while I went to college but he never wanted me to get into the business. Now I understand why. I rarely get a day off and the hours stink, but I like being my own boss."

The waiter brought our drinks. I peeled the paper from one end of my straw, and put the straw to my lips, the way you do when you're going to blow the wrapper across the table at your companion's nose. Instead of blowing the paper at Anne, I blew it into my hand. I didn't want to talk about bars anymore, and the thought of Anne benefitting in some way from Beth's inheritance brought my mind back to the case which was a good thing because I found my eyes straying to Anne's cleavage often enough to become embarrassing. So, I talked about my conversation that morning with the investigating officer, my idea about ACE being a partial license plate, and my later meetings with Rose Vanderslice and Jackie.

"So where does that leave us?" Anne asked.

"My secretary will have the NYSPIN printout in the morning, and I can meet you at Hooper's about one-thirty. Maybe you'll recognize a name or address. If not, I don't know. We may be at a standstill."

We left the restaurant at nine-thirty. The night air felt balmy, reminding me of Florida. I liked the feeling.

"Where's your car parked?" I asked. The neighborhood's unsafe, so I didn't want either of us walking around alone.

"Up the hill," she said.

"Mine, too." We crossed the street catty-corner. My Civic was half a block up. "Do you have to go back to work now?" I asked.

"Have something better in mind?" she asked, a smile on her lips.

"I was just curious." I could feel blood rush to my face and was glad for the cover of darkness, but as aroused as I was, I was also angry. Damn it, Anne, I thought, why are you doing this to me? I thought we had a deal. I began to wonder just why she had come to dinner dressed so seductively. What exactly was she trying to get out of me?

"I'm teasing you, Callie." Anne chuckled. Then she said, "You really do intend to keep this strictly business, don't you?"

"I'm trying, Anne." I took a deep breath. "But if you come any closer, I'll lose my resolve."

"And I'm not helping?"

I shook my head. "Not in the least. Not if you really want my help."

Anne stopped near a red Celica. "Here we are," she said.

"Very nice," I offered.

"Yes, it's Tink's. She loaned her car to me tonight because I still haven't replaced my Jeep."

"Oh, Anne, I'm sorry. I never gave transportation a thought when I invited you to dinner."

"That's all right, Callie. No problem." Anne smiled and extended her hand. "Good night, Officer Sinclair."

I took her hand and grinned. "I'll see you tomorrow."

As I drove home I thought about Anne's jumpsuit, the way the material fit so provocatively. Unlike me, she had dressed for seduction, and I wondered why. Was her attraction to me genuine or was that simply how she related as a bartender. Turning the ladies on just a bit, pouring another drink as she glanced across the brim of the glass, her lips pouting slightly, suggestively as she slipped the glass with its coaster over the smooth surface of the bar. An act? A habit?

I needed to learn more about Anne, her past, what made her tick. Hoping Tink might be able to supply some of those answers, I turned my car around and drove to Hooper's. I knew what I wanted to believe about Anne—or what she wanted me to believe—that she was sweet, innocent and sincere about her personal interest in me, yet I couldn't help suspecting a concealed motive.

Still angry with myself for becoming so captivated by Anne, I stomped out of my car and slammed the door, striding quickly across the street to Hooper's front door. I took a deep breath and prayed to my Higher Power that Anne not be inside.

My prayers were answered. Tink was behind the bar. She waved and smiled, beckoning me to a seat at the bar.

"The boss lady's already gone upstairs, C.J. Want me to tell her you're here?"

"No, Tink," I said, sliding onto a stool. "I want to see you, not Anne."

"Sounds groovy, but I'm still an hour away from closing. Can you hang around?"

"Sure," I said, swiveling around so I could catch the action on the dance floor.

"Still drinking whiskey sours on the rocks?"

I had forgotten that was my drink of choice. "A diet Pepsi will be fine."

Her voice became somber. "Oh yeah. I heard about that. How's it going?"

"Good, Tink. I've been sober ten years."

"Well, congratulations, I guess," she said with a shrug. "Be back in a flash."

I glanced around the room. Most bars are dark and smoky, and Hooper's was no exception. I was already resenting the fact that my hair and clothes would smell like cigarettes as I counted six women at the bar and maybe fifteen or so at the tables. Three couples were slow dancing to the music on the juke-box which was loud but not deafening.

Tink returned with my Pepsi and asked if I remembered a woman named Guzzy.

"Sure," I said. "Skinny, black hair. We played softball together. She could put away beer almost as good as I could."

"She's here," Tink said, pointing to a round table near the dance floor. "See if you can spot her."

I scanned the table Tink indicated, but none of the women looked like Guzzy.

"The fat one with bleached hair!"

"Oh my, she has changed over the last ten years..."

"So have you. Come on, I'll take you over. You can catch up on old times while I finish my shift." Tink ushered me to the table where five women were sharing a pitcher of beer. "Hey, Guzzy, look who I have here."

Guzzy squinted at me until recognition animated her face. "C.J!" She jumped up and bear-hugged me. "Don't hardly recognize you without a baseball cap on your head. Where the hell ya been? Last I heard you found religion."

I knew she meant A.A. Many people reject the program because the twelve steps talk about God or a Higher Power, not understanding that a Higher Power can be as simple as the air that dries the dishes after you've washed them.

"You must be wrong, Guzzy." I placed my Pepsi on the table and pulled up a chair, nodding to each of the women as Guzzy introduced me around.

"So, what brings you to Hooper's, C.J? Don't tell me it's the diet Pepsi they serve up here." She lit up a cigarette; I had forgotten she smoked.

Covering my real purpose, I just said, "Oh I ran into Tink earlier this week, thought I'd see what Hooper's was like. Do you come here much?"

"Once or twice a week. I like the peace and quiet. You go over to the other bars, you can't hear yourself think, let alone have a conversation. Besides I like the bartender."

"Tink?" I asked, dodging the smoke.

She smirked. "Hell no. I meant Anne, the dyke who owns this place. Too bad she's not on tonight."

My voice nonchalant, I said, "Oh yeah, I've seen her. Pretty."

"Hah! To say the least."

I wondered how well Guzzy knew Anne. "Is she involved with anyone?"

"Not now. Hey, don't go getting any ideas, C.J. You're not her type."

"Why's that?"

"She likes them young and fresh out of the closet. Well, that's what it was like before...She was getting it on with a nun, see, then they had a car accident and the nun got killed. Something about maybe Anne had been drinking which I don't believe, let me tell you. Not for one minute. Look at the sign over the door there, 'Who's your Designated Driver?' She'll never serve you if she thinks you've had enough. Anyway, she's in deep shit right now. But drunk, never. I've almost gone off the road a few times myself and it had nothing to do with drinking. Once I dropped my sandwich on the floor while I was eating and driving, and the other time was when I was having an all out fight with my lover. I hope she's got a good lawyer, you know, I'd hate to see her lose her liquor license."

Before I could ply her with more questions, a tall woman grabbed Guzzy by the shoulders. "Hey, Guzzy, let's dance."

"Excuse me, C.J., okay?" She stubbed her cigarette out on the ashtray under my nose.

"Sure, go ahead." I picked up my soda and walked back to the bar, feeling tired, annoyed with the cigarette smoke, and generally pissed because I was drinking Pepsi instead of a whiskey sour. I couldn't believe I was actually in a position so close to a drink. All I had to do was wave over to Tink and call out, "Whiskey sour on the rocks." Shit, I thought, I'd better call my A.A. sponsor.

Just the thought of Sadie strengthened me. The sponsors for straights in A.A. tend to be women for women and men for men to avoid romantic involvements. I knew several lesbians who were sponsored by gay men for just that reason too, but I knew I wouldn't be comfortable with that arrangement, allowing a man to be in a position of power over me. So I chose Sadie, straight, and an old-timer who had been in the program for thirty-four years. She was 'tough love' all the way. Whenever I started getting stupid I could depend on Sadie to smarten me up. I didn't want to think about what she'd say when I told her my ass was on a stool in Hooper's Bar.

"C.J., you look like shit and you haven't even been drinking." Tink interrupted my yawn.

"Thanks, Tink. How much more time till closing?"

"Half an hour, but we can talk now. Things are slowing down," she replied, watching as the group of women along with Guzzy getting ready to leave.

I felt a hand grip my shoulder. "Hey, C.J. it was good seeing you again." Guzzy was smiling at me, her eyes glassy. "Don't be such a stranger."

"Yeah, Guz. Take care." I waved to her friends as they strode out the door, joking over the responsibility of the designated driver who jangled her keys. I felt melancholy over how much of my youth I had wasted in bars like Hooper's, invariably drunk walking out the door with drivers in not much better shape than myself, and all the time lonely, eternally searching. What was I searching for?—love. How many more years had to pass before I learned that love is not finding the right person, but being the right person?

"So, what's the story, morning glory?" Tink poured herself a cup of coffee and came to sit next to me.

"Well, part of my job is to get background information on Anne, talk to the people who know her, find out as much as I can about her character so I can help her win this case."

"Cool. What do you need to know?"

"For starters, Tink, can you tell me about Anne's relationship to Beth?"

"Shit, yeah. Beth hung around here all the time for some months.

She kept saying she was in love with this other nun, but I knew she had the hots for Anne, know what I mean? I mean, who doesn't have the hots for Anne around here?" Tink smiled slyly. "But you probably noticed that yourself, right?"

I hoped my smile was benign because my heart was doing a dance, and I'm sure my cheeks were flaming. "Anne is very attractive," I acknowledged blandly while thoughts of her conjured words like erotic, sensual, passionate, and the feelings behind those words were propelling me towards insanity. "What is it about Anne that causes people to 'have the hots' for her, Tink? Does she come on to them?"

"She knows how to flirt, different with different people like she can size them up. Brash and off-the-cuff for some of the butchy dykes who come in, sometimes very femme, subtle. She told me once she watched how her grandmother tended the bar, real friendly like the bubbles in a chaser of soda water. It goes with serving drinks."

I guess I knew what kind of flirting she had done with me, and sat silently for a moment, thinking. Then said, "But it isn't just behind the bar that she does that. Does she...sleep around?"

"No way. More like playing hard to get and meaning it. There's a dyke who's been comin' around here lately, maybe once or twice a week. Name of Lee. Real truck driver, wears these damn blue overalls all the time and a cap down over her face sometimes like she was hiding or something. Real shy. Never picks anybody up. Leaves after Anne goes out. Anyway, this Lee just sits at the bar and stares at Anne all night long. Gives me the creeps, but Anne just laughs it off. She's as tough as they come. But when she falls it's like a ton of bricks, know what I mean?"

"Did she fall for Beth?"

"Yeah. She didn't tell me but I could see it. At first I think she felt sorry for her, mothered her. After a while it turned into something else, and all the time, Beth saying she was in love with Jackie. She was a ball of confusion, that one. And Anne wasn't keeping her distance any more."

"They became lovers?" Had Anne lied to me when she said they had only slept together once, and it was all settled?

"Is this just between you and me, C.J.?"

I knew that professionally I didn't need to know how many times they had slept together, but I had to know for myself. "Strictly confidential."

"Yeah, they became lovers. Beth wouldn't come in here any more, just go upstairs. At first Anne seemed real up, and Beth was acting needy because Anne talked to her on the phone a lot. But Beth was in love with Jackie, and so it was like she was using Anne to make Jackie jealous, trying to get her to leave the convent so they could be together."

"How did Anne handle Beth's confusion?"

"Anne was fighting with her on the phone about making up her mind what she wanted."

Hm, had Anne become jealous herself? Was she in a jealous rage herself that night she drove with Beth to Cobleskill, or furious that Beth was so messed up? "Did anyone besides you hear them fight on the phone?"

"Well, she was right at the bar. She didn't lose her cool or anything, turned away into the corner. More like trying to talk sense into the girl. That's the other thing, I think Anne was feeling funny about their age difference."

"So she never lost her cool? Do you think she was having second thoughts?"

Tink drained her coffee. "Anne's not very emotional, C.J. It's hard to tell what she's really thinking and feeling. She never confided in me, so to tell you the truth, I don't know how she handled it."

"What about relationships with other women, before that?"

"I guess she lived with someone before I worked here. Slept around on Anne all the time, so Anne gave her her walking papers. She came in here once when I was tending bar. Anne came down, saw her and told her to leave, all businesslike. That's the only reason I know about it. Before that, I don't know."

"What is she like to work for?"

"Tough." Tink smiled. "But fair. She doesn't let me hand her too much bullshit before calling me on it. She pretty much keeps to herself, and makes it a policy not to date women she meets in her bar. Beth was an exception, but then she didn't come in for a drink."

I digested that information while Tink began closing down the place. If Anne didn't pick up customers in her bar, she sure was cruising down at the probation office. One look at me and I was a goner. I chewed over that for a bit too, saying good-night to Tink.

SIX

The following morning I was awake before the clock radio. I prefer listening to the radio after morning drive-time, when you're likely to hear less talk and more music, so I turned the radio off before it had a chance to turn on. That explains why I was on my way to work before I heard the news.

"Our top story this morning…Rose Vanderslice dead at eighty-six." I increased the volume. "A spokesperson at St. Peter's Hospital confirmed that philanthropist Rose Vanderslice lost her battle with cancer during the night. Mrs. Vanderslice, long known as the area's leading patron of the arts, had been the principal benefactor of the Albany Symphony Orchestra…."

"Holy shit," I said. I was driving on Western Avenue, headed downtown, but when I got to Manning I turned right and made a beeline for St. Peter's Hospital. I didn't know what to make of Rose Vanderslice's death, but the little hairs on the back of my neck were prickling. Most days that's enough for me to start asking questions. What I wanted to know was, would there be an autopsy of Rose Vanderslice's body? Generally, when an 86 year old terminally ill patient dies in the hospital nobody wonders why.

I pulled into the visitors' lot and walked into the building, recognizing a young lesbian, whose name I had forgotten, standing near the reception desk. She wore a white lab coat. I flashed a smile and waved to her as I strode toward the elevators. When I got off at Rose's floor I went directly to the nurse's station and waited for the

RN on duty to look up from her notes.

"I'm Officer Sinclair," I said, displaying my badge. "I was here yesterday visiting Mrs. Vanderslice, and now I understand she died during the night."

The nurse, whose nameplate read Rhoda Flanagan, RN, did not confirm or deny anything, so I continued. "I'm investigating a manslaughter, and Mrs. Vanderslice was very helpful to me just yesterday. I must say I'm surprised she passed away so suddenly. Her death was unexpected?"

"I'm sorry, but I can't answer any questions about Mrs. Vanderslice. Patient confidentiality." She turned away, but I remained persistent.

"I don't want you to breach confidentiality, Ms. Flanagan," I said, smiling. "I wonder if you could just tell me the name of the private duty nurse who was with Mrs. Vanderslice during the night."

"That would be against rules," she said. "You'll have to speak with the head nurse."

"And what is her name?"

"Susan Trump. But she's not on the floor right now."

"Will she be back soon, do you think?"

"Possibly." One of the patient's rang for the nurse. I saw the room number light up on a monitor. Instead of trotting right off to tend to her patient she pushed an intercom and said, "May I help you?"

A feeble voice replied, "I need a bed pan."

"I'll be right there," she said. She clicked off, but didn't make a move toward the room. I thought about the poor guy having to pee, and instinctively stood with my legs together. "There's a waiting room down the hall," she said. "When Susan gets back on the floor I'll let her know where you are."

I was grateful the waiting room was empty, particularly of smokers. From the seat I chose I could watch people entering and exiting the elevators. After a few minutes the young lesbian I had seen in the reception area got off on my floor.

She smiled and peeked her head in. "Visiting someone?"

"No. I'm waiting for the head nurse." I glanced at her name badge. Ellen Cleavland, Ward Clerk. "Is this your floor, Ellen?"

"Yeah," she replied, coming all the way into the room. "I've been here six months. Pay stinks, but the benefits are okay."

"Maybe you can save me some time." I handed her one of my business cards. "I was in to see Rose Vanderslice yesterday about a manslaughter investigation. I was surprised to hear on the news that she passed away during the night."

Ellen gave me the same blank stare as Rhoda.

"She looked pretty strong yesterday. Did she have a heart attack?"

"I'm sorry, Callie," Ellen said. "I can't violate patient confidentiality. You'd have to talk to Susan."

"And she'll tell me the same thing, right?"

"Right."

"Look, Ellen, I don't want you to violate anything. Just tell me the name of the private duty nurse who was on with her last night. Can you do that?"

"I'm not supposed to."

"I know, but can you do it anyway?"

She backed up and peered down the hall. "I don't know if her chart's still on the floor."

"Can you check?"

"I'll try, okay?"

"Should I wait here?"

"No. I'll meet you in the women's room on the first floor. Give me fifteen minutes."

I took the elevator downstairs, stopped in the cafeteria for a diet Pepsi, then positioned myself in the first floor john and waited for Ellen.

"You're in luck," she said when she came in. "The chart was still there. The nurse who was on with her is Betty Amyot. Mrs. Vanderslice hired her through Nurseforce. That's all I can tell you."

I stuck my hand out. "Hey, Ellen. Thanks. You've been a big help."

She shook my hand. "Promise you won't tell anyone where you got that information. I'd lose my job."

"I promise."

When I went back downtown to my office Sid Kasselbaum was standing in the reception area, next to Marylou's desk.

"Hey, Callie, I've been looking for you."

I groaned inwardly because Sid is a pain in the ass. He has the habit of poking his nose into everybody's work, depending on his level of interest in a particular case. Whenever he expressed interest in one of my cases I could count on him peeking over my shoulder every step of the way, offering advice, and insisting that I take it, even if I considered his suggestion to be stupid, which I did on several occasions. Whenever I offered my opinion he barely listened, talking over me instead.

The other side of Sid is almost as bad, because when he's disinterested in a particular case that you want him to be interested in for whatever reason, he'd be difficult to pin down, or he'd practically fall asleep while you were talking about the case.

When Sid said he was looking for me, I offered a silent prayer that he would not ask about the Hollis file. "What can I do for you, Sid?"

"Not a thing, Callie. I was wondering if there's something I can do for you."

"What do you mean?"

"Do you need help with anything? Any of your cases giving you trouble?"

"Nope. Thanks for asking, though." Apparently this was just one of Sid's days to practice MBWA, Manage By Walking About, which was a management technique he read about several months ago.

"The case I gave you the other day. What was the name?"

I swallowed. "Hollis."

"Yeah. The Hollis file. Cut and dried. Right?"

"The case is going along fine, Sid." I was not above distorting the truth if lying would get Sid off my back.

"Good. If there's anything I can do you just holler, okay?"

"Sure." When Sid turned away I looked at Marylou and raised my eyebrows.

She shook her head. "Remember the time Sid read *The One Minute Manager?*"

I grinned. How could I forget? He wanted to motivate his staff, so he had half of us wearing little buttons that said, 'I got caught doing something right.' But it didn't work because everybody who didn't get a button got pissed off at everybody who did.

Marylou pointed to the computer printout that was perched on the end of her desk.

"Is that my list of partial plates?" I asked.

"All nine hundred and ninety nine of them. Enjoy."

When I got to my office I tossed the printout on my desk, figuring I'd get to it after lunch, then pulled my phone directory out of a drawer and began searching for the name Amyot. There were only twenty-two listed, and I didn't have to dial beyond the D's. Her husband's name was Duane. My phone call woke her up.

"Betty Amyot?"

"Um hum. Who's this?"

"My name is Callie Sinclair, Ms. Amyot. I'm sorry if I woke you. I understand you worked the night shift at St. Pete's."

"Are you from Nurseforce?"

"No. I'm from the Probation Department. I'm investigating a manslaughter and Mrs. Vanderslice was helping my investigation. I was in to see her yesterday and she appeared fine. I was shocked to learn of her death."

"Why would you be shocked? She was eighty-six years old and had cancer."

"I know, but when I saw her yesterday she looked so...strong. She also told me the doctors had given her three months to live."

"Well, predictions aren't always accurate," Betty stated.

"I learned that much from listening to the weather forecasts. Were you with her when she died?"

"Yes."

"How did it happen?"

"She stopped breathing." It was obvious from the sound of her voice that Betty Amyot didn't think my elevator went all the way to the top floor. "Who did you say you were?"

"Officer Sinclair," I said. "I'm an investigator with the county Department of Probation."

She didn't even try to stifle her yawn. "So what are you calling me for?" she asked. "I can't give you any information about Rose Vanderslice because of client confidentiality."

"I understand that, but I wonder if you can tell me if anyone had been to see her during the night?"

"I came on at eleven and I was alone with her until around three.

One of the doctors stopped in to see her then. Said there had been an emergency on the floor and he had just finished settling it. They do that sometimes. They'll stop by if they're in the neighborhood. That way they can charge the patient for a visit as long as they entered the visit on the patient's chart."

"Do you remember the doctor's name?"

"I don't, come to think of it. I took a break then. Got myself a cup of coffee and a smoke. When I got back the doctor was gone."

"And how was Mrs. Vanderslice?"

"She was sleeping peacefully."

"What time did she pass away?"

"Four-oh-three, exactly."

I thanked Betty Amyot for her help, then I called St. Pete's and asked to speak with Ellen Cleavland. When she got on the phone I asked her if she could check Mrs. Vanderslice's chart and give me the name of the doctor who visited at 3 a.m.

"I can't, Callie. Her chart has already been sent down to medical records."

"What does that mean?"

"It means the chart's gone. I can't access it."

"Shit." I chewed on my thumb and repeated the expletive. "Ellen, is there ever an instance where you can get a chart back out of medical records?"

"I suppose I could go down and tell them I forgot to make an entry."

"What are the chances of your doing that for me?"

Her sigh was audible. "How about if I call you back this afternoon? Would that be okay?"

"It would be wonderful."

I was hungry, so I stopped at Taco Pronto for a burrito on my way to Hooper's. When I arrived, Tink was tending bar and waved to me, then pointed toward the alcove where Anne was at the piano. She was playing 'Memory' from the musical CATS. I've always admired people who can play an instrument, any kind—piano, guitar, fiddle, harmonica. The only instrument I can play is a kazoo, and sometimes that even gives me trouble. I watched Anne's hands skip over the keys. She played with her fingers outstretched as opposed to curved. Her hands looked pretty, and I wondered what they would feel like against my skin.

"You make it look so easy," I said, when she was finished.

"All it takes is years and years of lessons and practice."

"You've been playing since childhood?"

"No, just feels that way." She laughed. "I started taking lessons three years ago, but I'm dedicated. I've wanted to play all my life, so once I made the decision to take lessons I made a commitment to be serious about it. And I am."

"Well, your hard work has paid off," I said.

"Thanks." She looked at the rolled printout I carried. "Is that the list?"

"All nine hundred and ninety nine vehicles with the prefix ACE."

Anne frowned. "That's a lot of cars."

"Yes, but the printout furnishes make, model, and color of the vehicle, in addition to addresses. If we knew a little bit about the car that was following Beth, we'd be able to narrow this down a bit. I've already gone through the list and crossed out all the plate numbers with expired registrations, although even those could still be on the road." I looked around. "Where do you want to sit?"

Anne led me to a table near the dance floor and called to Tink, "Can you bring us a couple of diet Pepsi's?" She turned to me. "Have you eaten lunch?"

"Yes." I placed the printout on the table facing Anne. "Why don't we start by seeing if any of these names sound familiar?" Anne put her reading glasses on and, while she was scanning the list, I walked over to the bar and picked up the drinks. "How are things going, Tink?"

"Not too shabby with me, C.J., but the boss lady, now that's a different story. She's scared she's gonna lose her liquor license over this."

I shook my head. "No way, Tink. That won't happen."

Tink shrugged. "Convince her of that."

I looked back at the table. Anne's head was bent over the list, concern creasing her forehead. I brought the drinks over and sat across from Anne. "Think back to your conversations with Beth about the car. Did she mention color? Or make? That could narrow the list down for us."

74

"I really don't think so," she said, slipping her glasses off. "I've got a pretty good memory, but I don't recall her saying anything about the car at all."

"Okay. Let me leave the printout with you this afternoon. Maybe we can talk later." I was considering what else I needed to do during the afternoon. If Ellen Cleavland could get me that doctor's name....

"How about dinner?" Anne asked.

"Sure," I replied, my mind not really focusing on Anne's question.

"At my place in Cobleskill?"

I glanced at Anne. "Huh?"

"We might get a lead," she said. "You know, if you drove on I-88, took a look at the reservoir..."

I narrowed my eyes. "You're serious, aren't you?"

"You bet I am."

I considered the validity of her suggestion. Maybe I was merely rationalizing how to spend more time with Anne, but the more I thought about her proposal the more sense it made. "Okay," I said. "Where and when?"

"I can get someone to cover for me here tonight. Why don't you pick me up at five? We can ride together, and I'll show you where the Jeep went off the road.

Instead of going back downtown I drove home and called my office as soon as I arrived. Marylou said there was a message to call Ellen Cleavland.

"Six West. Ellen Cleavland speaking."

"Ellen, this is Callie." I kicked my Reeboks off and stretched my toes.

"I was able to get the chart back," she said "but no doctor signed at three a.m. or any other time between eleven and seven."

"You're sure?"

"Positive."

"Why wouldn't he sign the chart? Doesn't that mean he can't charge for the visit?"

"Technically. What was this doctor supposed to be doing there in the middle of the night anyway?"

"According to Betty Amyot, he had an emergency on the same

floor and thought he'd stop by."

"Well, that does happen. The doctor may have been worried about her. Maybe it was a resident, just stopped in, saw she was okay. Not really a visit. After all, she was very ill."

"Well, if by some fluke you discover his name, do let me know." I leaned forward on my desk to hang up.

Ellen laughed. "Sure, Callie, but if you don't know the doctor's identity why do you keep saying 'he'? We actually have a number of women on staff."

"Oh, God," I said, embarrassed. "I can't believe I made such an assumption."

"Oh, Callie, I almost forgot. I heard the head nurse say that Mrs. Vanderslice was supposed to be released to go home today."

"What?" I couldn't believe I had almost hung up and missed that bit of information.

"Yeah, she had already started packing. Things like that often happen."

I looked at my watch, the time already after three on Friday afternoon. The Hollis file had been mine for a mere forty-eight hours, yet retaining everything that took place within that period made my head spin. I thanked Ellen, said, "I owe you one," and hung up.

I sat quietly for several minutes, trying to piece everything together, but there were so many details, none of which seemed at all conclusive.

I grabbed a legal pad from my briefcase and made a list of everything I learned so far, hoping that seeing it in black and white would yield something more tangible, but my list seemed to generate more questions than answers. Who was following Beth, and why? Was he, or she, the same person who forced Anne's Jeep off the road, killing Beth? What's the story with the anonymous caller who gave an account of the accident to the dispatcher? Who belongs to the license plate, if that is really what ACE represents? And on top of it all, Rose Vanderslice dies, and this last fact bothered me, enough so I wished I could get an autopsy authorized on her.

I wasn't any closer to finding who wanted the Jeep off the road than I was yesterday. Unless, of course, I considered Jackie a viable candidate, that there was some way she had managed it.

I decided I might have enough questions to pique the interest of Investigator Hughes. I dialed his barracks' number and was told he was out and not expected back before six. I left my home number with instructions that he call me any hour of the day or night during the weekend.

I filled a watering can and treated my house plants to a drink, snipping dried flowers from my African violets as I went along. I was in a hurry and pulled too hard on one of the plants, breaking a large healthy leaf from my favorite.

"Shit," I said, then touched the plant tenderly, feeling guilty for my carelessness. Then I checked my answering machine to be sure it was on. I didn't want to take a chance of missing Hughes' call if he returned to the station house sooner than expected.

I brought my portable phone into the bathroom with me and took a quick shower. The phone rang just as I was shutting the water off. I dried my hands and pushed the talk button.

"Hello," I said.

"Callie? Bill Hughes here. I got your message to call you. What's up?"

"Bill. I wanted to talk to you about the Hollis case. You told me to call you if I learned anything and, well, I think I have something you may find interesting." I told him about Rose Vanderslice's will, and the middle of the night doctor's visit an hour before her death, but somehow voicing my theory aloud to a police investigator had the effect of minimizing its significance. I wasn't surprised by his reserve.

"Rose Vanderslice isn't just any Jane Doe, Callie. If we have to ask for an autopsy on this one it's bound to get media coverage. Then what happens if nothing shows, which is probably what'll happen?"

"The media doesn't have to find out, Bill. Not if the autopsy is done right away." I felt embarrassed standing naked in the middle of the bathroom. "Can you hold on just a minute?" I squirmed into my white terry robe, then sat on the toilet seat with the lid down. "Are you still there?"

"Yeah, but..."

"Listen to me, Bill. Anne Hollis swears she was an innocent bystander during a homicide. And she saw someone standing up at the road, but was offered no assistance. Remember that dispatcher's statement you sent me a copy of?"

"Yeah, some guy called in the accident, thought it was a drunk driver."

"Yeah, but you and I both know that blowing a point zero five hardly rates as a D.W.A.I., let alone intoxication. Anne Hollis was not drunk. In my opinion, the caller could have been the perpetrator."

"You're jumping to conclusions..."

I ignored his interruption. "If Hollis' story is true, then why would a passing driver report seeing only one vehicle?"

"If she's telling the truth..."

"Let me finish," I said, running a hand through my damp hair. "When I began questioning Sister Beth's family I learned that she would have inherited half a million dollars if she hadn't died, but since she did die, someone else has become eligible for that half million, plus the other half million she was already expecting to inherit. Then what happens? The benefactor dies."

"But she's—"

"An eighty-six year-old woman dying of cancer, I know what you're going to say. But the doctor's gave her three months to live, Bill, and she was scheduled to be released from the hospital the day she died."

"They were sending her home?"

"Yes. St. Peter's has a hospice for cancer patients. In order to be admitted you practically have to guarantee you won't live beyond three weeks. If Mrs. Vanderslice was that sick don't you think they would have admitted her to the hospice?"

"No one can predict time of death with that much accuracy, Callie, but I hear what you're saying. Anyway, she was rich and must have chosen home care—obviously she could afford it. My problem with this is there doesn't seem to be enough here. Almost, but not quite."

"What will it take, Bill? Another death? Anne's, for example? I mean, the car had both of them in it. Weren't they both supposed to die? Look, you're going on the assumption that Anne Hollis is lying. Seeing it that way, of course there's not enough to warrant an autopsy. But what if she's telling the truth? What then?"

Bill was quiet for a minute. I let him take his time, think it over. Then I said, "Why not start with Rose Vanderslice's primary physician? Learn what his, or her, intentions are around an autopsy."

"If you're wrong the shit could hit the fan."

"Only if it leaks to the media." I crossed my fingers and said a little prayer.

"Okay," he sighed. "But I'll go directly to the medical examiner on this and try to keep it out of the D.A.'s office."

"Thanks, Bill."

"Don't hang up, Callie. I want to know who's going to inherit the million bucks."

"Her name is Jacqueline Prescott. Sister Jackie."

"What's her story?"

"She was Sister Beth's best friend."

"Yeah, well, right now she's a millionaire. If that's what she wanted, she has it now. I'd keep an eye on her if I were you."

I hung up feeling odd and disturbed. I even found myself looking in my kitchen cabinets, everything churning in my mind until I stopped and wondered what I was feeling. And then I knew.

Within moments I was frantically dialing up Sadie. "Hi, Sadie, it's me, Callie. Got a minute?"

"Sure, babe, what's up? Her voice was raspy, like too much liquor and cigarettes for too many years.

"I want to tell you about last night. I'm working on a case, and the woman I'm helping owns a bar. I went over there last night to conduct an interview and ran into some old friends, old drinking buddies."

"Uh huh. You have no business in a bar, Callie."

"I know, Sadie, but I was doing my job."

"Conduct your interviews somewhere else."

"I could tell you I won't go in there again, but I'm pretty sure I will have to as long as I work on this case. But I'm under some strain—"

"I can't argue with you about your job, but hear me good, girl. You are an alcoholic and you know what you gotta do. Have you been to a meeting today?"

"No, I got caught up in...."

"Don't make excuses, just get your ass to a meeting. Ten years does not exempt you from a slip, Callie."

I knew damn well she was right because I was shaking. I didn't quite know why, but I was. Anne, all by herself without being wrapped up in a case that was becoming stranger, would have been enough. I checked the A.A. directory and found a meeting for five o'clock on Western Avenue. With any luck I'd still make it to Hooper's by six-fifteen sober, and with a bit more sense in me. Then I called Anne to tell her I'd be late, knowing that I hadn't told Sadie everything, hadn't told her that job or no job, I was going off with Anne.

SEVEN

I double parked in front of Hooper's Bar at six-fifteen on the nose, a good deal steadier and less light-headed. And yet, for all the meetings I had gone to over the years—less and less as time went on—this time I had been scared enough to really need it.

Anne must have been watching for me because she opened the door and gave me a sign that she would be out in two minutes. It turned out to be three and a half, but who was counting?

The drive between Albany and Cobleskill is a particularly pretty one. The landscape is exceptionally hilly, towering above beautiful farmland. Even during rush hour, I-88 is lightly traveled, and unless the weather is bad, the ride is usually pleasurable. Having Anne next to me only heightened my enjoyment.

Instead of discussing her case, we talked about movies and literature. Anne preferred musicals and foreign films while I was happiest watching the bad guys getting gunned down by Dirty Harry. As far as literature goes, I admitted there was nothing literary about my preference for suspense and mystery novels. Anne, predictably, favored the classics. Obviously, we weren't going to be trading paperbacks.

I sensed a shifting in Anne's mood as soon as we passed the town of Central Bridge. She withdrew from our conversation and turned her attention to the side of the road.

"Are we close to where the accident happened?" I asked.

"Yes," she said. "Maybe two or three miles further." We drove the miles in silence, then Anne tensed visibly when the barricades came into view. I slowed down and pulled to the side, turning the engine off. Anne looked uneasy. "Maybe this wasn't such a good idea, Callie."

"Why don't you stay here," I suggested. "I'll just be a couple of minutes."

Anne nodded. I got out of the car and walked back a few yards. Repairs had not yet been made to the guard rails, and the tire tracks left by the Jeep and the tow truck were still visible at the bottom of the ravine.

I climbed over the rails, cautiously picking my way down to the bottom where the Jeep had settled. I wished I was wearing jeans and hiking boots instead of cotton twill khaki trousers and loafers. The terrain was slippery, and in some places so steep, I practically had to slide on my fanny to keep from toppling over. When I got to the bottom I turned and looked back up at the highway. Anne stood watching me, the mountain her backdrop. My car could not be seen at all and I could see Anne only because of the daylight. If this were the middle of the night I would have to rely on moonlight to tell me someone was watching, and even then I couldn't be sure.

Climbing back up to the road was not as easy as climbing down, and by the time I reached the highway I was breathing hard and my heart was pounding. Anne put her arm around my shoulder. "Are you all right?"

I took a deep breath. "I'm just old, that's all," I said, forcing a smile. "Can you imagine what shape I'd be in if I didn't walk four times a week?"

"The same shape I'm in," she said, grinning. "Are you up to seeing the reservoir?"

"Sure, let's go." We got back in the car and drove to Mineral Springs Road, passing Anne's property before making a left turn at the corner and driving up to the first dirt road to the right. The dust billowed around us. If our windows hadn't been closed we could have scrawled notes to each other on my dashboard.

"I think you're right about this being the road Beth took," I said. "My car's going to look like hers by the time we get there."

"The reservoir is just a little ways up." She leaned forward. "There. See the water?"

I parked the car, and Anne and I got out. We walked down to the water's edge. I wasn't impressed. The reservoir didn't look like a lake, the way the Tomhannock Reservoir does, but there were a few frogs croaking, and a small family of ducks swam along the water's edge. I sat down on one of the larger rocks and looked around.

"I don't think this is where she saw the car, Anne. Nobody can sneak up on you in here, and I doubt she would have come here after dark."

As we drove out, I was aware of how much dust was kicking up around us. Beth would not have been able to see anything through her rear view mirror until she got back out onto a main road. "Didn't you say she had been followed at night?"

"That's what she said the last time we talked."

"And the last time she was at your place...was that after dark?"

"Yes, by the time she left."

"This whole thing is so baffling," I said, feeling frustrated. "Why would somebody bother to follow Beth out here?"

Anne directed me back to her cottage, hidden from the road behind a stand of evergreens. I pulled in the driveway and parked, scanning the stone cottage. A stunning assortment of perennials adorned each side of the front door, some climbing on trellises, others fitting neatly below windows, reminding me of pictures I'd seen of English gardens. The blooms were a blend of pink, white, blue, and purple, with lavender roses climbing the white picket fence surrounding the small front yard. Anne's window shutters and front door had been painted mauve. "How lovely," I murmured.

"C'mon in," she said, opening the front door. "You're probably starved."

"Now that you mention it, I am."

I followed Anne into a medium-sized room decorated with white wicker furniture, the pillows fashioned from a printed material, mauve, turquoise, and purple swirls against a black background. French impressionist portraits of women decorated most of the walls, and the far wall contained large sliding glass doors which opened to a stone patio. Fern and spider plants hung from the ceiling in front of the doors, and several floor plants were placed among the wicker. An upright piano fit nicely into a corner.

"How do you keep all these plants alive while you're away so much?" I asked.

"I pay one of my neighbors to come once a week. She waters my plants, mows my lawn, and weeds the garden." Anne walked into the kitchen. "Sometimes she'll even shop for me if I call ahead." She pulled a package wrapped in butcher paper from the refrigerator. "How about charbroiled steak and a salad?"

"Sounds wonderful," I said. "Where can I get cleaned up a bit?" I was dusty from my climb down the ravine.

Anne pointed me toward the bathroom, and by the time I finished pulling myself back together she had already put the steak on the gas grill and was tossing a salad. The Nutcracker Suite was on the stereo, and a vase of flowers, fresh from the garden, decorated the glass-topped table.

"Can I pour you some wine, Callie? Or don't you drink at all?"

"Coke would be fine," I said, dodging the question.

She opened the freezer and pulled an ice tray from it. "You don't drink at all?"

"No."

"Did you ever? You must have, if you hung out with Tink at the Hudson Arms."

"That was a long time ago."

"And since then you quit drinking?"

"Ten years ago yesterday, as a matter of fact."

She nodded. "I thought maybe it was something like that. Does it bother you if I drink?"

"Not at all," I said, wondering if I was telling the truth.

"Will you let me know if it does?"

"Sure."

"Because I don't have to. Drink, I mean."

"Then why do you?"

She shrugged. "I think I was brought up that way."

I nodded. So was I.

She poured my coke and suggested I take my drink onto the patio. "Why don't you sit down and relax?"

I walked outside and sat on a lawn chair, taking a sip of my Coca Cola, then slipped my shoes off, enjoying the feeling of being barefoot. I wriggled my toes, and smiled.

Anne came out and checked the fire. "How do you like your steak?"

"Medium rare," I said.

"Me too," she said, turning the steak over. "This'll be ready in seven minutes." Anne sat on the chair next to mine. "I hate wishing my life away," she said, sighing, "but I'd give almost anything to have this whole ordeal over with. Then tonight could be a celebration instead of what it is...a friendly meeting between a probation officer and her defendant."

Is that what we were having, a friendly meeting? I closed my eyes and asked my Higher Power for the strength not to do something I would later regret, like pulling Anne into my lap and kissing her face a thousand times. The thought of it made me laugh.

"What's funny?" Anne asked, with a quizzical expression on her face.

"Nothing," I said, embarrassed. "I become silly when I'm ravenous."

"Then let's eat."

We ate inside, in front of the glass doors, the moon visible through the pines. Anne placed several lighted candles on the table and around the room. The mood was romantic, and I pointed that out to her.

"I think I'm romantic by nature, otherwise I probably wouldn't be so attracted to French provincial." She gestured toward the living room. "I find the delicacy...the femininity of the period romantic. Consider the women in the paintings, how gentle they appear to be, how lovely and pure in their white dresses...yet, there's a certain passion about them. Can you see it, Callie?"

"Yes," I agreed, fixing my gaze on a painting of a dark-haired woman with sultry eyes, lips the color of strawberries. "I can."

"Would you be more comfortable if I blew the candles out and put more lights on? Turned the music off?" Anne began to rise.

"Please don't," I said, touching her arm. "I wasn't implying that I'm uncomfortable. I think the candles are lovely." Besides, what was the difference? I was just as attracted to Anne in the middle of the day, beneath the fluorescent lights in my office, as I was here among flowers and candlelight.

I wanted to reach across the table and touch Anne's cheek. I'd spent more time fantasizing about how I might approach her when the time was right. Why can't life be more like books and movies, where one person weeps and the other consoles, and the next thing you know they're in each other's arms, making love? Too bad real life isn't that simple. And too bad I'm so fucking principled. Or am I simply self-protective?

Anne reached across the table, lightly touching my wrist. "Will you tell me about your alcoholism?"

Was it her touch, or her question, that caused me to tremble? "Talking about my addiction is difficult, Anne. Couldn't we discuss something else instead?"

"I suppose we could," she said, lightly. "What would you like to talk about? Movies? I hear Kathleen Turner is playing V. I. Warshawski. Do you know whether or not Paretsky wrote the screenplay?" Her voice was light, her stare penetrating. I got the message.

I sipped my Coke. "I started drinking when I was seventeen, hoping alcohol would give me the courage to deal with my newly discovered sexuality."

"And did it?" Anne's fingers pressed into my hand.

"No. Alcohol didn't give me courage, it gave me permission. I spent weekends in the gay bars. There was a place in Nyack called Fran Bell's...I drove up there every Saturday night, each week believing I would somehow be changed, feel comfortable. Of course, nothing changed, not the place, not the people, not me. I went on that way for years, anesthetizing my feelings in a bottle of wine. Holding onto things became difficult: jobs, relationships, friendships. But because I never realized alcohol was the culprit, I continued to drink every weekend. That's the insanity of drinking, Anne, an alcoholic keeps repeating the same behavior, each time expecting different results." A wry smile played on my lips, while fear danced a pirouette in my belly. How would Anne perceive me now that I revealed that part of myself? She squeezed my hand, but remained silent, the white space deadly. I cleared my throat self-consciously.

Anne stirred. "Oh! I was lost in my own thoughts for a moment." She shook her head. "I'm afraid I started to think about my culpability as a bar owner, Callie. How guilty am I? Dozens of young lesbians drink in Hooper's, and many of them get drunk all the time."

"You're not responsible for them, Anne. Certainly, my alcoholism was not the fault of my bartenders." I smiled. "Alcoholism is a family disease, Anne. My mother was alcoholic."

"You said, 'was.' Is she also in A.A.?"

"No, she died several years ago." Anne's face registered sympathy, but I ignored it, pressing on. "Mom was a heavy drinker, a daily drunk. She wouldn't quit, not even after her doctor warned that it would kill her." I drew a deep breath, leaning back in the chair. "I didn't drink with the same voracity as my mother, so it was easy for me to deny my alcoholism. Actually, I got into A.A. through the back door, after a year of group therapy for Adult Children of Alcoholics. The group wanted me to look at my own drinking, but I resisted for a long time. God, talk about denial."

"You didn't want to think of yourself as alcoholic?"

I shook my head. "I didn't want to think of myself as my mother."

"And now you're celebrating ten years of sobriety."

I flushed with pride. "Yes."

"I admire your courage," Anne said, "and your ability to be introspective. Without it you may not have conquered the demons." She moved the tips of her fingers around the rim of her glass. "I don't do much soul-searching, Callie, so chances are I wouldn't know I had a problem unless it came up and hit me in the head. Even then I'm not sure I'd have the determination to fix it."

"What do you call your current situation, if not a problem?"

"Oh, that." Anne's grin was self-conscious. "I was thinking more in the line of a personal problem, something deniable, like bulimia or alcoholism." Anne raised her glass. "To your ten years, Callie."

I lifted my glass of cola, tapping it against Anne's glass of wine, smiling at the irony of having my ten sober years toasted with a glass of Chablis.

After dinner Anne yawned and stretched cat-like, her arms reaching above her head. The material of her blouse pulled tight beneath her breasts. I felt my mouth go dry. "Are you in a hurry, or do you think I could take a few minutes to shower and change? I've been in these clothes since this morning."

"Go ahead," I said, casually. "I'll get the table cleared and do the dishes."

While Anne was in the shower I cleaned the table, stacked the dishes in the dishwasher, and changed the music on the stereo from classical to Barbra Streisand's Broadway Album. I would have liked to sack out on the couch for a few minutes, but how does one sprawl on wicker?

Instead, I strolled around the living room, picked out Chopsticks on the piano, and thumbed through a decorating magazine. Glancing at the titles on Anne's bookcase I found several which duplicated ones on my shelves—novels by Cather, Stein, Rule, and Forrest. The difference was that most of mine have never been read while Anne's copies were dog-eared.

I walked over to the sliding doors. The night air was very cool, so I pulled the glass doors closed. I didn't move away from the doors, although I could no longer see outside. The room behind me was reflected in the glass: the candlelight, the wicker, the plants, Anne.

Anne. I didn't turn around. Couldn't. Just stared at her reflection, barefooted, hair damp from the shower, wearing jeans and a T-shirt. I shut my eyes for a moment, feeling a tightness in my throat. My breathing had become shallow.

"Callie."

"Yes?" I answered without turning around. She came up behind me, standing close enough for me to smell the light fragrance of her cologne. I felt my back stiffen.

"It's pitch black out there," she said. "I hadn't realized how late it was."

I turned then, my face just inches from hers. "Are you ready to leave?" I asked, wondering if Anne could discern the tension in my voice, my stance.

"Yes. I just need to lock up." She reached behind my waist, pushed the lock closed. My breath caught in my throat.

"Do you have everything you need?" I asked. She looked directly into my eyes, and without saying a word, traced cool fingers across my cheek. My heart hammered against my chest. "Anne, I can't...I've never broken my professional code...."

She shook her head, her fingers silencing my lips. "I know this is forbidden, Callie. I'm sorry." She moved away. "I'll get my things."

I leaned against the door, closed my eyes. How could I have

believed that my coming here tonight was innocent, that we'd share a simple dinner like a couple of old school chums, maybe play a game or two of Scrabble, then, when we both began yawning, we'd simply pick up and drive back to Albany. Didn't I realize I'd want more, that Anne would want more? Yet, we had made a pact, an agreement, a promise, that nothing romantic would happen between us, at least not until Anne's case was solved.

And I wondered how she felt about Beth. Had they really settled things between them? How could she be turning to me so soon this way? Even though it made me suspicious, I was heady with a sense of recklessness.

"I'm ready, Callie." Anne stood at the front door, a backpack slung over her shoulder. "Will you turn that light off?" She indicated a lamp on the coffee table.

"Sure," I said, pushing off the wall, trying to appear composed as I crossed the room. When I reached the entrance, Anne opened the door, inviting me to exit first. I stood on the threshold, which seemed more like a precipice. I hesitated, then pulled the door closed, and turned back to face Anne. The room was in total darkness. I reached out to her and she leaned forward, pressing her soft lips to my mouth. She tasted of wine, and a dozen memories swept through my mind evoking fear, sadness, exhilaration, and longing. Something hot exploded inside of me. I drew her closer, my arm around her waist. She pressed me against the door frame, tightening her arms around me.

"Do you realize I'm jeopardizing my career? And your trial? I never..." My desperate lust so well-contained for how many years, forced all other thoughts from my head.

"Sshhh, Callie, please, no one will know."

I heard the lock snap on the door, then Anne struggled free of her clothes. My breath caught in my throat as she began unbuttoning my shirt. I heard her sharp intake of breath as she exposed my breasts. "Oh, Callie," she murmured, gliding the shirt down off my shoulders. I stood riveted, my body tense with desire, my nipples hardening beneath her touch. Her fingers struggled with the button on my slacks, tugging the zipper. "Take them off," she whispered. "I have to know how your naked body feels against mine, even if it's only once."

I slid my trousers and underpants to the floor and stepped out of them, kicking them away with my foot. Anne reached out to me and I walked into her arms, feeling intense pleasure as our bodies touched, breast upon breast. The sensation was delicious, and I wanted more. I hadn't loved anyone for such a long time, not since Jazz seven years ago. After breaking up with her, I swore I'd never trust anyone again, and had botched every budding romance since then. But not now; here I was—with Anne. More than anything I wanted to trust her.

"So soft," I breathed, moving my hand down her back, caressing her smooth contours. I brushed my lips over her mouth, her ear, her neck, my tongue gliding across the hollow of her throat. I felt a hunger deep within.

Anne slipped her hand into mine and led me to her bedroom.

"Anne, I can't do this. I can't go to bed with you." I stopped deliberately.

"I won't tell, Callie." Gently tugging, she pulled me to the bed where she lay down.

I sat beside her, tracing my fingers over her breasts, down her belly, and across the exquisite mound of pale hair. Anne pulled me down, her mouth seeking mine hungrily. Her kisses were long, slow, deep. I lowered my body over hers, my thigh between her legs.

"Anne—" I sighed, feeling her wetness on my leg. I slid down, kissing the inside of her thighs.

"Yes, Callie, yes," she moaned. Her fingers were in my hair, pressing my mouth against her. She thrust her hips, breathing rapidly, my tongue stroking her silkiness. I placed one hand under her, drawing her closer to me. "Please Callie, please believe in me. You are the only person I trust." I moved my mouth away and slid my hand between her legs. She was so wet, so silky wet. I thrust my fingers into her, gently at first, then harder as she undulated beneath my grasp, faster, and faster until the final vibration when she held her breath and shuddered.

My body still blazed with desire. I rolled onto my back, Anne turning toward me. "Let me love you, Callie. That's all I want. Someone who lets me really love. That's what I want, please."

"Oh, Anne, yes...more than anything I want you to love me..."

Had my body never felt such intense desire? Or was it that I had let it lie dormant for so long that now it burst out, drowning all my painstakingly nurtured common sense? She took my face between her hands, bringing her mouth down upon mine, passionately, her tongue sucking my tongue, darting in and out, in and out. She straddled me, her juices mixing with mine. I thrust my hips toward her as she knelt above me, both of us gasping for air. I reached for her breast, stroking the nipples until they hardened again. She held her breast to me, her face flushed with desire.

I moaned, no longer fighting to keep away from her. I had been kept too long from love.

She bent lower, placing her breast close to my lips. I sucked it, pushing my tongue against her nipple.

"I need you," she murmured. "Can't you see I need you to believe in me?" She slid her breast away from my mouth, bringing it down to my breasts, and rubbed it across my nipples until they stiffened, then she lay her head on my belly, and stroked me, dipping her fingers in the soft crevice between my thighs. "Open your legs, Callie," she whispered. "I want to please you." I spread my legs as Anne knelt over me. She thrust one of her breasts between my legs, stroking me with its nipple until my breaths came in quick gasps. My body arched and shuddered, and I fell back against the sheets, exhausted.

Anne collapsed into my arms, head nestled in the curve of my shoulder, her breath warm against my throat. I reached down and brought the sheet up over us. We lay there together for some time, I don't know how long, recovering.

"Should we get up?" Anne broke the silence of our slow breathing.

"I'm not sure I can move," I said, but my mind was saying we had to go, that we should have left long ago. Suddenly, I was overwhelmed with the knowledge that there was still a murderer out there, someone who could be dangerous to us, especially if we were lovers. I felt afraid. What if the murderer was onto us, had been following us, too. "We have to get back to town soon."

"Soon," Anne answered, but moved closer, flicked her tongue against my neck, sending delightful shudders through my body.

I held her protectively. "We may be in danger Anne, more now than ever. Do you understand?"

Her eyes widened. I knew she did. And I was afraid. My common sense seemed to want to come back in full force now, a voice scolding me in my head. You fool. A woman in a whole shit-load of trouble, and you fall head-over-heels for her. Here you are, feeling all protective, ready for another co-dependent relationship as if you can make it all better, messing around with a client who is not yet cleared of vehicular homicide! You're in for it now, so better hold on.

EIGHT

It turned out to be midnight when we got up, Anne going for a quick shower while I padded to the living room where I found my clothes still in a heap. Cotton doesn't hold up well when it's kicked into a mound. The bathroom door opened, and Anne peeked out. She saw me groaning over the wrinkles in my khakis.

"Don't worry about those, Callie. I'll give you something of mine to put on."

"Thanks," I mumbled, then winced as a sharp pain crossed my upper back.

"Are you okay?" she asked, coming out into the living room. She was drying herself with an oversized bath towel. Her face was still wet when she kissed me.

"I guess my body's feeling tense," I said, rolling my shoulders. "A hot shower will do wonders."

"It's all yours. I'll put some clothes out for you on the bed."

By the time I finished my shower the bed was made, and a navy sweatshirt and white sweatpants were laid out. I dressed quickly and joined Anne in the living room.

"There's hot water on the stove," she said. "I didn't know whether to fix tea or coffee."

"I'll make tea," I said.

"Did the shower help your tension?"

"Somewhat." I poured hot water over a tea bag, spooned two teaspoons of sugar into the mug. "How about you?"

"My teeth are almost chattering, but I'm not cold. Does that make sense?"

"Yes," I said, sitting next to her on the sofa. I looked across the room, at our reflections in the glass door, and shuddered. "I'm going to close the drapes, Anne. I feel as if we're sitting ducks in here."

"I'll do it." Anne rose and pulled the drapes across the windows, then dimmed the lights. "I've always felt so safe here, but now..." She shook her head, leaving the sentence unfinished.

"Until we know who the murderer is we'll need to take precautions. I think it would be smart for you to remain in Albany."

"You mean not come out here alone?"

"Not come out here at all, Anne, at least not until we know for certain."

"Okay. What else?"

"We should leave here right away, split up as soon as we get to Albany. Do you know what time it is?"

Anne held her watch up to me. "I can't see without my glasses."

"It's one-thirty," I said.

"What's on your agenda for today?"

I yawned. "Searching for the license plate, I think. Did you read over the entire printout?"

"Yes," she said. "But, I didn't recognize any of the names or addresses."

"Try not to be discouraged. Maybe I'll have better luck. Do you have the printout with you?"

"In my backpack."

"Good. I'll take it home with me." I held Anne's hand, silently wishing I could take her home with me, too. Yet, if we were being watched or followed, then being with me might place her in even more danger. "We'd better go now."

The ride back to Albany was quiet, almost spooky. There were few cars on the road. When one did come up behind us I'd ease my foot off the accelerator and let the car pass. Anne's uneasiness was evident in the way she kept turning her head to peer out the rear window, all the more reason for me to find out what happened that night.

When we reached Albany, I dropped Anne off in front of

Hooper's. Before getting out of the car, she handed me the license plate printout. "I want to kiss you good-night, Callie, but I'm afraid."

I nodded. "I'll talk to you in the morning."

Sleep would have been impossible for me, I was too wired. I took the printout to bed with me and spent a couple of hours studying the list, crossing out all of the unlikely ones, ending up with too many possibilities. The search was worse than looking for a needle in a haystack. At least in a haystack you'd know you were looking for a needle. I was looking for a connection, between the person who owned the partial plate, and Beth. About four o'clock I got out of bed and paced the rooms, wondering what more I could be, should be, doing. I got back into bed, scrutinizing the list until my eyes crossed. The quest seemed so hopeless, I finally pitched the computer pages onto the floor and pulled the sheet over my head. There was nothing more I could do on the Hollis file at the moment, so in frustration I turned to sleep.

The following morning as I drove to find breakfast out, an idea suddenly flashed in my head: wouldn't the car that pushed Anne off the road have left some of it's paint on Anne's Jeep? I couldn't believe the thought had never crossed my mind before. But why should it? I'm just a probation officer, not a detective, nor was I used to thinking like one.

I pulled off at Denny's, ordered scrambled eggs hard, with a side of bacon, then telephoned Anne. At the sound of her voice my heart did a somersault.

"Callie, good morning." Her voice sounded heavy, as if I'd awakened her.

"I'm calling from a pay phone, Anne. Listen, I had a thought...where was your Jeep towed?"

"To Shorty's Garage in Cobleskill. Why?"

I told her my idea about the paint.

"God," she said. "Why didn't I think of that?"

"Why didn't the police think of it?" I said, wondering if they had, but didn't find anything. "I'm going to drive out there now, and I'll call you as soon as I get home."

I felt almost too excited to eat, but I forced myself to relax during breakfast by reading; I tote whichever paperback I'm currently reading in my briefcase. Sometimes one can last me months.

The drive out to Cobleskill, or Coby, as the town is called by those who live there, took about an hour, but felt longer because I was alone, and anxious.

Guessing correctly that Shorty's garage was on the main drag, I pulled in and walked to the office. Shorty turned out to be about six foot-five inches tall and weighed about a hundred and eighty. I introduced myself, handing him my card.

"Any chance you still have Anne Hollis' Jeep here?"

"Sure do. The insurance company's been dragging its feet on the claim. Happens in the summer, y'know, with people bein' on vacations. You'll be looking for the white one out back. You can't miss it."

I trudged out behind Shorty's, where cars rested in neat rows like headstones in a graveyard. Anne's Jeep was against the fence on the right. What a mess, numerous dents and scrapes, most of them on the right side where the vehicle hit the guard rails. I began my search in the back of the Jeep, looking at every square inch of paint on the driver's side. And there it was, a narrow streak of black paint, about four inches long, behind the driver's rear wheel. Shorty loaned me a razor blade so I could scrape the paint sample into an envelope.

On the way back to Albany I prayed Anne wouldn't tell me the black paint had been there before the accident.

I called her as soon as I walked in the door. "My Jeep didn't have a scratch, Callie. Ask Tink. She'll tell you how I babied that car."

I told Anne I'd get back to her later, I wanted to do some work on the computer printout.

First, I crossed off all of the vehicles that were not black, which reduced the list dramatically. Then, remembering Anne's description of the vehicle as a large car, "an old jalopy," I removed all of the vehicles that were seven years old or less, then scratched off the ones that were obviously too small, such as compacts and sub-compacts. Finally, I eliminated all vehicles registered to people living outside of Albany, Schenectady, and Rensselaer counties. What I ended up with was a list of ten possibilities.

I was elated. I copied the list onto a legal pad and drove down to Hooper's. Anne's flush when I walked in said she was glad to see me. I held the legal pad over my head and smiled.

"Where can we talk?" I asked.

Anne pointed to a table in the corner. I sat down, facing the front door, and waited for Anne to join me. Watching her behind the bar, I wondered how I could have such strong feelings for a woman I'd only known for four days. "Get real, Callie," I said, under my breath.

In a few minutes Anne joined me, and I slid my list across to her, explaining how I eliminated all but ten vehicles.

"I'm amazed you were able to do this," she said, scanning the list. "But I still don't recognize any names or addresses. What will you do next?"

"I'll have to visit each person on the list, take a look at the cars...."

"That will be very time consuming."

"I know, and it has to be done outside of working hours. Luckily for us, today and tomorrow is the weekend and I can scout these out on my own time. I'll try to see how many I can check off by tomorrow night. With any luck we'll find the vehicle before Monday."

Anne reached across the table and touched my hand. "Callie, be careful."

"Promise."

And so that's how I spent the rest of the weekend—tracking down cars, and one after another, crossing them off. No black sedans. I also stopped in for an A.A. meeting to keep my head about me because I wanted to see Anne very badly. I made do with short phone calls to her, and since she was tending bar all Saturday night, I left one on her machine. What did I ever do on weekends before meeting Anne?

To help keep busy, I even went into my office on Sunday afternoon and caught up with paperwork so I could have more leeway if and when I needed it. There was a message on my machine from Bill Hughes. "Callie, just want you to know cause of death in the Vanderslice case...acute M.I. Myocardial Infarction. That means her heart stopped. Listen, babe, let me give you a piece of advice, okay? Drop it. Drop the whole smelly thing. That Hollis broad is feeding you nothing but bullshit and I sincerely hope you're not buying it. I figured that if the autopsy came up negative, it would prove Hollis a bullshitter."

Angry, I fled my office and looked for the next car on my list. This took me to Guilderland. When I arrived at the registrant's address there was no 1975 Ford in sight, but a late model Volvo was parked in the driveway. According to the printout, the Ford belonged to Jonathan Lindsay, date of birth January fourth, 1972. I noticed a garage behind the house, so I parked my car at the curb and rang the bell. An attractive middle-aged woman opened the door. She had dark curly hair, obviously permed, and wore a flowered sundress and sandals.

I smiled. "Hi," I said, "My name is Callie Sinclair. I'm looking for Jonathan Lindsay. Does he live here?"

"Yes, he does," she said. "But he's not here now. I'm his mother. Can I help you?"

"I'm not sure," I said, pleasantly. "Will he be home soon?"

"Not for another month," she said. "He's spending the summer in Spain. He was an exchange student last semester, and had the opportunity to stay longer."

"That's wonderful," I said. "So he's been gone awhile now."

"Since March."

"Well, then, maybe you can help me. Actually, I'm not really looking for Jonathan, I'm looking for his car. Does he still own a black 1975 Ford, license plate ACE 651?"

Her brow creased. "Yes, he does. We have it parked in the garage. What's this all about?"

"I'll explain in a moment, Mrs. Lindsay, but I wonder if I can take a quick look at the car?"

"My name's not Lindsay, it's Bennett. Jonathan's father and I divorced several years ago. I've since remarried." She made no move to show me the car, and I had a feeling that if I told her the truth about why I wanted to see it, she would refuse altogether, and the whole thing would get messy. So I decided to lie.

I showed her my badge and said, "Mrs. Bennett, I'm completing a pre-sentence investigation on a young man who was convicted of driving while intoxicated. He sideswiped several parked cars, and will be mandated to make restitution to their owners. My office was provided with a list of the cars involved, but where your son's car is concerned we had only a description and a partial plate number.

I just wondered if I could take a look at Jonathan's car to see if my client caused any damage. I'm sorry I have to bother you today but it has been quite an ordeal trying to get ahold of everybody."

Mrs. Bennett looked relieved. "I'll show you the car, but I doubt you'll be able to determine damages."

I raised my brows. "Oh, why is that?"

She laughed. "You'll see." She led me around to the garage, and as she lifted the door, said, "The only reason we keep it garaged is because it's such an eyesore."

It was an eyesore, for sure. There was no rear bumper, and three fenders were a mess of rusted dents and scrapes. "I see what you mean," I said, scrutinizing the vehicle's passenger side. There was a fresh scrape on the right front fender, but no visible white paint.

"Well," I said, shaking my head. "I'm afraid the defendant's going to get off the hook on this one. Seems a shame, though. But then again, if Jonathan's been out of the States, this is probably not the vehicle the young man hit after all." I looked hopefully at Mrs. Bennett as I took note of some blue coverall hanging on a nail in the corner of the garage. By the size, Jonathan had to be tall and slim. "Unless someone else in the household has been driving it."

"Not on your life," she said. "I wouldn't be caught dead in this heap, and neither would my husband."

"Do you have any other children?" I asked, sticking my head through the car's open window to see the inside.

"No. Johnny's an only child."

"The key is in the ignition," I said.

"That's in case we have to move it for some reason. You don't think we have to worry about somebody coming in here and stealing this wreck, do you?" She laughed.

"I guess not," I said. When she closed the door of the garage I didn't hear the lock click into place. She began to walk away. I said, "I don't think the door locked."

"The lock's been broken since last fall," she said. "I know we're probably stupid not to fix it, but my husband never seems to find the time."

I stuck out my hand. "Well, thank you for your time, Mrs. Bennett." As I said her name, I remembered why it sounded familiar to me, and my heart skipped a beat. "Mrs. Bennett...are you by any chance related to Sister Laura Bennett?"

"Why, yes," she said, enthusiastically. "Laura's my sister-in-law." She stopped in her tracks. "Say, I just happen to remember, you asked if anyone in the household has been driving Jonathan's car.... Laura borrowed the clunker when the convent car was being repaired."

"When was this, Mrs. Bennett?"

"Oh, six, seven months ago."

"Not more recently than that?"

"No, she hasn't mentioned it, so I still don't think this is the car that got sideswiped, if that's what you mean."

"Exactly." I wondered if she could have taken it without their knowledge, perhaps while they were away. "You haven't been out of town recently?"

"No, not since the holidays."

Too bad I couldn't connect Sister Laura to the car more recently, but it was definitely something to work on. "Well, I'll be on my way, Mrs. Bennett, thanks again for your time."

I drove home and changed into walking clothes. As soon as I stepped into the road, one of my neighbors jogged by and waved, leaving me feeling like a wimp. Screw it, I thought. I could jog if I wanted to, I just don't want to. I made a right turn out of the cul de sac and headed toward the condo development, thinking about Sister Laura. And the more I thought about it, the more it bothered me that I should be talking to a Mrs. Bennett whose son's old black sedan had a fresh scrape on its front right fender, and then find that she was related to one Laura Bennett!

Casting her in the role of murderer made me snort. Why would she want to kill Beth? I didn't buy Rose Vanderslice's absurd suggestion that the nuns need retirement money badly enough to kill for it. But I remembered Claudia Powell telling me Beth didn't like Laura, and wondered if Jackie could shed some light on their relationship. I made a mental note to call her as soon as I got to my office in the morning. I also decided to read Beth's diary again, in case it offered some clue to Laura having a motive. I certainly didn't have anything else planned for the rest of my weekend.

I speculated about the reaction Bill Hughes would have to my phone call if I dared to share my latest findings with him. He'd go wild if I asked him to obtain a sample of the paint on Jonathan Lindsay's car so the police lab could compare it with the paint I scraped from the Jeep. However, if the samples matched, he'd be forced to believe Anne's account of the incident. Of course, the police probably wouldn't be able to obtain that sample without a court order, so forget it. The only choice I had was to enter the Lindsay's garage and obtain the sample myself.

NINE

The time was seven forty-five on Monday morning when I parked my car across the street from the Bennett's house. Not directly across, but about four houses down. The Volvo was still in the driveway, chaperoned by a grey BMW. No wonder the Bennett's didn't want to be seen driving their son's junker.

At ten minutes past eight, Mr. Bennett emerged from the house carrying a briefcase in one hand and a travel mug in the other. I hunkered down in my seat, but he never so much as glanced my way.

Seven minutes later, Mrs. Bennett came out. She wore a pink and white pantsuit with white sandals. I speculated she was on her way to the Grand Union to stock up on supplies.

As soon as she drove away I started my car and pulled into the driveway. I got out of my car, walked up to the front door and rang the bell. No one answered. I stepped around to the back door and knocked. Still no answer. My heart pounding, I strode to the garage and lifted the door over my head. I quickly moved to the rear of the garage, and crouched down in the front of the car. Using a razor blade, I scraped some black paint into an envelope. The entire procedure took four minutes flat, and by nine o'clock sharp, I was seated at my desk, exhilarated, but nervous.

The first thing I did was put a call in to Foxmoor, requesting that Sister Jackie call me as soon as she arrived. The second thing I did was call Sid Kasselbaum to see if I could meet with him. We set it up

for 10:30. The third thing I did was call over to the state police barracks to find out what time Bill Hughes was expected in. I was told
three o'clock.

Beth's diary was tucked inside my briefcase. I brought it out,
and going to the page I had marked, sat and looked at it. I had
scanned her diary the previous evening for references to Laura
Bennett. I reread two of the entries from a year ago:

*May 24, 1990: Sister Laura knows! I had fallen asleep in Jackie's bed,
and at five a.m. I woke with a start. Sister Laura stood in the doorway of
our bedroom glaring at me. I was too frightened to move, breathe even.
After a moment she turned on her heels and disappeared. I don't think
Jackie woke up so I didn't say anything. Surely we will be separated tomorrow.*

*May 25, 1990: How baffling. Sister Laura greeted us at breakfast as if
she had not discovered Jackie and me together. Obviously I had only
dreamed she had seen us, but the dream (nightmare!) was so real!*

Sweat trickled from my forehead. I wasn't even hot. I tossed the
diary back into my briefcase, even more anxious to have a chat with
Jackie. Meanwhile, the least I could do was make an appointment
with Father Brannigan, so I called up St. Martha's Parish only to
find that he was out, but the secretary made me an appointment for
five o'clock. After that I concentrated on paperwork until it was
time to meet with Sid.

At ten-thirty I grabbed the Hollis file and marched down to Sid's
office. He was on the phone, but he waved me in. I settled in one of
the two visitor's chairs and tried not to eavesdrop on his phone conversation. Instead, I thumbed through Anne's file, trying to keep the
facts straight in my head.

When Sid hung up he frowned. "Is something wrong, Callie?"

"It's the Hollis file. I want to talk to you about it, but I need you
to listen to the whole story without interrupting me." I knew it was
beyond Sid's capabilities to be a good listener, but if you specifical-
ly asked him to listen he would make an effort.

"What's the problem? I thought you said it was cut and dried."

"You said it was cut and dried. I only agreed with you because I
didn't have time to get into a lengthy explanation."

"So tell me," he said, looking at me warily.

"First, I want to remind you that I've always followed departmental rules to the letter."

"Since when?"

"Since forever."

Sid shook his head. "Callie, you've broken every rule at least seven times, but if you're happy to think I haven't noticed, that's fine. Now get on with your story."

I told him everything, beginning with my initial meeting with Anne, my interviews with Sister Laura, Sister Jackie, and Rose Vanderslice, my conversations with Investigator Hughes, the autopsy findings, my search for the license plate, the black paint on Anne's Jeep, and finally, finding the car belonging to the partial plate and its connection to Sister Laura. The only thing I left out was my personal involvement with Anne Hollis.

Sid listened to the whole story, then asked, "Do you really believe a Mother Superior murdered someone? A nun, no less?"

"I think it's possible."

"What's her motive?"

I frowned. "That's the part I'm having trouble with."

"So what are you going to do?"

"The way I see it, there are two choices. One, I can contact Hollis' attorney and ask him to withdraw her plea."

"If you do that, the judge will set it for trial. Do you think that's a good idea, considering that she had been drinking? She'd most likely be convicted of a felony and serve jail time."

"I know. That's why I'm more comfortable with my second choice, which is to prove that Anne's drinking is not what caused the accident, that someone murdered Sister Mary Elizabeth. If I succeed, Anne Hollis' case will be discharged. I'm asking you to let me continue the investigation."

He scowled. "Let the police do it, Callie. Our department doesn't have the resources to put that much time and effort into a PSI."

"Sid, the police won't do it! They think Anne Hollis is lying. Either that or they're too goddamn lazy to go through the motions."

"If you weren't talking about a nun, a Mother Superior for God's sake, you'd have a better chance, but be reasonable, Callie, without a motive...." He shook his head.

My hands had become fists. "What makes you think nuns are exempt from murder? Don't you think they have emotions, passions? Joining a nunnery doesn't mean you stop feeling!" I leaned forward. "Listen to me, Sid. Human beings live inside those convent walls. People. They feel things...jealousy, ambition, shame, love. Sometimes, lust. They know anger and hatred, Sid, because they feel it! Let me look for a motive. Please. If one exists I'll find it."

"Too many other cases need your attention. You've already put excessive time in on this case."

"What if I do it on my own time?"

He squinted at me. "I recognize that stubborn look of yours, Callie. You're going to do what you want, whether I give you permission or not, but for the record, my answer is no. And I mean it. Don't let me hear one word of complaint about your snooping around. Not one word. Do I make myself clear?"

"Perfectly."

At three-thirty that afternoon I walked into the state police barracks and asked to see Investigator Hughes. I was carrying two sealed envelopes in my briefcase, marked A and B, each containing black paint samples. A uniformed trooper directed me to a room down the hall which looked nothing like the precinct rooms depicted on television. Instead of being a noisy space crammed with old wooden desks, green filing cabinets, and people wearing shoulder holsters, it was open and airy with modern furniture and floor plants. I asked one of the officers to point out Investigator Hughes. He did, and I was surprised.

Bill Hughes did not look like I had imagined him to look. He was beefy and completely bald, with a full mustache. And he was black. He sat at a metal desk, cradling the telephone receiver between his shoulder and ear while sorting through a file. Something the caller said made him laugh. The sound was deep and robust. He said, "You got that right!" just before he hung up.

His pen was poised over his notes when I walked over to him. He looked at me expectantly.

"Hi, Investigator Hughes. It's me. Callie Sinclair." I smiled and extended my hand.

"Well, well, well," he said, gripping my hand. "If it isn't the probation department's armchair detective, alive and in person." He smiled. "You don't look like you sound."

"Neither do you," I said. "I thought it might be better if I stopped by to see you rather than call on the phone." There was no visitor's chair near his desk. "Can I bring one of those chairs over here?" I asked, pointing to a pair of blue plastic seats across the room.

"Why don't we just duck into an empty office?" he said. "It's too busy in here to have a private conversation." He led me down the hall to what looked like an interrogation room. "Have a seat. Do you want coffee?"

"No thanks."

"Let me guess why you're here. You found startling new evidence that will prove your client is innocent beyond the shadow of a doubt."

Ordinarily sarcasm pisses me off, but coming from Bill it didn't bother me. I think I knew that I got under his skin more than he got under mine, which kind of evened things out. I pulled the two envelopes out of my briefcase. "Before I start, let me tell you that my supervisor and I met this morning, and I told him everything."

"I'm impressed. You know how to cover your ass."

I placed the envelopes on the table. "These are paint samples, A and B. What I'd like you to do is tell me if they match."

He eyed the envelopes. "I have to know what they are, Callie."

"One contains scrapings of the black paint I found on Anne Hollis' Jeep. The other is from a vehicle I believe was driven by the murderer."

Bill's eyebrows raised. "You've I.D.'d the murderer?"

"Possibly. I've discovered that Sister Laura Bennett, Mother Superior at Sisters of St. James, has access to the vehicle."

He whooped. "You telling me a Mother Superior is your prime suspect in a murder case?"

I gripped the arms of the chair. "Yes, I am. Laura Bennett is just as capable of murder as anyone else. The fact that she's a nun does not exempt her."

"I know that, Sinclair, but you have to admit it gives the case a certain...uniqueness." He picked up a pencil, twirled it in his fingers. "So, what's her motive?"

"That's the part that has me stumped."

"Callie, even if I believed this, which I don't, I'd be hard pressed to find anyone in the department willing to investigate without a motive. If I went to my superiors with what you've given me so far...." He shook his head, trailing off with a shrug.

"Fine, Bill, but can you do one thing for me? Can you have your lab analyze these paint chips, see if they're from the same vehicle? If we can prove the Hollis car was hit by another vehicle it may help her case."

He scratched his chin. "Your defendant would have to change her plea."

"I know."

"She'd have to be crazy to risk a trial."

"Maybe so, but will you do it anyway?" He shrugged and stuck out his hand. "Give me the damn envelopes, Callie. I'll see what I can do."

I smiled. "Thanks, Bill."

"But this is it," he said firmly. "Don't ask me for any more favors."

"I'll try not to," I said.

He rolled his eyes at me, as if he knew he hadn't seen the last of me.

On the way out of the barracks I stopped at a pay phone and called my office. Marylou told me there were no messages from Sister Jackie. I told her I would try reaching Jackie from home later. Meanwhile I drove across town for my appointment with Father Brannigan.

I knew something was wrong the moment I saw Father Brannigan; his face was pale and drawn, his eyes misty. "Officer Sinclair, what a terrible shock—"

"What is it, Father?" I grasped his hand. "What's wrong?"

"Come into my office." He turned and led me into a large dark-paneled room with wine-colored carpeting. Two green upholstered chairs faced the polished oak desk. "Please, make yourself comfortable."

I remained standing. "Father, what is it?"

"You're here about Sister Jacqueline Prescott, aren't you?"

"What about Jackie?"

"Why, she's dead."

His statement was like a blow to my stomach; I almost doubled over. "How?" I asked, falling into a chair.

"I assumed you knew, by now. The police said she closed herself in the garage, started the car and left it running, with the exhaust free to permeate the closed up space."

"God…" I tried to catch my breath. "I can hardly believe it." My head was spinning. Why would somebody who just inherited a million dollars commit suicide? And in the convent car? What if she didn't. What if she was murdered. Why?

"If you didn't know about Sister Jackie, why are you here?"

"I wanted to speak to you as candidly as possible about my investigation surrounding Sister Mary Elizabeth's death. I was hoping you could shed some light on my inquiries, but at the moment I'm in shock." I held my stomach with one hand, my head with the other. "Please give me a few moments to compose myself."

"Of course. Take your time. I'll get some tea."

"Thank you."

Jackie's death shook me as if she had been a friend, someone dear to me. I remembered my initial encounter with her at the picnic table, the sun highlighting her hair, then I recalled our last meeting, her tears, sobs. I choked back tears of my own, my throat aching from the effort. I moaned, "Oh Jackie, what happened to you?"

The office door swung open with Father Brannigan carrying in a silver tea service. He set it down gently on the desk. "Here we are, Officer Sinclair. Shall I pour?"

"Yes, thank you."

"Help yourself to sugar and cream. I apologize for those Oreo cookies, but they're all I have in the way of sweets." He sat heavily in the chair behind his desk. "I'm afraid my thoughts are rather scattered."

Sipping my tea, I squirmed in my seat, unsure of how to broach the subject when Father Brannigan did it for me. "No suicide note was found." He reached for a spoon and began stirring his tea. "And I'd be surprised if one popped up."

I gasped. "Then you don't believe she killed herself?"

He shook his head slowly.

"I was raised Catholic, Father, so I know suicide is a sin. Is that what you're thinking?—that a nun wouldn't commit such a grievous sin."

"No, it's more than that. Sister Jackie was very distraught over Sister Mary Elizabeth's death—they were very close friends—but I don't think her grief was so devastating that she felt she could not go on with her own life."

I spooned sugar into my tea and stirred. "I should explain my position to you, Father. My responsibility in this matter is to investigate the circumstances surrounding Sister Mary Elizabeth's death, then report those findings to the judge in charge of making a decision about Ms. Hollis' sentence. She is the woman who was convicted of vehicular manslaughter."

"Yes, I'm aware of her."

I wondered just how much he was aware of, but I didn't want to press, instead I detailed Anne's statement, stepping gently around the issue of Beth's sexuality and my belief that Beth had, in fact, been followed. "I'm in possession of Beth's personal diary, and at this point I have more questions than answers."

"I see." He leaned forward. "I don't know if I can help answer your concerns, Officer, but I'm willing to try. Does the diary reveal any facts pertinent to your investigation?"

"In my opinion, yes, but the reason I mention it to you is that one of the entries refers to Sister Laura requesting Beth meet with you, ostensibly to discuss her recent infractions. I wanted to know if that meeting ever took place."

"Ah." He sat back, crossed his arms over his stomach. "No. Sister Laura and I discussed the possibility, but the meeting never happened."

"Can you shed any light on Beth's problems at the convent?"

He rubbed his chin, pursed his lips. "She had gone AWOL, so to speak. She claimed Sister Laura had given her permission to spend the night with her sister, but Sister Laura says she did not grant permission. The incident caused quite a stir at the convent with everyone worrying about her whereabouts."

"Yes. Beth wrote about the incident in her diary. She said she found Sister Laura in a strange mood when she asked for permission to stay out overnight and was surprised when she was given permission."

"Hmmm," Father Brannigan murmured, "that's interesting."

"Yes, especially since it wasn't the first time something like that happened. In a similar entry that I found last night, Beth said she was in the kitchen when Sister Laura strode in and demanded that both Beth and Jackie see her in her office first thing in the morning, that she couldn't tolerate the way they behaved together. Beth thought that she and Jackie would be separated but when they went to her office, Sister Laura wasn't expecting them and dismissed them. What do you make of that, Father?"

"I don't know, Officer Sinclair. I've never experienced a communication problem with the Mother Superior. Maybe she just wanted to make them think about limiting their purpose in the convent."

I wondered what he would be willing to share about Laura. "How long has Sister Laura been Mother Superior?"

"Let's see, four or five years." He nodded enthusiastically. "A fine appointment."

"She's a good administrator?"

"Absolutely. She's astute about the sisters' personal issues and keeping the convent harmonious. I credit that expertise with the fact that Sister Laura was able to overcome enormous personal adversity in order to achieve her status within the church."

I shook my head. "I'm not familiar with her history...."

"She rose out of an impoverished and abusive family situation. Her mother was mentally ill and institutionalized for years. Laura had full responsibility for taking care of her siblings and running the household. Her father made her the surrogate wife," Father Brannigan's face colored, "in every way. But Laura was able to face this suffering when she turned to the Church. Fortunately for her and for us, she at last found her place as a nun. An exemplary one."

I reached for an Oreo to keep composed, and said, "I see. Yes, that is a great deal to overcome without intensive psychotherapy— for us lay people. Does the church provide such counseling for its clergy and nuns?"

"Yes, of course. But I couldn't disclose any information about whether Sister Laura had any, even if I knew. Preparing for vows is an arduous and cleansing process as it is. If anything, she would demand the same thoroughness from her novitiates that she went through, but I have always found her sensitive and fair."

Frustrated, I chomped on the Oreo cookie, knowing perfectly well that if Sister Laura had had any personal problems along the way, he wasn't going to tell me. Politely I concluded my interview with the Monsignor. I was all the more anxious to pay a visit to the convent.

Within fifteen minutes I was on the convent doorstep. The doorbell was answered by a short, plump woman with grey hair and a pleasant face.

"I'm Office Sinclair," I said, showing her my badge. "Is Sister Laura in?"

"No, I'm sorry, she's out, but she'll be back soon."

"I wonder if I might speak with someone else in the meantime? Do you live here?"

"I'm Sister Roseanne," she said. "C'mon in." She led me to the same room where I met with Sister Laura earlier in the week. "Is Sister Laura expecting you? It's not like her to be late. She had to run an errand, but she said she'd be back in a few minutes. Who else did you want to speak with?"

Sister Roseanne was a regular little chatterbox. I liked that in an interviewee. "I'd like to speak with you if you have a few moments."

"I guess that would be okay, but I'm not sure what I can do. You see, we had a tragedy here today." Her eyes filled. "One of our sisters passed away." She pulled a hanky out of her pocket and blew her nose.

"That's the reason I'm here," I said. "I've been investigating the events surrounding the death of Sister Mary Elizabeth, and Sister Jackie had been most helpful to me. In fact, I was hoping to meet with her this afternoon to discuss a matter pertaining to the case. I'm very sorry to hear of her passing."

"Thank you." She lowered her head. "Her death was such a shock. I was the one who found her. We hadn't heard the motor running." She made the sign of the cross. "It was my turn to do the grocery shopping, so I was going out to the garage for the car. As soon as I opened the garage door I knew something was wrong. I could smell the exhaust. The car doors were open and Jackie was slumped over in the front seat. I screamed and ran into the house. Sister Laura called an ambulance, but it was too late. Sister Jackie was dead."

"Sister Roseanne, I know it's probably difficult for you to talk about it, but I wonder if you can tell me whether or not Sister Jackie left a suicide note."

She shook her head. "We haven't found one. Are you Catholic, Ms. Sinclair?"

"Yes, I am." I said.

"Then you know that suicide is a sin?"

"Yes," I said, "that's one of the things that surprised me so much. That and the inheritance."

"Well, a million dollars to a nun isn't such a big deal, you know?"

"Why is that, Sister?"

She snickered. "We're allowed to accept patrimony...that's what they call it when a nun inherits money...but it's controlled by the Order. If Sister Jackie wanted to spend any of her money, she'd have to get permission first."

"Can you tell me what Sister Jackie's state of mind has been lately? What I'm getting at is, has she been so depressed that she would resort to suicide?"

"I didn't think so, but apparently she was. She hadn't been the same since Beth died. Did she tell you how close they were?"

"I understood they were best friends."

Sister Roseanne nodded. "Like this." She held up her hand, two fingers tight together.

I felt myself hesitate before asking my next question because I thought it might be considered inappropriate. Since when did that ever stop me? "Sister, what about Beth and Jackie's relationship with Sister Laura?"

She blinked rapidly. "What do you mean?"

"How did they get along?"

"All of the sisters get along well."

"With Sister Laura? Does, did everyone get along well with Sister Laura?"

"Most of the time."

"What is Sister Laura like as a Mother Superior? Is she stern, agreeable...."

"Sister Laura has always been strict." She frowned, then brightened. "But very fair. That's what a Mother Superior is supposed to be."

"I see. What about lately? How has she been lately?"

"Lately?" Roseanne giggled. "Well, she has been forgetting things lately."

My interest was piqued. "What kind of things?"

"Well, like last week—she left me a note to pick up a gallon of pistachio ice-cream. I bought some and served it for desert at dinner the next night. She didn't eat hers, said she hated pistachio. When I reminded her about the note, she got mad, not that she said anything but I could tell because she stomped out of the room."

"So how do you explain that?"

Sister Roseanne laughed. "Too much on her mind! It certainly isn't her age because I'm older than she is. But others have commented too...little things. She forgets what she said to you before, contradicts it."

I began wondering if Sister Laura was suffering from early senility, unless she was under some sort of strain. "Sister, when was the last time you saw Jackie yesterday?"

"Oh, in the morning. I didn't actually see her last night. She wasn't with us for dinner. With her parents. She came home in the evening but went to her room. I was going to bed when she got a phone call, around eleven. Sister Genevieve answered the phone and called up the stairs."

"Did you hear what it was about?"

"No." She shook her head. "The phone is downstairs."

"And where was Sister Laura?"

"Why, in her room of course." Sister Roseanne looked at me baffled. "We all were going to bed."

I was just about to ask Sister Roseanne if it were possible that Sister Laura could have gone out without her knowledge, but the front door opened and Sister Laura strode in, her face tense. When she saw me sitting on the couch she blanched. I was feeling a bit weak at the knees myself, suddenly finding myself face to face with my nightmare. I stood and walked towards her. "Sister Laura, I'm so sorry to hear of your loss."

"Ms. Sinclair." Her gaze swept the room, settled on Sister Roseanne.

Sister Roseanne jumped to her feet, her face crimson. "She was asking me some questions about Sister Jackie and Mary Elizabeth...."

I wanted to kick her in the shins and tell her to be quiet. Instead, I said, "Sister Roseanne has been most kind to keep me company while waiting for you. I arrived just a few minutes ago." I hoped my smile looked engaging.

Laura appeared stricken, her voice frail. "Why are you here?"

"I came as soon as I heard about Sister Jackie," I said. "I was expecting to meet with her this afternoon at Foxmoor."

She walked to the couch and sat down, her hands at her sides, her eyes red and puffy. I followed, sitting across from her. Sister Roseanne scampered from the room.

"If this is a bad time for you, Sister...."

She dismissed my concern with a wave of her hand. "You said you were planning to meet with Sister Jackie. Didn't you see her the other day?"

"Yes, but I had more questions." I reached into my briefcase and brought Beth's diary out. I watched Laura Bennett's eyes as she followed the path of the diary to my lap. "We were going to talk about this today."

She focused abruptly on my face. "What is it?"

"Sister Mary Elizabeth's journal," I said. "I was hoping Sister Jackie could help me understand the meaning of some of the entries." I tapped the diary against my knee, then sighed, and returned it to my briefcase. I felt sure the diary would burn through my briefcase, or that Laura would tackle me. "I wonder if you would let me take a look at the car in which Sister Jackie died?"

"Absolutely not," she stated emphatically, drawing herself to a standing position. "I'm afraid I'm going to have to ask you to leave."

Her manner had changed so quickly. One moment frail, the next, forceful. I hesitated. "Sister, I want to remind you that I'm a probation officer investigating a manslaughter, and in that capacity I have the right to make inspections relative to the case. I was being polite by asking you to show me the vehicle. If you refuse to cooperate, I'll find my own way to the garage."

The Mother Superior opened her mouth to speak, but was interrupted by the doorbell. She spun on her heals to answer it. I heard voices, but couldn't make out the words. A minute or so later Sister Laura returned to the parlor with a tall beefy black man in tow.

"Well, well, well," he said with a tight grin. "We meet again. What a surprise."

"Hi, Bill," I said smiling.

Sister Laura said, "Investigator Hughes, I take it you are acquainted with Ms. Sinclair?"

"I sure am."

Her smile was sly. "Perhaps then you can enlighten me as to whether Ms. Sinclair, in the course of her investigation of a recent manslaughter, has the right to examine the vehicle in which Sister Jackie died?"

"Well, now," he said, rubbing his chin. "I don't see what harm it could do. The police and pathologist have finished up." He turned to me. "Why don't you come out with me, Officer Sinclair? We can examine the scene together." He turned back to Sister Laura. "If you'll excuse us, Sister?"

Hughes frowned as soon as we stepped outside. "What the hell are you doing here, Sinclair?"

"What are you doing here, Hughes? This isn't your territory. Since when does a state trooper make house calls."

"We don't, but when I heard there was another death at this convent, and since we are in consultation with each other over Hollis, I thought it might not hurt to take a look."

"You mean, maybe I'm not crazy after all?"

"Oh, I wouldn't go that far, Sinclair. You might say I'm trying to keep you out of trouble. Let's go take a look." We walked around to the garage and opened the doors. A blue late model Chevy sat with its driver's door open. "I had a long talk with the detective in charge. Told him this case might relate to one of mine.... Don't go lookin' at me like that, Callie, I just said that so I could find out what I wanted to know from him."

I nodded. "I don't know what I expected to find," I said sadly. "One of the other nuns said there was no suicide note." I heard a scraping noise behind us and turned. Sister Laura had followed us. She stood outside the garage, her manner congenial as if she had carefully collected herself.

"I owe you an apology, Ms. Sinclair," she said softly. "You, too, Investigator." She shook her head. "This...tragedy. I'm afraid it's made me...difficult. Please forgive me."

Bill's voice was gentle. "No need to apologize, Sister. Suicide is especially difficult to accept."

Sister Laura bowed her head, her voice almost a whisper. "I don't believe it was suicide."

"What?!" I exclaimed in complete surprise.

"Sister Jackie was a good nun," she explained, "a good Catholic. Suicide is a sin against God. You must believe me...Sister Jackie would never have killed herself! Never!"

I couldn't believe my ears. I said, "If it wasn't suicide it had to be murder. Do you find that more within the realm of possibilities, Sister Laura?"

Bill shot me a look of disbelief which quickly turned to irritation. Sister Laura didn't reply, just stared at me.

Bill interjected. "Sister, when the police were here this morning, did you express your views about the suicide at that time?"

"I certainly did, but I don't think they agreed with me. I overheard them saying it looked pretty cut and dried."

There was that damn term again. Cut and dried. Nothing about this case had been cut and dried, right from the beginning.

"I know you've been over this numerous times already, Sister," Bill said softly, "but would you mind repeating the events for our benefit? We understand Sister Jackie was found this morning by Sister Roseanne. Did anyone see Sister Jackie earlier?"

Sister Laura shook her head. "No. We all assumed she was still asleep. Jackie's bedroom is at the far end of the upstairs hallway, and there was no reason for any of us to look in on her. She's the only one in the household who works second shift, so we're used to her sleeping late."

"What about last night?" I asked. "Anything unusual happen?"

"Jackie went to her mother's house for dinner and arrived home about seven. I was the only one downstairs when she got in. She was very upset, but that's not unusual for Jackie when she's been visiting home." Sister Laura's voice lowered conspiratorially. "Her mother can be a problem."

Bill asked, "Did you speak with her when she got in?"

"No. She went directly to her room and closed the door. She remained there until just before eleven when the telephone rang, waking the household. Sister Genevieve answered it. She said it was

Jackie's stepfather calling for her. Jackie took the call, but I don't know what, if anything, happened after that. We were all in our rooms."

"Could you hear anything she was saying on the phone?" I asked. "Was her voice angry, frightened, anything unusual?"

"I couldn't hear. The telephone is on the first floor. All of our bedrooms are on the second."

"Did you notice if she came upstairs after the call or if she went directly out?"

"I think she came back up. She must have. I remember seeing her walk past my bedroom on her way downstairs, wearing a night-shirt. When we found her this morning she was fully dressed. I must have fallen asleep. I never heard a thing."

Bill asked, "Does this car belong to Jackie personally?"

"No," Laura replied, "It belongs to the convent. Jackie used it more than anyone else because Foxmoor is not on a bus route. She works the second shift, so the other Sisters have access to the car the early part of the day. Sister Roseanne was planning to use it to shop for groceries this morning."

I got behind the wheel of the car and sat there, thinking. The key was still in the ignition. "Bill, would the police lab have dusted for prints this morning?"

"I'm sure it's standard procedure. Why?"

"I was just wondering whose prints they're going to find on the ignition key."

TEN

As Bill Hughes walked with me to my car, I asked, "So, what do you think?"

"I think Sister Jackie committed suicide."

I raised my eyebrows. "You must be joking. Why would you think that?"

"Why wouldn't I?" he said, irritation in his voice.

"Because Jackie's death doesn't feel right."

"You know what your problem is, Callie? You're pissed because Sister Laura stole your thunder. You came over here today to expose this suicide as a murder...a murder that you believe was committed by the Mother Superior...only to have that same Mother Superior say she didn't think it was a suicide!"

"I can't explain why she said that." I paused in front of my car.

"Well, I can. She said it because she believes it."

"Maybe she's trying to throw us off," I said, without conviction.

He shook his head. "We'll see what the lab comes up with, but I think you're wrong."

"What happens in the meantime?"

"Nothing. Unless the lab finds something suspicious."

"Will you keep me informed?" I opened my car door. "Let me know about prints, etcetera?"

"I'll tell you what I can, when I can, but not unless you promise to lay off."

"I don't make promises I can't keep, Bill. Let's just take this a day at a time, okay?" I slid behind the wheel of my car and pulled the door closed. Bill knocked on the window, so I rolled it down.

He stuck his face through the opening. I felt his breath on my cheek when he said, "You stop playing detective. It's dangerous!"

I started the engine and the radio blared, the noise deafening. I didn't turn the volume down. Bill backed away, and I pulled out of the parking space. I saw him in my rear view mirror, staring after me. He was pissed.

I drove home and rummaged through my briefcase to find the notes I made during my last conversation with Jackie. I remembered asking about her parents, but I couldn't recall their names. I pulled the Hollis file out of my attache and it fell to the floor, sheets of lined yellow paper floating across the room. I scolded myself for not having a better system as I waded through a dozen pieces of paper before I found the note: Pam and Dr. Harry Loomis, Guilderland. I grabbed the telephone directory and looked them up. Surprise, surprise—I discovered that Dr. Loomis and his wife were next door neighbors of the Bennett's! I could hardly wait to get back into my car and drive out to Guilderland to pay my respects.

I parked right in front of the Loomis' house, a two story brick colonial, and walked up the driveway. Before I got to the front door, movement in the backyard caught my eye. Someone was working in the garage.

The door was open, so I peered inside. The garage was oversized, allowing for a Saab and Corvette to share space, while leaving enough room for heaps of equipment, tools, and spare parts. If I didn't know better, I'd think the garage was a commercial establishment rather than a hobby shop.

"Can I help you?" A tall well-built man emerged from the house behind me. He looked to be about fifty, with dark hair, grey at the temples. He wore a white shirt, sleeves rolled to his elbows, black jeans, and an old pair of docksiders, without socks. He didn't look pleased to see me prowling around his private property.

"Hi," I stuck out my hand, but he ignored it. "I'm Officer Callie Sinclair from Albany County Probation. Are you Dr. Loomis?"

"Yes," he said warily. He was carrying a container of car polish and a clean white cloth.

"Please, don't let me interrupt you," I said, turning toward the garage where the silver Saab was waiting for a shine. "I just stopped by to offer my condolences to you and your wife on the loss of your daughter."

"Thank you," he said, loosening up. "It's been a terrible shock. Mrs. Loomis is presently under sedation." He moved toward the front of the car, and I followed him, noting the size of his shoulders. I had a feeling he lifted weights. He looked over his shoulder and said, "How did you know Jackie?"

"I met her recently when I began investigating a manslaughter. She was personally acquainted with the victim and had been very helpful providing information to my department."

"You must be talking about Beth." Dr. Loomis dabbed some car wax on the Saab's hood and began rubbing in a circular motion. "Jackie took her death very hard," he said. "They were very close friends, you know."

"I understand Jackie was here for dinner last night?"

He stopped polishing. "Yes, she was."

I said, "When Jackie arrived home she was upset. Can you tell me why?"

"At the risk of sounding impolite, may I ask what business that is of the probation department?"

"I'm sorry, Dr. Loomis, I'm used to asking impertinent questions all day long, and I think it's become a habit. I hope you'll forgive me, but I do need to ask them." I smiled feebly. "You see, I've been working rather closely with the police on the manslaughter case, and well, quite frankly, I'm trying to rule out a tie-in with Jackie's death."

"But of course there's a tie-in."

My eyes widened. "You think so?"

"I believe it was Beth's death which prompted Jackie's suicide."

Dr. Loomis had missed my point, but maybe that was just as well. I continued carefully. "I was told she didn't leave a suicide note."

"That's right."

"I understand you talked with Jackie last night, sir, just before eleven o'clock. Can you tell me if she said anything that would indicate her state of mind?"

He hesitated before replying. "I can't think of anything specific.

She hasn't been herself since Beth died."

"Are you aware that Jackie left the house after your telephone conversation?"

"No." He laid the can of polish on the ground and wiped his hands. "Do you know where she went?"

"I'm not sure she went anywhere, Dr. Loomis. We don't know time of death yet. Sir, why did you telephone Jackie last night?"

His jaw muscles flexed. "Our conversation had to do with a family matter. Now, if you'll excuse me, I'd like to tend to my wife."

I might not have excused him, but I happened to hear a car pull in next door, at the Bennett's. I politely thanked Dr. Loomis for his time and scooted down the driveway.

"Mrs. Bennett!" I called cheerily. "Hi there."

She seemed surprised to see me emerge from the Loomis' driveway. "Hello," she said, smiling. "Did you need to see Johnny's car again?"

"No. Actually I stopped by to pay my respects to Dr. and Mrs. Loomis. I was acquainted with their daughter, Jackie."

Gloom wiped the smile from her face. "A disaster," she remarked, shaking her head. "Jackie was such a dear girl."

"Have you known her long?"

"Five or six years. Ever since her mother married Dr. Loomis and moved next door. I can't believe she did such a thing. She wasn't the type to commit suicide, don't you agree? Did you know her well?"

"Only for a short time, Mrs. Bennett, but well enough to agree with your observation."

"Please, call me Mary." She stood with her key in the door. "Why don't you come in for a minute? Have a cup of coffee."

"Thank you, I will," I said, following her into the house. "What a beautiful room." The beige carpet was so thick my feet sank in practically to my ankles.

"Thank you. We had a decorator in. All I did was tell him my budget, then sign the checks. He did the rest. Come on into the kitchen."

She had a breakfast nook, which I adore. Makes me feel as if I'm eating at a diner. "Please don't pour coffee for me," I said. "But I'll take a diet soft drink if you have it."

She pulled a bottle of cola out of the fridge, and poured a huge glass of it. It wasn't Coke or Pepsi, so I figured it was going to taste like cough medicine. I tried not to grimace with my first sip.

"I'm sorry, I don't remember your name," she said.

"Callie Sinclair."

"Callie's an unusual name, but very pretty."

"Thank you."

"How did you become acquainted with Sister Jackie?"

Well, so much for my cover. "I'm the investigating officer in the manslaughter case involving her friend's death, Sister Mary Elizabeth."

Her eyes widened. "Oh, yes. She was a sweet girl, too. I remember meeting her two or three times when I visited Laura at the convent residence. Laura Bennett, my sister-in-law?"

"Yes, I remember." Then lowered my voice for effect. "Mary, I'd like to confide something in you if I may?"

Mary Bennett leaned forward. "Of course. What is it?"

"I'm wondering about a connection between Beth's accident and Jackie's suicide."

"Oh, you mean because Jackie's been so distraught over it?"

"Yes...."

"Pam Loomis told me how broken up Jackie's been."

"Well, I think there's more to it than that. I understand Jackie was visiting her mother last night for dinner, and that when she left she was extremely upset. Would you know anything about that?"

She colored. "How would I know?"

"Well, you are friends with Pam Loomis. Perhaps she mentioned something."

Mary spooned sugar into her coffee and stirred it. "No, she didn't."

My glass was sweating, making rings on the table top. I reached for a paper napkin and slipped it under the tumbler. "Did you know about Jackie's inheritance?"

"Yes, Pam told me. I think leaving all that money to a nun is crazy, don't you?"

"I'm not sure, what makes you say that?"

"Well, according to Pam, the convent won't let you use your own money without permission. Something to do with the vow of poverty. So even though she'd be a millionaire, she wouldn't live any differently. Harry thought that would be a waste, and I quite agree with him."

"Yes, I see what you mean. So what was he suggesting she do? Leave the convent?"

"Heavens, no!" she exclaimed. "He wanted her to turn the million over to her mother. You know, so they could invest it for her."

"I wonder how Jackie felt about that."

"She disagreed with him. Maybe that's why she left so upset yesterday. Pam told me that Harry and Jackie got into quite an argument over his suggestion. Jackie said she hadn't decided what to do with the money, but implied she might turn it over to the Sisters' retirement fund."

"If she couldn't splurge on herself, why not?" I said. "I understand the nuns don't have a retirement plan. Or not in their control—they get to be placed in some Catholic aged nun's home, or rely on being taken care of by younger nuns in the convent. Besides, her parents seem to have enough money."

"Hah!" Mary Bennett laughed. "No one has enough money, my dear. No one." She walked to the counter and poured herself a second cup of coffee. "What you said about the retirement plan is true, the nuns don't have one at this convent. Laura's the Order's financial officer, that's how come I know."

My heart leapt into my throat. Finally, a possible motive for Sister Laura—if she knew that Jackie had changed her will already. Was Sister Laura going to make sure Jackie didn't have time to change it yet again under pressure from family? My mind wanted to run in ten different directions, but I forced myself to maintain my focus on the Loomis'.

"I've never met Pam Loomis," I said. "What's she like?"

"She's very nice," said Mary, so carefully that I knew she was hiding something. I also knew she knew I knew, and I was sure she wanted me to know more.

"Nice is such a benign description," I said, grinning. "Don't you think? I mean most of us are nice, but that's not what we're really like. For example, I'm kind, gentle, and considerate when I'm not being pushy and overbearing. See what I mean?"

"I guess so, but Pam really is nice most of the time."

"And when she isn't being nice she's…" I wanted Mary to fill in the blank for me, and she did.

"...a drunk."

"Pam Loomis is an alcoholic?"

Mary nodded. "She must be. She goes off on these toots every so often and poor Harry has to go looking for her. There have been times when she's ended up at some pretty sleazy joints."

"What a shame," I said. "I guess that explains why Jackie chose to work in the field of alcoholism."

Mary Bennett continued. "The saddest part is there were many times Pam didn't want to go home when Harry found her, so Harry would call Jackie and she'd have to go out to the bar to talk her mother into going home."

I wondered if that was where Jackie was headed last night, and that Harry didn't tell me because he wanted to keep the family secret.

"Rescuing her mother must have been especially difficult for Jackie," I said. "As an alcoholism counselor she knew that by doing so, she was enabling her mother to continue drinking."

"Yes, but if she didn't rescue her, God only knows what could have happened to her in those bars!"

"That's probably what made it so difficult," I said. "She knew that if her mother were forced to hit bottom she might have sought treatment. I understand some people would rather commit suicide than quit drinking." I shuddered, remembering my own mother, and the dozens of times I drove through the city searching for her. Not long before she died I found her in an alleyway, passed out in her own vomit.

I bent over, making a fuss of opening my briefcase, rapidly blinking back tears. "Mary, do you know if Pam went out drinking last night, after Jackie left?"

"I know that both she and Harry went out together, and this was at least two hours after Jackie left. They didn't get home until one-thirty." I asked how she could be so sure of the time. "Our bedroom overlooks the Loomis' driveway. When they slammed their car doors, the noise woke me up. I noticed the time on my digital clock radio."

"Did you hear anything they said?"

"No, but I could tell Pam was looped because she was hanging all over Harry. I went to the window to close it, and watched them go into the house. Pam could hardly stand, let alone walk. Harry practically had to carry her."

It was raining by the time I left Guilderland. As soon as I got home, I called Anne and told her about Jackie's death. Her reaction was similar to mine, disbelief and sorrow. We agreed to meet for dinner at nine and catch up. I showered and changed into jeans and a striped rugby shirt, then slipped my feet into soft leather moccasins, ran a brush through my damp hair, and sprinted out the door. Hooper's Bar was a comfortable fifteen minute drive from my townhouse, but that night I made the trip in ten, anticipating Anne waiting under the awning by the front door, rain splashing on the sidewalk in front of her and me sweeping her away in my chariot.

No such luck. She wasn't even in the bar.

"Boss lady's still upstairs," Tink said in the middle of some concoction with the blender. "Can I get you something to drink in the meantime?"

"No thanks." I contemplated going out to wait under the awning myself, realizing quickly it was much too conspicuous a spot with customers coming and going, mostly coming. I chose the furthest bar stool from the door and plunked myself down on it, already feeling that my palms were clammy. And I didn't even want a drink, did I? Sadie had been right to warn me. I muttered a prayer to my Higher Power that I wouldn't run into any more Guzzies from my past, and had barely finished the thought when I discovered I must have asked for a Growth Opportunity instead.

"Well as I live and breathe." The voice next to my ear was unmistakable. I closed my eyes, willing this ghost away. "Callie, baby, aren't you going to say hello?"

I turned to face the woman I had taken a good four years to get over and another three to forget. "Hello Jazz."

Still busty and full figured she wore skin tight stretchpants with an oversized white shirt, and over that a chic leather jacket with studs. Her short hair was spiked and she had ear cuffs all up and down her ears. The heavy eye make-up was a new touch. So it wasn't exactly déjà vu. Jazz was always one for dress-up and the latest style. What I could see was that seven years had indeed transpired because she had a completely different look.

She kissed me on the cheek, gushed, "Oooh, baby you look terrific, just like you did before."

That was a non-starter for sure; I said nothing, just gave her my best blank look.

"You're not drinking again are you, Callie? No, no!" She wagged a finger at me, clicked her tongue, reminding me in a flash of the infinite mockery and sarcasm I had always put up with.

And what the fuck is it to you, I thought as I said, "Just waiting for someone."

"Oh, and I bet I know who." Jazz rolled her eyes, giving me a secretive, gloating smile. "Anne Hollis. Can't say I blame you. I've had the hots for her myself."

My heart was pounding, my hands shaking as I kept them glued in my lap. How was it possible for her to be standing there, talking so casually with me as if we had never had that intensely awful relationship? "What makes you think I'm here to see Anne?" My voice sounded a bit high-pitched, but Jazz didn't seem to notice.

"Tink, who else?" She said with a big wink.

I glanced down the bar, narrowing my eyes. Tink always did have an awful big mouth. For someone so concerned about confidentiality the other night, she sure was one for gossip. Ah, but then, what did she know of Jazz? Tink had been my drinking and softball buddy before sultry old Jazz came along. Still, I wanted to chop Tink up into little pieces using that blender.

"It has been too long, much too long, Callie. I've missed you." Jazz leaned closer, that pout on her lips now, with the little girl voice while her hand found its way conveniently to my thigh. I felt my face flush, my pulse quicken. Was it an old spark of lust or pure rage? I didn't know, but I pulled away.

"Cut it out, Jazz. I'm not interested."

She laughed with her head tilted back, full-throated. "Since when?"

"Ever since I found you fucking with someone else in our bed, and pretending you just couldn't figure out how she got there." I didn't bother explaining how the only way I had finally purged myself of that ordeal after she had moved out, was to buy a new futon bed. I wasn't going to waste my moment of triumph on her.

Jazz batted her eyelashes at me. "You aren't still mad, are you?"

I shrugged. "What difference does it make?"

All sincere now. "It makes a difference, Cal. I wasn't lying when I said I've missed you. In fact, I've been thinking about you a lot lately." She sat on the stool next to me, swung her leg around so her knee rubbed against my thigh. "Do you ever think about me?"

I shook my head quickly. "Not in a long time."

"Well, maybe I can change that," she drawled. Before I knew it, she had reached over and covered my mouth with hers, brushing her tongue between my lips before I even had a chance to tighten them in defense. She moaned, low and smooth, "Oh God, Cal."

"Callie?"

I swiveled in my bar stool, realizing immediately just who that kiss was meant for. She must have seen Anne behind me. "Anne..."

"Hi, Anne," Jazz said, that slow innocent smile shaping her lips. "Cal and I go way back, don't we, baby?" She stood up, placed her hand on my shoulder and whispered in my ear. "It can't be better in bed than we were."

I flushed, jerked my shoulder from her grasp. A look of disappointment shadowed Anne's face, but I didn't know how to fix it. I was too flustered to explain the whole story in a nutshell or pass Jazz off as being her usual old self.

"I didn't know you knew Jazz?"

"I wish I didn't," I said, pulling myself together. "Are you ready to leave?"

"Yes."

I grabbed her arm, more for dear life than as a suave escort, and led her outside. We paused under the awning as rain poured down in torrents on the sidewalk in front of us.

"Anne, my car's across the street. Lets make a run for it."

"I hope you weren't waiting long."

"Just a minute or two."

After we got into the car she squeezed my hand. "God, it's good to see you."

"Yes," I agreed, pulling out of the parking space, checking my rear view mirror. "But I'm not sure this is a good idea."

"What isn't? Our having dinner together?"

"In a public place. I'm afraid we'll be seen together."

"By Sister Laura?"

"Yes." And I began telling Anne about my visit to the convent.

"Callie, do you still think Sister Laura is guilty of murder?"

"I'm not so sure. She seemed sincerely distressed over Jackie's death, and I don't think she was acting, yet I later learned that there's a possible motive. Sister Laura is the Order's financial officer. That position would certainly give her access to Jackie's million if Jackie's will had left all her money to the convent, and providing that Laura knew that. It isn't clear to me what the status of her will is, or if she had time to speak to her attorney." I looked over at Anne, her expression hopeful. "Wait, there's more," I said. "I drove over to Jackie's parents' home, and, oh, get this, Anne, Doctor and Mrs. Loomis live right next door to the Bennett's. Can you believe it?"

"The Bennett's are the people whose son owns the black car, right?"

"Right. The people who are related to Laura Bennett. They're friends of the Loomis'. Mary Bennett was telling me that Dr. Loomis wanted Jackie to turn her inheritance over to her mother!" I was so excited to be able to tell Anne what I learned that I was practically jumping up and down behind the wheel. For just a second I was aware that every ounce of my professional demeanor had gone out the window.

"He wanted her to turn the entire million over? What is he, crazy?"

"Well, in a way I could see his point—as a nun, Jackie couldn't really spend the money, and Loomis feels the Order shouldn't control all those resources. I kind of agree with him on that point, but for some reason, Jackie didn't. She told them she wanted the money for her retirement. Maybe Loomis knew the status of her will. Maybe he killed her before she could turn the money over to the Convent." The rain slowed to a drizzle making the wipers go 'scritch–scritch–scritch' across the windshield.

"So what are you saying, Callie? That Jackie's stepfather murdered her?"

"If Jackie's will was not changed he had the motive and the opportunity. I'm just not positive about the means. And to complicate things further, the police believe Jackie's death really does appear to be suicide. We'll have to see what the lab has to say. In the meantime I'm going to check on her will."

"Any word yet on the black paint?"

"Not yet, and I don't dare press Hughes. He's not exactly thrilled with me poking my nose into what he considers police business."

I pulled into CoCo's parking lot. It was crowded as hell so I had to drive behind the building to search for an opening. I found one along the fence, parked, and turned the engine off.

The rain began coming down harder. "Do you want me to drive you to the door? I don't have an umbrella in the car."

"No, it's okay," Anne said, placing her hand on my thigh. "Maybe we can sit here just a minute to see if the rain lets up."

The rain made it almost impossible to see out of the windows, and, I reasoned, just as impossible to see in. I leaned over and brushed Anne's cheek with my lips. She turned her head, pressing her lips against my mouth, then just as quickly pulled away. "Callie...I know I have no right to ask, but why were you kissing Jazz?"

"I wasn't kissing her!" I retorted too hotly. "She was kissing me, purely for effect. She's like that—manipulative. She knows I'm involved with you—don't act surprised, Tink said something. We've got to put a gag on that girl. How do you know her?"

"Jazz? She slept with my ex, and just about anyone else she can get into bed with."

Anne's words stung. Had I been that stupid back then, or had Jazz's sexual appetite increased since we split?

"So she comes to Hoopers a lot?"

Anne shrugged. "Pretty regularly for a year and a half."

"She's drinking?"

"Scotch on the rocks with a twist."

"Anne..." Headlights swept across the windshield, causing me to flinch. "Damn," I said. "This isn't going to work. We're too exposed." I shifted my car into first gear and stepped on the accelerator. Anne slid closer to her window.

"Where are you taking us?" she asked.

"Well, first we're going to drive around for a few minutes, until I'm sure no one is following us. Then we're going to my place."

129

Rain pelted against the bedroom windows as Anne came into my arms. "Hold me," she whispered, urgently, burying her face in the hollow of my neck. "I need to feel safe tonight."

I pulled her against me. "You're safe now. No one knows we're here." I tugged at her shirt where it tucked into her pants, freeing it so I could slip my hands underneath, slowly gliding them across the smooth contours of her back, around to her flat belly, and finally to her breasts. I was warmed by her compelling need to make love, excited by the musky smell of her cologne. My heart beat a staccato as I unfastened her buttons, sliding her shirt from her shoulders. Once again I discovered the smoothness of her skin, the fullness of her breasts. "I will always keep you safe," I murmured, drawing her closer.

Anne placed her hands at the back of my neck, pulling my head towards her, her lips against my ear. She whispered, "Take your clothes off, Callie."

My breathing was quick, urgent with desire. I pulled my shirt off, and together we pushed our jeans over our hips, stepped out of our panties, and stood facing each other. "Do you want me to turn the light off?" I asked. Anne nodded. "Don't you think we should?"

"Does the darkness make you feel safer?"

"Yes, somehow it does."

I dimmed the light, pulled the bedspread onto the floor. Anne sat on the bed and moved to its center. "I wanted to take time with you," I said, following her, lowering myself on top of her naked body, "but..." Anne pulled my mouth down to hers, kissing me deeply, her tongue searching. My need for her was so great, the pain between my legs insistent. I pulled my mouth away from hers and bent over her breasts, taking one at a time into my mouth, stroking her nipples with my tongue until they grew hard.

Anne moaned, "Oh, God, Callie, I can't wait." She pushed my head gently down her belly, spreading her legs so that my breasts were against her mound. She was so wet, so exquisitely wet. I moved down and ran my tongue against the inside of her thighs until she quivered with anticipation, and then I kissed the softest part of her, hungrily, wantonly, lustfully, her legs trembling, her hips grinding into the mattress. "Yes, Callie. Yes...Yes...Yes!" She gasped with desire, my tongue unrelenting, my fingers finding the deepest part of her. She groaned with pleasure as they slipped inside her, moving in and out with deliberate slowness until she cried out, moving her hips rhythmically, moaning, "Oh, God, oh, God, oh, God...." until her back arched in a final spasm of ecstasy.

Anne rolled onto her side, cradling my head against her breasts. I entwined my fingers in hers and closed my eyes, overpowered by the intensity of my feelings for her. We lay that way for several minutes, quiet, tranquil, fulfilled.

I thought of how little I knew about Anne, yet how much she'd been willing to share in my arms.

"Why are you alone, Anne?" I asked, my voice muffled against her body.

"I'm not alone," she breathed. "I'm with you."

I straightened my body, pulling the sheet along with me, and moved in such a way that we faced each other, my hand lightly stroking her arm. "You know what I mean...."

Anne sighed. "I think living alone has become a habit with me. I was in a relationship for several years with a woman named Lucy." Anne brushed her lips against my forehead. "It ended about a year ago."

"What happened?" I asked, fingertips gliding lightly over her breasts.

"Mmmm, that's nice." Anne smiled. "I think the temptation of all those lesbians gathering in one place was too much for her—

especially Jazz. She decided she wanted an open relationship, and I didn't. I guess I'm too old-fashioned."

I touched my lips against her shoulder. "I'm glad...I'm old-fashioned, too."

"Why are you alone?" she asked.

"I'm not alone," I teased. "I'm with you."

Smiling, Anne raised herself to a sitting position. "You can tell me all about it while I'm rubbing your back."

I turned over, arms in surrender position, my cheek against the sheet. Anne straddled me, and as she leaned down to kiss the nape of my neck her breasts brushed against my back, sending shivers down my spine. She ran the tips of her fingers lightly over the muscles of my back. I flushed with excitement as she bent forward, flicking her tongue along my spine. I groaned, arching my hips, and as I did so she moved herself against my buttocks. She lay her body on mine, our hips moving together in a pulse of rapture until I thought I would burst.

"Dear God, Anne, let me turn over." She raised herself over me so I could turn onto my back. Her face was radiant with excitement, her hands, her lips, her tongue caressing my body.

"I could do this forever," she said, gliding down my body, a hundred kisses blanketing my breasts. "Can I kiss you here?" she asked, her hand between my thighs, her voice hushed.

"Oh, yes," I moaned, "but I don't think I can...."

"We'll see," she murmured, stroking me until my breaths were coming in short quick gasps. She lowered herself to me, her tongue thrilling against my thighs. I moaned as her mouth paralyzed me, dissolving me into erotic pleasure, my body trembling, quaking, in a final orgasmic contraction.

I lay exhausted, my heart hammering, struggling to breathe. "Anne," I choked, laughing, "that was wonderful."

She smiled and took me into her arms. "I don't want this night to end. Being with you here, I feel so protected."

"You are protected," I said, snuggling closer, hoping I could keep my promise to her, keep her safe.

"The strain of the last two days is beginning to take its toll on me, Callie. I lie awake at night listening to the building's every creak and groan. Last night, one of my cats darted across my path and I shrieked, which is totally out of character for me."

"I know it's upsetting, Anne, but I'd rather have you a bit nervous than feeling so secure that you get careless."

"Don't worry. I've been double latching my doors, and my windows!"

"That's a precaution you should take anyway," I said.

"Callie, I live on the second floor. Who's going to come in my windows?"

I bit my tongue to keep from saying, "The Flying Nun." Instead, I murmured, "You can't be too careful."

Anne sighed. "I know, but for right now, can we change the subject? You were starting to tell me why you're not currently in a committed relationship...."

"I don't know why," I said lazily. "My friends would tell you I'm too fussy, and maybe they're right, but I don't want to get involved with someone just for the sake of being in a relationship. You know how it is with lesbians: we meet on Tuesday, fall in love by Wednesday, and move in together Saturday morning. Two years later we've stopped making love, and three years after that another Tuesday comes along and it's all over. We fight over who gets the cats, or the dog, or the stereo." I closed my eyes. "I'm so afraid of that."

Anne traced her finger along my jawline. "If you're afraid of making a commitment," she said, "how do you get your needs met? Casual sex?"

I laughed. "God, no. Anne, I can't remember the last time I made love." Which wasn't true. I remembered the last time with Jazz all too clearly, the way she moved beneath me, the way she tasted. Seeing her again brought it all back, sickening me, reminding me of how long I had cried burning tears over her—or out of self-pity. I was unable to carry off any attempt at casual affairs after that, for fear of the same repeated scene. Until Anne—but Anne wasn't casual sex, my body knew this all too well.

Anne rolled onto her back and made a place for me in the crook of her arm. I nestled against her as she whispered in my ear, "If I have my way, you'll never stop making love with this woman."

I felt my heartbeat quickening. I didn't know what to say to her. I was falling in love with Anne, but I wasn't ready to tell her that. I thought she saw me as her white knight, her protector. She was vulnerable, and I was the only person who believed in her complete innocence. Once this investigation is over, I thought, whether she's sentenced or released, she'll no longer need me, will she?

Anne propped herself on an elbow. "Callie, what do you think it is I feel toward you?"

"I think...you're in lust with me."

Anne laughed. "You're right, I am. And I want to make love to you again, but not until I've had a shower." She ran her hand over her body. "God, I'm sticky."

"Go ahead. I'll take one after you." While Anne was showering, I called to have a pizza delivered, then flipped through my record albums to find a few I thought Anne would enjoy. I chose two Lucie Blue Tremblay's, one Johnny Mathis, and three Roberta Flack's.

My back deck overlooks a small forever wild area of the pine barrens. I threw open the sliding glass doors and put the outside lights on so we'd be able to watch the rain splash against the deck through the screen door. My six foot privacy fence assured me we'd be safe from any would-be spectators.

When Anne emerged naked from the bathroom, I handed her a light cotton ankle length robe, then I ducked in, showered, dried, and put on a robe before Lucie Blue began to sing *Voix d'Enfant*.

As I stepped out, she said, "I toured your house while you were in the shower. I hope you don't mind."

"There's not much to see. Unfortunately I don't have your knack for room design." I apologized over my newly constructed two-bedroom ranch-style townhouse. My white stucco walls are decorated with framed posters surrounding contemporary furniture, accented with lots of foliage. I have a fairly decent stereo system with a compact disc player I detest. I much prefer the now obsolete LPs. Also, my television is hooked up to a VCR so I can tape my favorite shows during the week for whenever I get a night on my couch.

"Have you really read all those mysteries?" Anne asked, pointing to my long book shelf which runs the length of one wall in the living room.

"Yes," I laughed. "Want to borrow one or two?"

"Hardly." Anne ran her hand over the spines, picked one at random, reading the back cover. "Here's one about a beautiful young woman found murdered in a luxurious penthouse. The only clues are a steamy collection of erotic love letters and thirty-two separate knife wounds. No wonder you're so paranoid, Callie. If I read stuff like this I wouldn't be able to sleep at night."

"Then put the book down, darling, I wouldn't want you to have nightmares."

The doorbell rang, and I jumped, then laughed because I didn't want Anne's assessment of me to be true. "It's only the pizza!"

Anne busied herself pouring Pepsis and lighting candles while I paid for the delivery.

"I'm sorry I don't have anything alcoholic here." I said as I carried the warm box over to the coffee table. I blew on my fingers as I tried to get some pieces apart.

"No problem. It won't kill me to eat pizza without beer."

We sat on opposite ends of the couch and devoured the entire pizza, barely uttering a sound. Afterwards I reached over and put out the light, leaving us bathed in the glow of candlelight. I closed my eyes and listened to Roberta Flack's seductive voice sing about love and desire.

"Mmmm, this is wonderful," Anne murmured. "Rain is so sensuous."

"It's the first chance we've had to really relax," I agreed, snuggling against the cushions.

"This is the first time I've been able to feel calm around you."

I opened my eyes. "What do you mean?"

"Every time we've been together, I've been on edge."

"Oh, of course," I said, thinking I understood. "This case...."

"That's not what I mean. The case has me uptight, I'll agree with that, but from the moment I saw you, there's been this tension, a sexual tension I suppose. Whenever I've been with you, or we've talked on the phone, or even when I've thought about you...which seems to be constantly..."

My heart began hammering. "Like I said, you're in lust with me."

"Yes, Callie. I'm in lust with you, but there's something more. Something to do with trust."

We sat for a long while, listening to music, watching the rain.

After awhile, Anne slipped her hand between the buttons of my robe and embraced my breasts. When she spoke again, her voice was husky. "I can't keep from touching you."

I looked into her eyes and was startled by their intensity. The atmosphere in the room was overpowering: candlelight, raindrops, music, and Anne's body, like silk, against mine.

Another of Roberta's albums dropped onto the turntable, and as she sang, I wanted to say the same kind of words about moving in, about being together. I felt frustrated, thinking I would never be able to say that to Anne.

As if Anne could read my thoughts, she said, "I want to get to know you better...spend more time with you like this." She kissed me. "I want to be alone with you for days on end."

"I'd like that, too," I said. "Just as soon as the case is resolved."

"I feel so stifled!"

"I know. So do I."

Anne drew a deep breath. "I was just thinking about Beth and Jackie. What must it have been like for them to feel so much for each other and not be able to express their feelings?" She shook her head. "Imagine how much shame they felt."

I shuddered. "I don't want to imagine it, Anne. I came out nearly twenty-five years ago, yet the memory of shame still haunts me." I sipped my cola, thoughtful for a moment. "How are you dealing with your feelings about Beth? You were so close...." I wondered how close besides the sexual encounter. Had Anne been in love with Beth?

"I cry a lot, Callie. When I'm alone at night, in bed, I think about Beth and I cry. I feel the loss of a loved one, a very special person, and I cry for myself...but I also cry for Beth...for the years she spent in self-denial, the years spent loving women who couldn't, or wouldn't, return her love. Her life was very lonely."

"Yes," I agreed, "I got a sense of that from her journal entries."

"Accepting her death is hard enough, but accepting the fact that someone planned to kill us both...." Anne's body tensed, her hand balled into a fist. "I'm angry, Callie. Sometimes I think I'm going to scream at the top of my lungs. If there was someone for me to hit, I would hit him..." Anne's fist pounded the mattress. "...or her! I almost think that if it were possible for me to avenge Beth's death I would do it in a heartbeat. Can you understand, Callie, or do I sound crazy?" Anne didn't wait for my reply, just plunged ahead. "Years ago, a friend and I went to see one of the Charles Bronson vigilante movies. I'd never seen a movie like that, so I didn't know what to expect. In the beginning, I was horrified, then I became angry, and, with every atrocity, my anger just kept building and building and building until, finally, Charles Bronson's character began executing the villains, one by one. And with each vigilante killing I felt more and more relieved, until, finally, I left the theater feeling...mollified." Anne drew a deep breath. "The movie frightened me, Callie. But my feelings frightened me more. And they're the same feelings I have now, towards Beth's murderer."

"Anger over the death of a loved one is normal, Anne. Even the thought of an eye for an eye, but I don't...."

"But that same murderer might also have killed Jackie," Anne pressed, "and for all we know he, or she, is still crazy enough to be planning to kill me, to kill us. I don't know about you, Callie, but I'm becoming damned frightened and damned angry!"

I reached for her, and she fell into my arms, anger exploding into tears. "Oh, God, Callie," she sobbed, her body trembling. "I'm so afraid."

Eight o'clock the next morning I was lying in bed thinking about Jackie's purported suicide, wondering if Jackie had ever called on my friend Maggie Delgado for help after I gave Jackie her phone number during our last meeting. Maggie's a former nun who left the convent about ten years ago. She finished school, became a licensed psychologist, and recently shared a holy union ceremony with Jan, the woman she had been living with for eight years.

I reached for the phone and dialed Maggie's number, and chit-chatted with Jan until Maggie picked up on the bedroom extension. Anne stirred next to me in the bed.

"I hope I didn't wake you, Maggie."

"It's okay," she said, stifling a yawn. "I had to get up anyway. We're driving down to Poughkeepsie to visit Jan's parents. It's their forty-third wedding anniversary. Can you imagine? Forty-three years together. It's wonderful. Jan and I will have to live well into our eighties to have that much time together." Maggie always sounded the same. Calm, serene, and tranquil. I wondered if they taught the technique in social worker school. "So, Callie, it's good to hear from you, even at eight o'clock on a Sunday morning. Tell me what's happening."

I looked over at Anne who was pulling herself into a sitting position against a pillow. "Maggie, you wouldn't believe it if I told you, so I'll save it for another day. The reason I'm calling is to ask if you were contacted last week by Sister Jackie Prescott."

"Yes. The nun who committed suicide on Friday. I talked with her...which day was it?" I gave Maggie a moment to search her memory. "Thursday morning. I can't tell you what a shock it was to learn of her death. She told me you referred her to me. We had set up an appointment to meet this week. Tuesday, I believe."

"Then you never really talked with her?"

"Just for a few minutes, Callie. We didn't get into much on the phone."

"Could you tell if she was depressed?"

"I'd say so. She said she recently lost her lover."

"She said that? Referred to her as her lover?"

"Not exactly. I was paraphrasing, but she did indicate the woman who died was someone she loved very much. Why are you asking, Callie?"

"Because I don't think Jackie committed suicide."

"What are you saying?"

"I'm saying she was murdered."

Maggie whistled through her teeth. "I wish I could help you, Callie, but I don't know how. When Jackie called she sounded depressed, but depressed enough to commit suicide? I didn't get that impression. If I had, I would have given her an immediate appointment."

"So you're saying she wasn't in crisis."

"Not on Thursday morning. No."

"Maggie, can I see you about this? Tomorrow?"

"What more can I tell you? I only spoke to the young woman for what, maybe three minutes?"

"I know. Humor me, okay?"

"Do you want her Tuesday appointment? It's at four." I shuddered as I jotted the note in my pocket calendar. "See you then," I said. I put the receiver down and looked at Anne.

"Were you listening?"

"Yes. It sounds as if your friend Maggie was just as surprised as we were. What else are you planning to talk to her about?"

"I'm not sure, Anne. I just have this funny feeling that keeps nagging me. I can't even put it into words. Maybe by the time I see Maggie on Tuesday I'll have a better idea of what it is."

"I hope so," Anne said. "In the meantime, do you think we could try for a couple of hours of serenity?"

"Yes, of course we can," I said. "I'll cook breakfast while you read the Sunday comics."

Anne laughed. "I don't read the comics."

"No kidding?" I said, slipping into a robe. "I don't think I've ever known anyone who doesn't read the comics."

"Now you do," she said, following me to the front door to retrieve the *Sunday Times Union.*

I opened the door and stepped out onto the walkway, my gaze sweeping the driveway. "Son of a...."

"What's wrong?" Anne asked.

"My car! Look at it!" All four tires were flat. I ran barefooted into the driveway, scrutinizing the tires. "They've been slashed," I said, and peered into the driveways on either side of mine, and across the street. "Maybe a bunch of teenagers went on a tire slashing spree through the development."

"No one else's car appears to have been vandalized." Anne pointed out.

I looked again at the flat tires in disbelief, touched the wounds made by the knife. "I'm calling the police," I said. "Come on." We strode back into the house, and I stomped into the kitchen, lifting the telephone receiver. I hesitated, then placed it down. "I can't call the police," I said in frustration.

"Why not?"

"Because whoever did this is probably the same person who killed Beth and Jackie, and it's probably their sick way of telling us to quit snooping around or we're next."

"All the more reason to call the police."

"Yes, under normal circumstances, Anne. But how would I explain to the police that the murderer is coming after me?" I looked into Anne's eyes. "You're not supposed to be here, remember?"

"The police don't have to know about me. I'll leave right now!" Anne stood in the kitchen, her fists clenched, her cheeks flushed. "Callie, he used a knife! You've got to call the police, please!"

"Okay, okay, I'll call them." I put my arms around her, pulled her close. I could feel her body trembling, or was it mine? "We shouldn't have done this, Anne. We can't see each other again until this case is solved."

"Oh Callie, I'm afraid something dreadful is going to happen to us."

"Shh, Anne, nothing's going to happen. I promise." I offered a silent prayer that I'd be able to keep that promise. It made me think of Beth's desperate praying.

Anne left by taxi, but not until we phoned Tink, arranging for her to take Anne in and watch over her for the next several days. Good old Tink, she said she wouldn't let Anne out of her sight. We asked her not to talk about it. If she could hold to that, she'd be able to hire herself out as a bodyguard.

At ten the next morning I was pacing my living room, waiting for the service station to call and say my car was ready. I wanted to be in my office in case Hughes phoned with the autopsy report.

Once again, I went over everything I knew or wondered about in my feeble attempt to be a detective. I felt frustrated because I didn't have the power to make things happen the way I thought they should, which was to assign a couple of police officers to canvas the convent's neighbors to ask if they noticed anything suspicious on the night Jackie died. I made a mental note to ask Hughes to check on this and Jackie's will. It could prove that Dr. Loomis had the motive and the opportunity, but what about the means? What means did he use to kill his stepdaughter? I thought about the different possibilities.

Possibility A—He didn't kill her. Sister Laura did. After Jackie got the phone call from her stepfather, she was upset. Laura heard Jackie crying, fixed her a hot chocolate laced with sleeping pills, then took her out to the garage and put her behind the wheel of the car while it was running. She would be implicated if there were any drugs when Hughes called with the toxicology report.

Possibility B—Dr. Loomis telephoned Jackie and told her to meet him somewhere. But when she got to the garage he was waiting for her in the shadows. He hit her over the head and put her body behind the wheel of the car.

A blow to the head would show up in the autopsy.

Possibility C—Dr. Loomis telephoned Jackie and told her to meet him somewhere, but when she got to the garage he was waiting for her in the shadows. He held a gun on her and forced her to get behind the wheel and turn the engine on, then ran a hose from the exhaust pipe through the window of the car. He then stood outside the closed car, waiting for her to die.

Even I couldn't buy that one. If Jackie knew he was really going to kill her, it seemed likely she would have taken the risk of being shot rather than stay to die in the car. Wouldn't she?

Possibility D—He didn't kill her. Jackie actually committed suicide. She was feeling distraught over Beth's death, guilty about her sexual orientation and breaking her vow of chastity, frustrated with her mother's alcoholism, angry over the argument with her stepfather, and disillusioned about her inheritance.

This made sense, even without a suicide note, so why couldn't I buy it? Because Jackie was Catholic. Yet if she had broken one vow already, why not this sin too? Conceivably, if her world had broken apart, nothing would hold her back any longer. Perhaps she felt that much despair.

TWELVE

By ten-fifteen the garage phoned to say my car was ready. I walked the mile and a half to pick it up, and drove to the office on four new tires. I wasn't at my desk more than ten minutes when Bill Hughes burst in. "What's this?" he roared, slamming a manila envelope onto my desk. "Go ahead, open it..."

I grasped the envelope, feeling my color rise even before seeing the contents.

"...I found it in my mailbox this morning," he continued. "Sent to me anonymously. That's a picture of you with your client, Anne Hollis. What were you doing sipping drinks on her patio, Sinclair? This could get us in real trouble!"

"Calm down, Bill," I said, relieved that the photograph was so innocent. "Let me explain. I drove out to Cobleskill to take a look at the scene of the accident, then Anne showed me the reservoir where Sister Mary Elizabeth had spent a lot of time. The reservoir is just around the corner from Anne's house, and she invited me for dinner." I shrugged my shoulders in a gesture of innocence.

"Was that the only time?"

"Yes," I lied, convincing myself that if the photographer had more provocative shots the envelope would have contained them. And yet I felt uneasy. My tires had been slashed. Would more photographs be mailed soon, photographs taken over my fence somehow? I groaned inwardly at the thought of Anne in my robe, how the light was on over my deck. And Anne said I was paranoid. A little good sense would have told me to keep my curtains drawn.

"Well, make sure it doesn't happen again, Callie. Come on, use your head. It's unethical, not to mention the possible legal complications, and not to mention egg on our faces. I hope you're smart enough not to associate with Anne Hollis at all, not even questioning until the case is closed."

I bristled. "Hughes, it's my job to supervise persons placed on probation by the court." But I, too, realized the danger of our association and realized he was warning me as a professional, and yes, a friend. "I don't intend to fraternize with my client, Bill."

"Good." His face relaxed, genuinely relieved while I was wondering why the person involved sent the pictures to him. "Now, I got a message that you called me." He sat down in the visitor's chair.

"Yes." I told him about the tire slashing.

"Why do you think the incident is related to the case?"

"I can't give a logical reason, Bill." I tapped my stomach. "But I feel it here. And now there are the pictures too."

"Then we're dealing with a crazy."

"Somebody's trying to warn me off, and that makes me think I'm getting close to something." I swiveled my chair, looked out the window. Rain clouds were moving in fast. "Bill, do you know if Jackie changed her will in the last few days?"

He frowned. "Why?"

"She told me she left everything to her mother, but suppose she changed it and made the convent her beneficiary. That would either be like a suicide note or a cause for murder, especially since she argued with her stepfather about the money the night she died. She threatened to leave it to the convent—maybe she already had."

"I'll check it out. A million dollars is a lot of motive." He pulled out his notepad.

"Another thing. The Loomis' next door neighbor—she's Laura's sister-in-law! Her kid owns the vehicle that I think was involved in the Hollis case. I gave you a paint sample, remember?"

"Hey, yeah. So this guy Loomis had access to the vehicle that may have been used to kill the nun, the first nun."

"Right." My heart was beating like a tin drum. "But so did Sister Laura."

"I'll call the lab on the paint samples, tell them to put a rush on it," he said quietly.

My mind switched back to Jackie's death. "What are the chances of the Albany police canvassing the convent neighbors, to see if anyone witnessed a Saab parked nearby the night Jackie died."

He pulled on his lower lip. "We'd have to justify the manpower." He pulled some papers out of his inside jacket pocket. "I received copies of the preliminaries this morning."

"You have the autopsy reports?—Well?"

His voice sounded tired. "Jackie's autopsy showed bruises on the upper part of her left arm, but she could've gotten that by bumping into a door frame. No other bruises. No contusions. Nothing inconsistent with suicide."

I leaned back in my chair, arms limp at my sides. "Nothing suspicious at all?"

"Pathology isn't thinking anything but suicide. But I'm not so sure anymore."

I felt a glimmer of hope. "What's changed your mind?"

He crossed his legs and folded his hands behind his head. "That someone is trying to scare you off. And I'm intrigued that Loomis had access to the car. I guess you could say I'm feeling something in my gut too. But don't get your hopes up that pathology will find anything incriminating because they can't find something they aren't even looking for." He put both feet on the floor and leaned forward. "This isn't television, kiddo. What happens in the real world is this—an overworked medical examiner looks at an apparent suicide and determines cause of death based on the obvious."

"You mean if Jackie was injected with a sedative the medical examiner wouldn't find it?"

"Maybe, maybe not. If a fresh needle mark were clearly visible, then they would run a toxicology report...."

"This sounds hopeless," I said, running my hand through my hair.

"Yeah, well if we want the Albany cops to treat this as a homicide, let's give them more than we've got. If Loomis had the motive and opportunity, how did he do it?"

"How would you do it, Bill?"

"Whatya mean? If I was him, how would I have gotten her in

that car without her kicking and screaming?"

"Exactly."

He stoked his chin. "Hmm. Without hitting her over the head or trying to inject a sedative into her bloodstream..."

"Right. But you've got to knock her out fast even though she knows you and has no reason to be alarmed."

Bill snapped his fingers. "Chloroform? What else?"

"What if he injected her with something that wouldn't show in a toxicology report...like potassium chloride which is untraceable."

"Where'd you learn that?"

"I read a lot of mysteries."

Bill let out a guffaw. "A mystery novel?"

I narrowed my eyes. "Yeah, so what? Potassium chloride is just one chemical that won't show up in an autopsy. Maybe there are hundreds of others. The point is, we're never going to know for sure, so what difference does it make?—Unless we can get Rose Vanderslice's nurse, Betty Amyot, to identify the doctor who came in the middle of the night as Dr. Loomis!"

"So where are you going with all this?" He put the autopsy report back in his pocket. "You think Loomis killed all three?"

"Yeah. He killed Sister Mary Elizabeth. Her death would have looked like an accident if Anne Hollis had died, but she didn't, and he knew that. He saw her scramble after Beth once she was thrown clear of the Jeep. So he made it look like manslaughter by calling the dispatcher and saying Hollis was driving like a lunatic. He didn't want the police to fall for whatever story she was going to tell."

"Okay, so after he kills the nun, he has to kill Rose Vanderslice in order for the second nun, his stepdaughter, to inherit the full million. Then in order to get his hands on the money, he has to kill her too? That's your scenario?"

"That's it, Bill."

"Now, let me punch a few holes, okay? First, did Jackie tell him about the Vanderslice will, and when exactly? That has to be established. Second, why couldn't he just wait for Vanderslice to die from natural causes? Third, we have to show a match on those paint samples, and prove he had access to that vehicle at the time of the accident. Fourth, we have to prove he killed Vanderslice, which I'm going to tell you right now we're not going to be able to do. And fifth—this is the biggie, Callie—if he didn't know about the money, what reason would he have for killing Sister Beth in the first place? And why would he have chosen such a dubious method. How'd he know she was going to die in that crash?" I was about to open my mouth in protest, but he stopped me. "Before you say anything, maybe we can make him squirm a little bit by getting a positive I.D. from the nurse. And if you feel sure that Loomis killed Jackie, is Sister Laura still on your suspect list?"

"I guess not. The evidence, however circumstantial, points to Loomis. That is, as long as Jackie never changed her will."

I noticed Bill was using a lot of "we" pronouns, and I wondered what that meant. Since Jackie's death occurred within the City of Albany, the case was outside of his jurisdiction, and as a probation officer performing a PSI I was really stretching my authority.

"What can I do to help?" I asked.

He hesitated. "I don't know. Let me make a few phone calls, and I'll let you know. Do you have anything else for me?"

"No, I think that takes care of it."

"Okay. Jackie's wake is tonight, and I'm planning to be there. Let's see who shows up. How about meeting me around eight at O'Hare's Funeral Home in Guilderland?"

I told Bill I'd meet him there, then spent the afternoon on projects which had nothing to do with the Hollis file, but they needed to be done. Also, I knew their completion would not only make Sid Kasselbaum ecstatic, but convince him that I was living up to my end of the bargain by working on the Hollis case solely on my own time.

I couldn't help but think of Anne, her scent, her skin, and then all the awful details surrounding her and us. I stayed in the office until six-thirty, grabbed a burrito grande from Taco Pronto on my way home, and changed into grey pants and navy jacket for Jackie's wake.

I met Bill Hughes in the parking lot. He looked even more uncomfortable than I did. "I hate these things," he said, tugging on his collar. He wiped the sweat from his bald head with a big white hanky.

I held the door open. "Shall we?"

We were greeted by a distinguished looking man in a black suit who asked who we were visiting. Bill told him, and he directed us to The Serenity Room.

I hesitated at the door, not wanting to go in. The room was fairly crowded, the casket positioned along the wall on the right. I wondered how I could get through this without looking at Jackie. I didn't want to view her body in death; I felt it would be an intrusion.

Before I had a chance to back away, Bill grabbed my elbow, guiding me toward the casket. Faces turned to stare at us, no doubt wondering who we were.

I knelt at the casket, Bill standing behind me, and made the sign of the cross. I forced myself to look at Jackie's face impassively, but inside I was oatmeal. I wanted to gather her in my arms and comfort her, the way I couldn't the day she was sobbing in her office. Dear Jackie, I thought, I'm so sorry this happened to you. I pray that you and Beth are together now, in a place where bigotry doesn't exist, where you have the freedom to love each other. You chose to serve God, and in serving God you believed you had to give up yourselves and your love. I'm sorry you didn't know that your kind of love is also a part of God. I pray you know that now.

I stood up and walked over to where Dr. and Mrs. Loomis were seated. I introduced myself to Pam Loomis, then introduced Bill to both of them. The doctor's demeanor was about the same as it had been on Friday, which could be best described as detached. Mrs. Loomis, on the other hand, was warm and friendly, despite the fact that her daughter was lying in a casket four feet away. The smell of alcohol on her breath was pungent, and I hoped she wasn't taking sedatives along with the Dewars.

From what I know all too well about alcoholism, I've always found that drunks pretty much fall within a few categories: The angry drunk who, after a few drinks, gets into a brawl or else beats on his or her lover either physically or emotionally; the sorrowful drunk who gets a crying jag; and the sleepy drunk who nods off in a beer. There's also the drunk who becomes seductive after a glass or two of wine, and finally, the happy drunk, the one with the legendary lamp shade on his or her head.

I placed Pam Loomis into the category of seductive drunk. She had that look about her, the cling of her dress to her hips—the type who swung her hips suggestively as she walked—and the way she carried her breasts, high and proud. She was a Sophia Loren type, long dark hair, dark smoldering eyes.

I don't mean to imply that all seductive drunks exhibit a raw sexuality—I for one didn't and I certainly fell into that category. I remember sitting in a bar one weekend in Patterson, New Jersey, and after I had a few drinks, I began to feel horny, so I started to make eye contact with a cute blond dyke seated at the other end of the bar. She began returning my stares and before I knew it, we were giving each other those special signals that meant, 'Your place or mine?' Luckily, my friends hauled my ass out of the bar before the blond's lover decked me.

"Did you know my baby well?" Pam Loomis asked, jolting me out of my own awful nightmare.

"Jackie?" I rallied. "No, I met Jackie very recently. She was helping me investigate the case involving Sister Mary Elizabeth."

Mrs. Loomis' eyes filled with fresh tears. "Poor Beth," she said. "I can't believe we've lost both of them."

I glanced at Bill Hughes, my eyes imploring him to engage Dr. Loomis in some inane dialogue, and he obliged. I touched Pam Loomis's shoulder and said, "Mrs. Loomis, I know this is a bad time for you...."

"Please, call me Pam."

"Thank you. Pam, I wonder if, after the funeral, I could call on you to talk about what happened to Jackie. I was thinking of Wednesday morning. Would that be convenient for you?"

"No, I'm sorry, but Harry's taking me away for a small vacation...to the Bahamas for a week or so. Maybe when we get back?"

I knew I had to get her alone, but where? How? The detective in me hit on an obvious approach. I made my face look real disappointed. "Gee, Pam, I hate to say this, but I don't think this can wait that long. You see, I'm still investigating Beth's accident, and there's a small possibility that what happened to Jackie may be related in some way. We need to clear it up."

Pam chewed her lower lip and turned to Harry for support, but he was being stonewalled by Bill Hughes. "How long do you think this will take?"

"Five minutes," I said. "Maybe less." I looked directly into her eyes and said, "I have to go to the ladies' room."

Pam, easily suggestible, decided to come along. She turned to her husband and stage-whispered, "I'm going to the ladies' for a minute. I'll be right back." She picked up her purse and began walking down the aisle. I followed behind. Harry took two giant steps to catch up with her. He whispered something in her ear, then made a grab for her purse. She clutched it even tighter to her chest and pulled away from him. He shot me one of those If-Looks-Could-Kill looks, but I didn't care.

I followed Pam into the ladies' room, waiting near the sink while she did whatever she had to do in one of the stalls, something which I suspected, had more to do with ingesting liquid than voiding it. When she emerged her eyes were just a trace glassier.

"I'll be as brief as possible," I said. "As I started to tell you, I'm investigating the incident in which Beth was killed, and I'm not convinced it was an accident."

Pam frowned. "Jackie told me it was manslaughter. The woman behind the wheel was driving recklessly."

"That may not be true, Pam. New evidence points to the possibility that another car pushed theirs over the guard rails."

"My God." Her hand went to her throat. "On purpose?"

I nodded. "We think so."

"How do you think that relates to Jackie's death?"

"We're not sure. Has Sister Laura spoken to you?"

Pam rolled her eyes toward heaven. "Oh, sure. Soon as we got here. That Laura's a real pill, isn't she?" Her fingers tapped a beat on her purse. "I guess I shouldn't be so harsh, but a part of me blames her for what's happened to Jackie."

"What do you mean?" Did Pam think Laura was the murderer?

"Sister Laura took an interest in Jackie ever since Jackie first thought about the convent. She reminded me of one of those army recruiters."

"Did she mention her thoughts to you that Jackie's death wasn't...intentional?"

Pam closed her eyes. "Yes."

"I understand Jackie was very depressed, maybe so depressed that an accident happened."

Fresh tears formed at the corners of her eyes. "I think that may be true."

"Jackie was at your house earlier that evening, having dinner with you and Dr. Loomis. Can you describe her mood when she left?"

Pam shrugged. "I think she was okay. She seemed a bit subdued all evening, but at the time I didn't think she was depressed."

"Did she and Dr. Loomis have a conversation about her inheritance?"

The light went on. "Oh," she said. "Yes, they did. Harry thought it was ridiculous for the church to control Jackie's money because she wouldn't be able to spend it without asking permission. Jackie said she had joined the convent to renounce worldly goods and didn't want control of the money."

"Did you agree with your husband?"

"Well, in a way, I guess I did. A million dollars is a lot of money to give to a bunch of nuns. Lord knows what they'd do with it. Harry wanted to invest it for her, in case she ever decided to leave the convent."

I raised my eyebrows. "Do you think that was likely?"

"I doubt it. Jackie wanted to be a nun her whole life. I think she was really happy that way, although for the life of me, I can't understand why. You know, all those women...." She rolled her eyes again and chuckled.

"How long had you known about Jackie's inheritance?"

"We never heard a peep about it until Beth died. Harry and I were thrilled...." She colored. "Oh, I didn't mean that the way it sounded. When we found out that Jackie was going to inherit we were happy for her, but Jackie, she couldn't have cared less."

"I just have one more question, Pam. Friday night, after Jackie left, did you and your husband go out?"

"Yes, we did. He took me to Thirsty's. I remember being surprised because Harry hates to go out. He's usually a real couch potato. But Friday night he was hot-to-trot...."

A pounding on the door. "Pam, Pam...."

I opened the door. Dr. Loomis stood outside. He ignored me and glared at his wife. "Father Edwardsen is here, Pam. He's going to lead us in the rosary."

"Oh, Harry, sure. Just let me take a quick pee, okay?"

I turned on the faucets while she slammed into a stall. I sensed confusion if not fear in her response to him.

I dried my hands, then walked out in search of Bill Hughes. I found him in the vestibule surrounded by nuns. I looked around for Laura Bennett, then spotted her in a conversation with the priest. I strode over to Bill and whispered, "Can we get out of here before the priest starts?"

"Amen," he said, looking relieved. When we got outside, I filled him in on my conversation with Jackie's mother. He said, "He doesn't leave us much time, does he? If Loomis is leaving the States in two days we'd better bring him in for questioning tomorrow right after the funeral."

"Bill, I'd like to be there when he's questioned. Do you think that can be arranged?"

"We don't have enough on him, but, I'll see what I can do, Callie." He turned toward his car. "Talk to you tomorrow."

I got behind the wheel of my Civic and drove out to Thirsty's. I hesitated getting out of my car, wishing I had asked Bill to come along. It's one thing to walk into a lesbian bar, quite another to enter a straight establishment where I'm even less comfortable.

I walked in and sat at the bar, mildly surprised to find more than two dozen people there on a Monday night, except that they were watching baseball. When I ordered a diet Pepsi I asked the bartender if he had by any chance worked Friday night. He said he had.

"Do you remember Dr. Loomis and his wife being here that night?" I began to describe them but he stopped me.

"I know who they are. Mrs. Loomis drops in from time to time."

"Do you remember what time they were here?"

"Why are you asking these questions. Are you a cop or something?"

I replied by retrieving my wallet from my shoulder bag, and flipping it open, revealed my identification. I was hoping he wouldn't look too closely, assume I was a plainclothes detective, and open up to me. No such luck. He pulled out his reading glasses from his breast pocket and hooked them over his ears. He reached for my wallet. "Probation, huh?"

So much for that. "I'm investigating a case which may involve the Loomises. Can you remember what time they were here?"

He squinted at me. "Mrs. Loomis is a good customer."

Sighing, I reached for my wallet again, this time extracting a ten spot. I laid it on the bar. "Do you think you can remember what time they were here on Friday night?"

"Sure, they arrived about nine-thirty, left after midnight." He folded the ten dollar bill and slid it into his pocket along with his reading glasses.

"Do you remember Dr. Loomis making a telephone call from the payphone?"

He shook his head. "Sorry, I was busy. I wouldn't have noticed."

"Would you have noticed if he had left the bar for awhile?"

"Sure. I noticed that."

"You did? You saw him leave?"

"Just before the eleven o'clock news came on. He left a twenty on the bar for his wife, but I don't think she noticed he was gone. She was in her cups by then."

"I see. Do you remember when he returned?"

"I didn't notice at the time, but he wasn't gone very long. Maybe half an hour."

"How did he look when he got back?"

The bar tender pursed his lips. "He was sweating."

About nine-thirty, I thought about driving downtown to Hooper's instead of going home, but I knew I had to stay away from Anne for both our sakes.

Aside from thoughts of safety, I was exhausted. I felt bone tired, and uncomfortable. I was still wearing a bra, and my feet hurt. So I drove home, showered, changed into shorts and a tee shirt, and flicked a rerun of *Hogan's Heroes* on the tube. Ten minutes into the program, I dialed Tink's number to say good-night to Anne.

THIRTEEN

Somebody told me once that any question could be answered within four phone calls, and unless the calls are to a government office, I've found that to be true. As soon as I arrived at my office I dialed Ellen Cleavland, the ward clerk from St. Peter's Hospital, to see if there was anything she could tell me about Dr. Harry Loomis.

"The name doesn't sound familiar," she said. "But I'll ask around. When do you need to know?"

I looked at my watch. "In about three hours."

"Callie, I don't think—"

"I know," I said, interrupting her refusal, "I keep asking the impossible, but this is important. Dr. Loomis may have been the doctor who visited Mrs. Vanderslice the night she died."

"What do you need to know?"

"See if you can find out where he has privileges, what his specialty is, whether or not he's respected by the medical community...."

"Gotcha. Where can I reach you?"

"Call my office. If I'm not here they'll beep me." An hour and forty minutes later, Ellen called back.

"Callie, what I learned about Dr. Loomis came mostly from the gossip mill. I can't verify it."

"Let's have it."

"Dr. Loomis is a plastic surgeon, but he's not considered a very good one. He's had malpractice suits filed against him, causing him to lose privileges at this hospital."

"Can you tell me anything about the malpractice?"

"The word is, he'd been injecting women's faces with silicone. You know, to give them the high cheekbones look. After a period of time, the silicone began to shift. I hear it's extremely painful, and eventually causes disfigurement."

"How awful," I said. "Did all the malpractice suits involve silicone injections?"

"This same source told me Dr. Loomis disfigured a woman's mouth. Something about using acid to remove a blemish on her upper lip. But, I don't know how true that is."

I shivered despite the warmth. "If he had lost privileges, how could he have gotten into the hospital after hours?"

"The guards wouldn't know about the lost privileges, Callie. If Loomis was wearing a lab coat with his name tag on it, that would have gained him entry. All he'd have to do is walk into the ER area and enter a stairwell."

"But wouldn't someone have stopped him on the floor?"

"No. Because of his specialty, most of the floor nurses wouldn't know him. Even if they did, they probably wouldn't question him."

"I see. Anything else?"

"Just that he's been sleeping with his receptionist."

"Uh, huh." I looked at my watch. "How am I going to repay you, Ellen?"

"No need, Callie. Maybe I'll need a favor from you someday."

After we hung up, I immediately placed a call to a friend of mine in the insurance business, who referred me to a colleague of hers who underwrites medical malpractice insurance, and he referred me to his girlfriend who works for the Albany County Medical Society. Within those four calls, I had discovered a wealth of information about Dr. Harry Loomis, learned all I needed to know about malpractice insurance, and verified that the rumor-mill at St. Peter's Hospital was right on target.

I skipped lunch and met with Bill Hughes and Detective Dan Southern at police headquarters. The purpose of the meeting was to plan a strategy for questioning Dr. Harry Loomis.

We met in the police interrogation room, a small place with a conference table and six chairs, unplugged video and tape recorders. Dan sat at the head of the table, Bill and I flanked him on each side. I chose the seat facing the door.

"I need to know what we have here," Dan began. He was a young cop, blond-haired and blue-eyed, and looked as if he could be Union College's star quarterback. "Callie, Bill tells me you have some interesting theories here, I'd like you to run them by me, see how much is circumstantial, how much we might be able to prove."

"I'll start by telling you what I learned from my interviews with Jackie Prescott's mother and her mother's next door neighbor." I referred to my notes, then explained what had happened the evening Jackie went over to her mother and step-father's house for dinner, about their argument over the money.

"And what made Jackie think her stepfather would use the money himself?" Dan pressed.

"Because Dr. Loomis had enough malpractice suits filed against him to make his insurance virtually unaffordable. I maintain that Jackie was so angry over his desire to control the money that she threatened to give all of it to the convent retirement fund. If she had done that, the money would have been inaccessible to him forever. He was pissed to say the least, so he goes to his garage to work on his car and let off a bit of steam. There, he conceived of a way to get Jackie's million.

"Later that night, very out of character, he invited his wife to Thirsty's Bar for a few drinks. Thirsty's is located on New Scotland Avenue, just two and a half blocks away from the convent where Jackie lived. Loomis made a phone call around eleven, then left the bar, leaving his wife behind. According to the bartender, Mrs. Loomis didn't seem concerned about his absence. She was quite busy drinking and chatting to other customers—"

Dan interrupted, "You think it was Jackie he telephoned from the bar?"

I nodded. "We have a confirmation from one of the other sisters that he did call. We can't know for sure what he said on the phone, but my guess is that he told her something like her mother, upset by their argument, went to the bar and got drunk and could Jackie please come help get her home.

"Jackie said she would, but she'd have to get dressed again, which gave him time to leave Thirsty's and drive the two blocks to the convent. He parked down the street, quickly walked to the convent garage and let himself inside. Probably the first thing he did was make sure all the car windows were open.

"When Jackie entered the garage he lunged at her from the shadows, grabbing her from behind, knocking her out somehow, quickly—maybe ether on a handkerchief over her mouth and nose. How could she scream? As soon as she was unconscious he could have yanked the garage doors closed, then dragged her to the car and lifted her into the driver's seat and started the engine. If she had started to come to, he could easily have administered more ether. Then he let himself out of the garage and returned to Thirsty's, confident that Jackie would succumb to exhaust fumes before she was found."

Dan raised his eyebrows. "That's quite a story, Callie. We still don't have evidence of homicide. The preliminary autopsy hasn't shown any sign of chemicals."

"Not yet, but I'm sure they would if we asked them to look further. I know most of this is circumstantial—"

"All of your evidence so far is circumstantial."

"Okay," I conceded, "but how do we get material evidence in a case like this?"

Dan sighed. "We probably won't, Callie. Look, I'll level with you. The only reason I'm going along with the interview is as a personal favor to Bill. We go back a long way." He turned to Bill, a tight smile on his lips.

Bill nodded and said, "Our only hope is to shake him up, rattle his cage enough to see if he opens up, gives us a clue."

"Dan, did you learn anything about Jackie's will? Was her money left to her mother?"

"That's correct."

I brightened. "So Loomis does have a million dollar motive."

A uniformed officer poked his head in the doorway. "Investigator Southern? There's an Elizabeth Amyot here to see you. She's up front."

As Dan left to fetch her, Bill asked if I really thought this was a good idea.

"I do, Bill, short of putting him in a line-up, right? It's an easy way to find out whether or not Betty recognizes Loomis as the doctor who showed up in Mrs. Vanderslice's room, and at the same time it'll give Loomis a hint that we're tying her's and Jackie's death together. I hope that seeing Amyot will shake him up enough so that when we start questioning him he'll make some mistakes."

Dan walked back into the room. "This is Betty Amyot."

We all shook hands, then Bill waved me to speak.

"Betty, you and I and Bill will wait here for Dan to come back with a man. We'll have the door open a crack so we can see them coming. Then as they reach the door, you will step out as if you were just leaving a meeting. If you recognize the man as the doctor you saw the night Mrs. Vanderslice died, please acknowledge him. If you don't, just keep walking."

Bill added, "If he's our guy it'll unnerve him to see you, Betty. He'll wonder what you're doing here, and if you were interviewed. We hope."

Dan shrugged. "It's your show. Just remember, this is an interview about his step-daughter's death, not an interrogation. He isn't under arrest. Yet. And no, Sinclair, we aren't going to tape it but I'll take notes, and later prepare a statement for him to sign, if necessary. Let's proceed."

I stopped looking at the tape recorders, wishing I could plug one in. Then, at one p.m., Bill and I positioned ourselves in the interview room with Betty Amyot while Dan went up front to meet Loomis.

Just as planned, as Loomis and Southern were about to enter the room, Betty Amyot got up to leave. In the doorway she stopped, looked at Loomis, and said, "Good afternoon, doctor."

He looked momentarily stunned, then mumbled, "Hello."

Bill said,"Thanks for coming in Mrs. Amyot.We'll be in touch."

I turned to Harry Loomis and held the door open. "Please come in." I was ecstatic! We had something.

Bill pulled a chair out for Dr. Loomis at the head of the table, the seat farthest from the door. He sat to Loomis' right, Dan to the left. I made myself comfortable at the opposite end of the table near the door.

Dan cleared his throat and said, "I've invited Officer Sinclair and Investigator Hughes to join us. They're both investigating a separate case, but may find some of what we talk about here relevant to that case. Before we begin," Southern continued, "I'd like to inform you that you have the right to have your attorney present during questioning."

Dr. Loomis frowned. "Why would I need my attorney present? I thought this meeting was regarding my stepdaughter's suicide."

"Simply formality, doctor," said Southern. "You're not being charged with any crime. We just want to ask you some questions."

"Go right ahead, Detective," he replied. "Although I don't know how much more I can add. I've already answered questions put to me by the police, and by Ms. Sinclair."

"Try to bear with us, Doctor," Hughes suggested. "In order to close this case, we need to have a few more answers."

Dr. Loomis sighed. "Very well."

Southern referred to the contents of a file. "Doctor, your stepdaughter, Jackie Prescott, joined you and your wife for dinner the evening she died. Is that correct?"

"That's correct."

"And how would you describe her mood during dinner?"

"She was melancholy, Detective. Her best friend died recently in a car accident, and Jackie was still mourning her."

"That's understandable, Dr. Loomis. I wonder, though, to what extent her grief took her."

"I'm afraid it drove her to suicide."

Southern continued, "Dr. Loomis, to your knowledge, did your stepdaughter have a history of mental illness?"

"Not to my knowledge. No."

"To your knowledge, had she ever been treated for clinical depression?"

"Not to my knowledge."

"As a doctor, do you think you would have been able to recognize the symptoms of clinical depression in your stepdaughter?"

"Jackie and I never entered into a discussion of her symptoms, Detective. Obviously, she was depressed over the death of her friend, but I wasn't unduly concerned."

"So, in your professional judgment, Jackie was not depressed to the extent that you felt treatment to be advisable."

"I'm not a psychiatrist, Detective."

"I see. What is your specialty, Doctor?"

"I specialize in plastic and reconstructive surgery."

"You're a plastic surgeon." It was not a question.

Dr. Loomis shrugged acknowledgement.

"Do you mind?" Hughes asked Southern, indicating he would like to question the doctor.

"Not at all."

Hughes scratched his head and shuffled through some papers in his file. "I'm confused, Doctor. Something in my notes...yeah, here it is. We have a report from a nurse...the nurse who greeted you in the hall just a few minutes ago, as a matter of fact." Bill continued his shuffling. I knew full well it was for effect. "Just a minute, I'll find the report...."

Loomis' brow furrowed, but he sounded bored as he asked, "Are you talking about Mrs. Vanderslice's nurse out in the hallway? I'm afraid I don't remember her name."

"Betty Amyot," I said, surprised at his easy admission, my heart sinking at his obviously relaxed arrogance.

He waved his hand dismissively. "Names elude me, but I never forget a face."

"Dr. Loomis," Bill began, clearing his throat which indicated to me that he was changing tactics, "Can you tell us why you were visiting Rose Vanderslice in her hospital room at three in the morning?"

The doctor chuckled. "Yes, it does seem an odd hour for a visit, particularly because she wasn't my patient. Actually I looked in on her as a favor to Dr. Litowski, Guy Litowski. We're friends, you see, ever since our residency together years ago. He and his wife had asked me and mine to join them for dinner the evening before I visited Mrs. Vanderslice. I'm sorry, I can't remember the date, but the Litowskis were celebrating their twenty-fourth wedding anniversary. We had dinner at the Beverwyck, then went out afterwards for a few drinks. I don't remember the name of the bar, but it's not far from St. Peter's. Anyway, as we were leaving, Guy complained of feeling ill but said he couldn't go home until he had checked on a patient he was concerned about."

Right, I thought grimly. You knew perfectly well Mrs. Vanderslice was under his care, and you got him drunk.

"Of course the hour was past two a.m., and we told him so, and that surely they would beep him. But he was very insistent, saying he was worried about Mrs. Vanderslice because she was very ill and was supposed to be released the next day. He felt he had to check in on her in case he had to change her release date. Finally, I told him I'd have a look at her." He chuckled again. "It's an old habit with us to cover rounds for each other if necessary."

Right again. You cover for each other, and I'll bet he'll back your story. I sat back in my chair, restraining my impulse to tap my pen on the table impatiently. Then I remembered what Betty Amyot had told me on the phone. "Excuse me, Doctor, you didn't see any other patient on any other floor?"

Startled, he shook his head. "No."

"Mrs. Vanderslice's nurse said you were attending to an emergency and while in the vicinity, thought you'd check in on Mrs. Vanderslice."

Did he pale slightly? I knew I had some small thing on him.

He paused. "Then she was mistaken. As I was saying, I was doing Guy a favor. He and his wife went home, and my wife waited in the car while I visited the patient...." More gruffly he snapped, "What does this have to do with my stepdaughter's death?"

Bill appeared unruffled. "You'll have to admit, Doctor, that it struck us a bit odd. A doctor visiting another doctor's patient in the middle of the night at a hospital in which this doctor who happens to be a plastic surgeon, lost his privileges. We were wondering why he would visit a patient who was terminally ill with stomach cancer."

"Now you know." Dr. Loomis composed again, smiled broadly. "And I ask again, what does this have to do with my stepdaughter's suicide?"

Hughes didn't answer him. Instead, he said, "Dr. Loomis, when did you learn of your stepdaughter's inheritance?"

"Let me think." He stroked his chin. "Ah. I remember. My wife and I were told by Beth's sister, Claudia, during the funeral services for Beth. The news came as quite a shock. Jackie never said anything about it to either of us."

Bill and I exchanged glances. How could we accuse Dr. Loomis of Beth's death if he wouldn't admit to knowing about the will beforehand? And what about the car that pushed the Jeep off the road? Surely he had access to Bennett's car, but without physical evidence we'd never get him to admit it.

"Doctor," Bill tried again, "Let's go back to your stepdaughter's dinner visit, shall we? You mentioned that she was depressed during dinner. Was she also depressed when she left to go home?"

Loomis hesitated. "I suppose so, yes," he said quietly.

"Wasn't she angry, Dr. Loomis?" I pressed.

He turned to me with a cold hard look. "Why should she be angry?"

"Because you and she had an argument about inheritance." I pointed at him with my pen. "You wanted her to turn her million dollars over to you."

Loomis dismissed me by turning to Bill. "I wouldn't call it an argument. We had a discussion about Jackie's inheritance. Her mother and I wished to invest the money for her future rather than allow the Order to control her funds."

Bill leaned forward. "I understand Jackie refused to turn any money over to you or your wife, is that true?"

Now Loomis bristled. "I don't care for the implication of that statement, Investigator. The disagreement was a simple case of me asking Jackie to make a wise financial decision. Unfortunately, Jackie had a different plan, which was to place the capital in a retirement fund." He shrugged. "But it was her money to do with as she wished."

In my opinion Loomis was still too controlled, and in control of us. I wanted to shake him up, get him angry. Maybe then he'd slip, say something incriminating.

"Why did she refuse to allow you to invest her money?" I asked sharply.

Loomis replied blandly. "I don't know. She didn't say."

Not so easy, I thought, asking, "Could it be that she was afraid she'd never see the money again?"

His cheeks colored. At last. "Detective Southern, I agreed to come here today because you said you needed to explore the events surrounding my stepdaughter's suicide so you could close your case. Now suddenly I feel as if I'm on trial here."

Southern turned to me calmly. "Do you think you could rephrase your question in such a way as not to offend the doctor?"

I smiled politely. "I'll try, Detective. Dr. Loomis, I understand malpractice insurance makes it very difficult for doctors to continue practicing medicine profitably."

He pulled on his cuffs. "Your understanding is correct."

I directed my next statements to Southern and Hughes. "Medical malpractice insurance works the same way as insurance in general—it's experience rated. The insurance company takes the number of claims and the cost of those claims and weighs them against the premium, continuously increasing the premiums to ensure a profit to the insurance company." I turned to Loomis. "Did I explain it correctly, Doctor?"

He moved his shoulders as if to get the kinks out. "I'm not an insurance agent, but your explanation sounds right."

"You're not an insurance agent, Dr. Loomis, but you certainly have thorough knowledge of medical malpractice insurance. You've had enough malpractice suits filed against you to make your insurance virtually unaffordable, so it seems to me that a million dollars would come in handy—"

"That's enough!" Loomis stood up, knocking his chair against the wall.

Exactly what I wanted. Well, sort of. He still hadn't slipped.

Southern reached over and straightened the doctor's chair. "Please sit down, Dr. Loomis."

"No. I will not sit!" Beads of sweat broke out on his forehead. He was ripping. "This is supposed to be an investigation into the suicide of my stepdaughter, yet this woman..." He pointed to me. "...is making accusations which are totally irrelevant and out of place!"

I sat back in my chair. 'This woman,' huh. Well, at last he'd come out and said it.

Bill stood, placed a hand on Loomis' shoulder. "Please, sit down, Doctor. I think we need to clear up a misunderstanding here."

"That's right," Southern said. "Officer Sinclair never believed Jackie's death was suicide, and although we're inclined to agree with her, theorizing murder and proving it beyond a reasonable doubt are two different things."

"That's absurd," said Loomis, his eyes bright. "How could she have been murdered? The police said it was clearly a suicide. Why, even the autopsy reports agree."

"The preliminary reports agree, Doctor, but the department is willing to explore the possibility that someone rendered Sister

Jackie unconscious, then set it up to look like a suicide." Loomis slumped back in his chair as Southern added, "May I remind you, Dr. Loomis, that you may have your attorney present during questioning."

Loomis' voice cracked. "Am I being charged with a crime?"

"No, sir." Southern shook his head.

"I don't believe this!" Loomis ran his hand through his hair.

I cut in quickly. "Dr. Loomis, I understand you and your wife were at Thirsty's bar the night Jackie died."

"We were."

"And that you called Jackie from the bar." I expected him to deny it but he didn't.

"Yes, I called to apologize for the argument." By his tone, he seemed to have gathered himself together again.

"Did she accept your apology?"

His manner was smug again. "Yes, as a matter of fact she did."

"After the phone call, what did you do?"

"What do you mean? I went back to my seat and had another drink."

"Didn't you leave the bar for a short time, Dr. Loomis?"

He blinked several times. He looked at me then back at Southern, straightened his back. "If you have further questions for me at this time I would like my attorney present."

"Bill? Any more questions?" Southern raised his eyebrows.

Bill shook his head.

"You may leave, Doctor, but I advise you to cancel your trip and stay in town until I get back to you."

Hm, he just didn't make his vacation plans soon enough, I thought as we all stood up. So sure of himself. Take the upset wife off for a while, so caring. Bill had to move out of Loomis' way as the doctor bolted out of the room.

"Why'd you let him go? I was just getting somewhere." I complained to Dan.

"We don't have anything to hold him on. I think we've got him sweating. It'll keep. Anyway, he asked for his attorney. We'll see what pathology turns up. And we need statements from any witnesses. I'll put my men out, maybe someone saw his car parked near the convent."

"Start with the bartender at Thirsty's." I grumbled. "And get a statement from Betty Amyot."

"Hey, Callie." Bill thumped me on the back. "Don't look so hang-dog. What did you expect, a confession?"

I nodded. "Yeah, I did. Or at least some slip up."

Dan laughed. "Just like in the movies."

Consoling me, Bill said, "I'll call you as soon as we get something."

On my way back to the office I stopped near the Empire State Plaza, bought a hot dog and soda from one of the street vendors, then found a shaded park bench where I sat and thought about the case, wondering why I was feeling so uneasy. I was ecstatic that Southern agreed with Bill and me about Loomis' probable guilt, but something still nagged me. Both Harry Loomis and his wife said they had no knowledge of Jackie's impending inheritance until after Beth was dead. Of course Harry could have been lying, probably was lying. But still...I had to admit it was hard to imagine Dr. Loomis premeditating Beth's murder in order to eventually end up with Jackie's million. I also felt the odds were against seeing him charged in Beth's death unless I could physically connect him to the Bennett's car. And until that happened, Anne's case would not be discharged.

These thoughts were making me anxious once again and I was suddenly impatient to get back to my office. As soon as I reached my desk, the phone rang. "Callie, it's Bill. I've just learned something I think you should hear. Dr. Loomis couldn't have been responsible for Beth's death."

I winced. "Come on, Bill, let's not go around on this again."

"Callie, I know you don't want to hear it, but it's true. My people just confirmed that Loomis and his wife were still attending a medical conference for plastic surgeons in France on the day of Beth's accident."

"Damn!" I hollered, slamming my hand against the top of my desk and wondering how I was going to break this to Anne. "So where does this leave Hollis?"

"Same place she's been all along, Callie. In a very tight spot. Look, I know you get pissed whenever I mention it, but don't you think it's about time to admit your client is guilty?"

I closed my eyes, tightened my hand around the receiver. Is it possible, I wondered. Could it be that Anne is guilty after all? My head started to spin, grasping at straws. What about my tires? What about the pictures of Anne and me? What about—? "Bill, give me one last shot...the paint samples. Do they match?"

"Oh man, I knew I forgot something. Let me put you on hold, see if I can find out anything."

I remained on the line, grateful there wasn't any muzak, just plain old silence while Bill called the lab. What the hell more could I do for Anne if the samples didn't match. As I waited, an even worse possibility popped into my head—what if they did match?

The line clicked. "Callie, you still there?"

"I'm here."

"I've got it, but I can't explain it. The suckers match."

I drove home before my four o'clock appointment with Maggie Delgado. I wanted to be out of my dress and into something comfortable.

As I entered my front door I stooped to pick up what I thought was an advertising flyer which had been jammed between the doorknob and the doorjamb. My stomach flipped when I read the handprinted block letters in blue ballpoint on white paper:

MIND YOUR OWN BUSINESS OR YOU'LL BE NEXT.

Oh God, I thought. This can't be from Dr. Loomis, can it? I stuffed the note into my shoulder bag, changed into jeans and a tee shirt, then drove to Maggie's office, all the while feeling sick to my stomach.

FOURTEEN

Maggie Delgado's office is located on the first floor of an Albany two-family. Entering the front door I stepped into a waiting room furnished with contemporary-style sofa chairs mixed with Native American pottery, sculpture, and weaving, their colors a calming blend of mauve, turquoise, and sand.

Maggie stepped out to greet me, striking in a long peasant dress, offset by multiple strands of liquid silver mixed with turquoise beads. Her long black hair was braided into a chignon. As usual, she was barefoot. "Callie," she said, opening her arms. "It's such a delight to see you!"

I hugged her. "You feel good."

"C'mon in. You've never seen my space, have you?" She led me to the room she uses for therapy sessions. Two upholstered chairs sat facing one another.

"Where do you want me to sit?" I asked.

"Whichever one seems most comfortable," she said.

I selected the chair facing the window, and sat down, wondering if the chair selection process was indicative of any personality traits.

I didn't lose any time telling her. "We think Jackie's stepfather murdered her."

"Oh, how horrible," Maggie said, grasping her throat. "Tell me about it." Maggie sat opposite me, pulling her legs up, yoga-style, into the chair.

I filled her in on everything that happened during the last week and a half. She smiled when I talked about Anne, and frowned profoundly over everything else. When I finished she asked if I thought she could help me process my feelings.

"I don't want to process my feelings!" I exclaimed. "But maybe you can help me discover what it is that keeps niggling at my subconscious. You see, all along I thought it might be Sister Laura, that was responsible for Beth's death, but it's driving me crazy that I can't come up with sufficient motive. She did have access to the vehicle that rammed Anne's Jeep...." I ran my hand through my hair and sighed. "Today I was able to drop a net of suspicion over Dr. Loomis, showing he had motive, opportunity and the means to kill two people, Jackie and Mrs. Vanderslice. But the murder I most want to solve, so that Anne would be free of suspicion, is still unresolved." Frustration mounted until I felt like screaming. I stared past Maggie's head into the branches of the tree outside her window.

"Maybe you need to back away from it for awhile, Callie. Think about something else...tell me more about Anne."

"If you think focusing on Anne will get my mind off this case, you're wrong. All I can think about is saving her, Maggie. I don't want to fail."

"What's the worst that will happen?"

"Anne will be placed on probation, will have a record."

"That would be unfortunate, but not earth shattering.

I hesitated. "I may lose her."

"Why is that? Is your friendship with Anne that shallow?"

"No, of course not! I'm sure we'd still be friends...maybe. It has to do with trust." Maggie watched me, silent, knowing I'd ultimately say what was true. "I'm in love with her, Maggie. I daydream about sharing my life with her, but what kind of a chance do we have if her innocence isn't upheld? Not to mention the fact that whoever did it would get away with it and still be free. No matter what I believe, what I've tried to do for her—it would hardly be the basis for a sound relationship if we fail at this point—"

"Callie, we've talked about this before...your projections...."

I put up my hand. "I know exactly what you're going to say. Why don't I just take it one day at a time, as I do everything else."

Maggie smiled, as if to say, "Well?"

"For starters I only met Anne about a week ago, but it seems like a month, so much has happened. And she's a client! But I was drawn to her at once. She's charming, intelligent, pretty." I stood up and walked to the window. "She drinks." I shrugged, not having intended to talk about my personal feelings. "She isn't an alcoholic. I haven't seen her drink to excess, but I'm uncomfortable."

"Does Anne know you're recovering?"

"Yes. And she has offered not to drink around me. But that's not the point. It's just that to start a relationship with that issue would be enough. When Anne has been drinking, and I've kissed her, I've found it comforting somehow, arousing even, much more intense than if there isn't alcohol on her breath."

"And that makes you anxious? Are you afraid it will make you want to drink again?"

I shook my head. "All I know is that I'm afraid, but I'm not sure what of. Does that make sense to you, Maggie?"

"Callie, think for a moment. When you were a little girl, who fed you, rocked you, sang to you?"

"My mother," I said, adding sarcastically, "when she got around to it."

"Was she sober?"

"Probably not."

"Would you say her breath probably smelled of alcohol?"

"Yeah...most likely," I said, finally understanding why instead of feeling repulsed by the scent of alcohol on Anne's breath, I was soothed. Especially with all the anxiety over the case.

"Do you think you can keep from confusing your feelings for her, your desire, from those earlier feelings of comfort you sought from your mother?"

I closed my eyes for a moment, memories of my mother flooding me, good ones—the two of us laughing, sharing a joke. Bad ones—my mom sitting at a bar ordering a double whiskey. Tears threatened. I rubbed my eyes. "I can't afford to think of my mother right know. I'm not sure what I'm going to do with the information but it helps to know where those feelings are coming from. Obviously, I can enter therapy with you and work it out sometime," I added too bitterly. "Right now, unfortunately, it isn't the issue in my relationship with Anne—by comparison I wish it were. First things first, Maggie! I have to prove somebody else killed Beth, that's priority one."

Maggie's hands gestured matter-of-factly. "Is your only suspect Sister Laura then, if Jackie's stepfather is ruled out?"

"I'm afraid so. At this point I don't have any other leads. But it seems to me the woman is too wrapped up in her role as defender of morality to fall victim to ordinary human..."

"Tell me. About her."

I took a deep breath. "She's assertive, aggressive and cold really, very much in control. You know the type...remember Dixie, the ex-Marine I lived with before I met Jazz?" I shook my head. "God, what a tyrant. Went crazy if I folded towels the wrong way. Living with her made my life hell. Somehow that's how I picture life with Sister Laura."

"Is Sister Laura a lesbian?"

Her question startled me. "I doubt it. It's certainly prohibited by her rules. Imagining her in an intimate relationship is difficult...."

"You're hesitating."

"I was just thinking...there is something seductive about Laura—her position of power and control. I can see how a young, naive nun may be attracted to her." I found myself groping for the right words to express the nagging feeling I'd been having, but I was at a loss.

Maggie leaned forward, her look intense. "Do you think Sister Laura was involved with Beth?"

"No...there was no mention of Laura in that context in Beth's diary."

"What about Jackie? Could there have been an involvement there?"

I sighed. "Anything's possible, but I doubt it. She did have strange moods, Maggie. All of a sudden her expression would change, her voice take on a different tone. It was unsettling."

Maggie rested with her elbows on her knees. "Go on."

I shrugged. "What else is there. She's forgetful...."

"In what way?"

I explained about the diary entries. "I get the sense that the one hand doesn't know what the other is doing."

"Do you know anything about her background?"

"According to Father Brannigan, she had an abusive childhood, possibly an incestuous relationship with her father."

"Is she seeing a therapist?"

"He wouldn't reveal anything, just that becoming a nun is some sort of equivalent. He wouldn't tell me anything."

"Of course not," she said bitterly. "She is a person of authority in the Church. When I was in the convent I saw quite a bit of dysfunction, enough to guess that Sister Laura could be suffering from a serious personality disorder, but as long as she can function, keep it under control, the Church will look the other way. And she has—obviously—she made it to Mother Superior."

"What kind of disorder?"

She shook her head. "Drawing a conclusion based on our short conversation, never having seen or spoken to Sister Laura, would be impossible really and unethical."

"I can respect your principles, Maggie," I said, frustration rising in my throat, "so long as you're not talking about some kind of disorder that might place Anne or me in danger. But we have been followed, and threatened." I told her about Beth being followed, about the slashed tires, the threatening photos of Anne and me and the message left under my door.

Maggie's inner struggle was obvious in her expression, but she said nothing.

"Come on, Maggie," I pleaded, "no one will ever know what we talked about."

"All right, but you must understand this is pure conjecture."

"Of course."

"Multiple personality disorder is one of the possibilities."

I smirked. "Sister Laura as Sybil? I don't think so, Maggie."

She put her hand up. "Wait. You're thinking about the most sensational cases. What you're not realizing is that multiple personality disorder is quite common. A person may have two or more personalities, each dominant at a particular time. These personalities would come complete with their own unique behavior patterns and social relationships, often each with personality traits and behaviors not acceptable to the other."

"Do these personalities know each other?"

"One personality knows and remembers, but the other or others often have no knowledge."

I stood up and began pacing. "This is crazy, Maggie, but it's beginning to make sense. The other Laura, would she have a different name?"

"Not only that but she may have a different life entirely."

That link was getting closer. Somehow I knew this was the key. "This is so confusing. You mean this other Laura might even be living the life of an out lesbian." I couldn't help but laugh. It seemed so absurd. "Surely she would be recognized."

"With treatment, a person suffering from this disorder could reintegrate and be able to function relatively well, live what appears to be a normal life. It's happened."

I was feeling restless, tired of talking about Sister Laura, anxious to see Anne, something I wasn't supposed to do. I rubbed my hands over my face and stood up. "My head is spinning."

"With good reason." Maggie also stood, reached her arm out and grabbed me around the shoulders. "Come, give me a hug before you leave."

I wrapped my arms around her, pulling her close. "Thanks for your help, Maggie. I'm grateful for our friendship."

"Me, too, Callie. Call me any time." She released me. "Listen, one last word...don't forget the fact that Sister Laura's a nun. You know what I'm saying?"

I felt brain dead. "No."

"Treat her as you would any other suspect, Callie. Give her the same emotions, ask the same questions you would of any other woman, but then remember that she's also entered the convent, made certain vows, cast off certain ideals, hopes, even fears, and taken up others."

"I'll keep that in mind," I said, wondering what the hell Maggie was talking about.

I got into my car and began driving uptown, heading towards home, thinking about Maggie's parting words, speculating about Sister Laura's dual personality, and the part they might have played in Beth's death. Could she have murdered Beth because Beth was a lesbian? Surely that wasn't a motive for murder, yet the prickling sensation was at the base of my skull again. What was it trying to tell me? I made a U-turn on Western Avenue and impulsively headed back downtown. I had to see Anne.

I walked into Hooper's, surprised to see it so busy on a weekday night until I noticed the sign offering drinks at half price during Happy Hour. Tink was tending bar and told me Anne had left for Cobleskill.

"More than an hour ago, C.J. What's up?"

My pulse quickened. "Why the hell did she go out there? I thought you were supposed to be keeping an eye on her?"

"She's not spending the night, just needed a couple of hours of peace and quiet." Tink pointed to the ceiling at Anne's apartment above. "She said the juke box reverberating through the ceiling was driving her nuts—"

"I need to use the telephone." I strode behind the bar, picked up the house phone and dialed Maggie's office number.

"Maggie," I said when she answered, "what did you mean about Laura? You were trying to tell me something, but it went over my head."

"It occurred to me that Sister Laura may have been jealous."

"Jealous?" I rolled the word around in my mouth, tasting it, feeling its texture. "Of whom?" I asked. "Beth or Jackie?"

"Possibly neither. Because she had control over them."

The jukebox blared, causing me to shout, "I don't get it, Maggie. Who else could she have been jealous of?"

"Why, Anne, of course. Consider the possibility that Laura or her other personality had known of the 'particular friendship' between Beth and Jackie, but didn't see it as a threat until Anne, the big bad lesbian, suddenly appeared on the scene...."

I felt the color drain from my face. "If what you're hypothesizing is true, Laura must have intended for Anne to die in that car crash along with Beth..."

"Possibly...."

"...and if she had wanted Anne to die, then Anne is still in danger!"

I slammed the phone down without saying good-bye, and ran out to my car for my briefcase which contained the telephone numbers related to the Hollis file. I dialed the convent first, recognizing Sister Roseanne's squeaky voice as soon as she said, "Hello?"

"Hello, Sister Roseanne? This is Officer Sinclair." Little Richard was still screaming on the jukebox, I had to put my finger in my other ear in order to hear myself. "You may remember me. We met...."

"Of course I remember you, dear. Are you calling for Sister Laura? Because if you are she isn't here."

I hollered above the noise, "Do you know when she'll be back?"

"I really don't. I couldn't say. My, but you play your radio loud."

"Did she take the car?"

"No, Sister Genevieve has the car. I heard her say something about dropping her off."

"Did she say where she was going?"

"Not exactly, but she did say she may be going to visit her brother."

I slammed the receiver down. My hands were shaking as I dialed Bill Hughes' number. A voice I didn't recognize answered and told me Bill was not expected back for another hour yet. I left Anne's Cobleskill number, indicating that my need to talk with Investigator Hughes was urgent.

I then dialed Anne's number. There was no answer and the answering machine didn't pick up.

"Tink, did Anne mention if she was making any stops along the way? Grocery shopping or whatever?"

"No. She shopped this afternoon."

"Did she get any phone calls before she left?"

"No, I don't think so." Tink squinted her eyes. "Wait a minute! Lee came around looking for her."

"Lee? Who's Lee? "

"You know, the truck driver with the hots for Anne. Haven't seen her in a while. I was surprised she came back."

"What does she look like?" I demanded shrilly.

"Tall, short brown hair, always wears blue coveralls."

Coveralls. Which bell was that ringing? "Did you tell her where Anne went?"

"I don't know. I might have." Tink placed her hands on her hips. "Somethin's wrong, ain't it?"

Of course—there were blue coveralls hanging in the Bennett's garage!

Next I dialed Mary Bennett, praying she was home. She was—

just barely back from shopping.

"Listen, Mary, this is Callie Sinclair. Please, this is urgent. Go look in the garage and see if your son's car is there." I couldn't bear the precious time it took for her to find out.

"Well, wouldn't you know," She sounded amazed. "It's gone! How did—"

"Thanks. It's a police matter. I'll get back to you." I left the phone dangling for Tink to hang up, picked up my briefcase, looked at my watch—ten minutes before six. "I'm going out to Cobleskill."

"I'm comin' with you," Tink said, untying her bar apron.

"No, you're not," I said. I scrawled Bill's number on a napkin. "It'll take me an hour to get there. Keep trying this number. When you reach Investigator Hughes, tell him where I'm headed, and that Sister Laura may already be there!"

I hurried out to the car, and made an illegal U-turn in front of Hooper's, heading downtown to pick up the Interstate to the Thruway. Once I got onto I-88 I drove eighty miles an hour all the way to the Cobleskill exit. I pulled into Anne's driveway so fast that the tires on my Civic sent a spray of stones onto the grass. Tink's car was the only one parked in the driveway. I shifted into neutral and jumped out of the car, racing up to the front door. "Dear God, let her be safe," I prayed, ringing the doorbell.

The door swung open and Anne stood in the entrance, smiling. "Callie! What a wonderful surprise!" She grabbed my arm, pulling me into the house. "What are you doing here?" Placing her arms around my waist, she whispered, "I've missed you so much."

For a split second I noticed with pleasure that she hadn't been drinking, and somehow the relief that flooded me struck me in a new way. But then I pulled back.

"What is it?" she said, alarmed. "Something's wrong."

"We have to leave," I said. "Being here isn't safe."

"Why?"

"Anne, Dr. Loomis isn't our problem…"

"…I don't understand…."

"…Sister Laura is. Come on." I grasped her hand, pulling her towards the front door.

"Wait a minute," she said, jerking her hand free. "Tell me what this is all about."

"I'll explain it all in the car. Laura's had an hour jump on me as it is."

"What are you saying?" The color drained from Anne's face. "Laura's on her way here?"

"I don't know...I think so...Has Bill Hughes phoned?"

"No, no one."

"I tried calling you before I left."

"The phone hasn't rung."

I crossed to the table and lifted the receiver. "Maybe I'd better try phoning Bill again." I punched in his number, but it didn't ring. I pressed the clear button and waited for the dial tone. "This is absurd," I said. "The phone's dead."

"It happens all the time out here," she remarked, unconvincingly.

"Let's go," I said. This time she didn't object, just took my hand and followed me towards the front door. There was a sound, like a loud WHOOSH, and we looked back towards the glass patio doors. A wall of flames flared against the outside of the glass.

"Oh, my God!" shouted Anne, her face of mask of terror.

"Come on!" I grabbed her arm, pulling her towards the front door, but it was too late. Flames raged against the door, danced against every window.

"What's happening?" Anne cried.

I peered out one of the windows, saw Sister Laura spilling gasoline onto a pile of rags. She was dressed in blue coveralls.

"Anne, come here," I yelled, pointing to Laura. "She circled the house with gasoline!"

"I know her!" Anne sobbed. "That's Lee."

"That's Sister Laura! We've got to get out of here!"

Anne screamed, "We're trapped!"

"Wait a minute," I said, panic mounting, my heart skipping beats. "We need to think this through, stay put. We're in a stone house. Someone will see the flames, the smoke, call the fire department. Surely help will be on the way."

Anne stood in the middle of her living room, flames visible from every window. "The roof isn't made of stone, Callie. It will catch fire and collapse!"

"Let's find some blankets, Anne. We can wet them, use them for

175

protection." As we entered the bedroom, the window shattered and a torch was hurled through the splintered glass, landing in the center of the bed where the quilt immediately ignited. "Where are the blankets!" I shouted.

Anne opened the closet, tossing a woolen blanket into my arms. I spread it low, over the burning bed, and the lack of oxygen to the flames extinguished the fire instantly.

A moment later, another crash. Thunderous. One of the glass patio doors had been smashed, and a lighted torch had been thrown through the opening onto the floor where it rolled several feet across an area rug, but did not catch fire. I scrambled after the torch, hurling it back through the patio door. Seconds later, Sister Laura used it to break a small window. When the glass smashed, Laura pushed the torch through the window, catching the drapes on fire.

"Now what?" Anne shouted. Smoke was rolling in through the broken windows.

"Wet these blankets, Anne. We have to get out of here!" I stood near the patio doors, trying to pinpoint Laura's location. "Where are you, Lee?" I shouted. A surge of smoke doubled me over in a choking spasm. When I regained control of my breathing I peered through the flames and caught sight of Laura standing beneath a tree. Her posture was tense, determined. She held a lighted torch in her hand.

Anne returned with two quilts she had drenched under the bathtub faucets. We pulled them over our shoulders and headed for the front door. As we passed the kitchen, Anne grabbed an oven mitt.

"I'll open the door," she said. "You go first."

"Together, Anne." The blankets were pulled over our heads. Anne grasped the doorknob and pulled the door open. The heat and smoke struck instantly, freezing us in our tracks.

"I can't," Anne cried.

I couldn't either, until I turned around and saw the murky smoke filling the house. "Let's do it!" I shouted, pulling Anne's blanket over her face and pushing her through the searing blaze.

We landed in the gravel, several feet from the house, both of us scurrying on all fours away from the heat.

"Listen," Anne said. "Sirens."

I had heard them, too. I had also heard footsteps running

towards us from the side of the house.

"She's coming," I said to Anne. "Run!" I scrambled to my feet, sprinting in the direction of the road.

"Wait," Anne groaned, trying to stand. "My ankle."

I stopped, turned, just as Sister Laura rounded the corner. She held a can of gasoline and the lighted torch, and without a moments hesitation, she flung the gasoline at Anne, splashing it over her legs and across her back.

Anne screamed, then began to scramble backwards. I rushed forward, grabbed her beneath her armpits, and pulled her away from Sister Laura, just as Laura was preparing to throw the torch.

"Don't!" Laura shouted. "She killed Jackie!"

"No," Anne sobbed. "I didn't kill Jackie!"

"Liar." She spat. "Jackie killed herself because of what you did to Beth. You turned her against the convent. You should have left her in the closet!" She swung the can of gas menacingly.

How could I distract her, keep her from throwing the torch?

"Lee!" I shouted. "The night Beth died—was it you or Sister Laura who ran her off the road?"

"It was an accident," she hissed, her eyes narrowing. "I was only going to follow them here, spy on them."

"Why?" I kept an eye on the hand holding the can of gas.

"Jackie, of course! I wanted her to know the truth about Beth, but I lost my temper. I hit that bitch's Jeep."

"So you're the one that killed Beth."

"Shut up! She's the one who went off the road."

I reached for Anne's hand. The sirens were getting closer. If only I could keep Lee talking until help arrived.

"You've been hanging around Hooper's bar, Lee. Why? Were you interested in Anne or was it just an act?"

She shook the torch at us. "I thought I told you to shut up."

Then she dashed forward, her feet sliding on the wet grass, and down she went, kicking the can still dribbling gasoline on the lawn. The instant the torch fell from her grasp Laura was ablaze.

"My God!" Anne screamed.

I ran to the wet quilts we had discarded moments before, and flung them over Laura's body, rolling her, patting her, until I was certain the fire was out.

Fire engines and a rescue squad vehicle roared up the driveway. Anne flung her arms around me and sobbed, "What if you hadn't come?"

"Don't think about that," I said softly, felt her body trembling. "We're safe now."

FIFTEEN

"Better late than never," I wisecracked when Bill Hughes stomped into the hospital's waiting room. Instead of a plainclothes suit he was wearing his state trooper's uniform, complete with heavy boots.

"How's Hollis?" he asked, scowling.

"She'll be fine," I said. "Just a sprained ankle. She's having it taped now."

"So what the hell happened, Callie? I hear they've got Sister Laura in here, too. Care to enlighten the state police or are you planning to crack this case wide open all by yourself?"

"As tempting as it is, Bill," I said, smiling, "I'm gonna let you share in all the glory." I filled him in on everything that happened from the time I arrived in Cobleskill.

"Damn," Bill muttered. "She sure had me bulldozed."

A nurse walked into the reception area and Bill called to her. "Nurse, I need to get a statement from Sister Laura Bennett. Is she able to talk?"

"You can try, but just for a few minutes."

"Hey Sinclair, ready to wrap this up?"

"You bet." I turned to the nurse. "If Anne Hollis is released before I get back, would you ask her to wait here."

"I'd be glad to."

Bill and I walked through the Emergency Room entrance to the small cubicle where Sister Laura lay on a gurney. Bill pushed the curtains away and entered. Her eyes were open, staring at a point beyond the hospital ceiling, her blue eyes seeming to reflect the color of heaven. Her voice was hoarse as she prayed, "Hail Mary, full of grace..." She was hooked to an I.V. and a nurse was at her side, taking her blood pressure.

Bill said, "We're here to get a statement. How's she doing?"

"She's being monitored for shock. I'll have to remain in here with her."

I turned to Bill and whispered, "Let me talk to her first."

He nodded and moved to the other side, standing almost behind Laura, beyond her view. I bent over Laura's bed as the nurse moved away, busying herself with Laura's chart. "Sister Laura, it's me, Callie Sinclair."

Her eyes expressed fear as she chanted. "Hail Mary, full of grace. Hail Mary, Hail Mary, Hail Mary..."

Who was praying, I wondered, Laura or Lee? I glimpsed at Bill. He raised his eyebrows, questioning, and looked down into her face.

There were no burns on her cheeks or forehead, but the flesh on her neck looked charred, and her hair was scorched above her ears. The smell was sickening.

"Hail Mary, full of grace...."

I hesitated before speaking again, deciding that if it was Laura and not Lee praying, she would be utterly confused, perhaps even in shock, having no idea what had happened to her or how she came to be burned."Lee," I said, reaching toward her shoulder. I didn't know where to touch her. Her body was covered with a sheet. I called the name again. "Lee...."

Her voice quieted. Nothing moved but her eyes. They looked into mine.

"Anne is safe," I said.

She closed her eyes, as if against my words, tears spilling down her cheeks.

"Why did you do it?" I asked. "You killed Beth and today you almost succeeded in killing Anne Hollis. All I want to know is, why?"

She moved her head from side to side, her eyes still closed.

I balled my hands up into fists, fighting the urge to strike her.

"The police are here," I said, my voice quivering.

"Sister Laura," Bill began. "I'm going to read you your rights." He pulled a small printed card from his pocket and began reciting Miranda, then asked, "Do you waive your right to an attorney?"

She shook her head.

"Ma'am, I need to hear your answer. Do you wish to have an attorney present during questioning?"

"No, I have nothing to say."

He asked again. "Do you wish to have an attorney present?"

"No."

What could I say that would shock her into speaking?

"Already, they're saying Sister Laura tried to kill Anne because she was jealous of her, that she was part of a love triangle."

Her head jerked. She narrowed her eyes, hissing, "That isn't true."

"What is the truth? Tell me! Laura hates Anne Hollis because she's a lesbian, isn't that the truth?"

"No!" she shouted.

"Sister Laura was jealous of Anne's relationship with Beth...."

"No! Laura never accepted that part of herself. She doesn't even know she's one of us."

I peeked up at Bill, caught sight of his raised eyebrows before turning back. "Why did you do it, Lee?"

The woman's face crumbled and she began to whimper, "I'm thirsty...Please give me some water."

I turned to the nurse who nodded, bringing a cup with ice. She helped Lee take a small piece into her mouth. Lee swallowed with difficulty, fighting to regain control of herself.

I reached again towards her shoulder, barely touching it. "Please, Lee...for your own sake, for Laura's sake, tell the truth." I closed my eyes, unnerved by the fact that I was interviewing a dual personality, gazing into Laura's eyes while speaking to her in the third person.

Tears threatened Lee again. "When she was part of the novitiate...this was many years ago...there was a postulant she was close to. Sister Margaret..." Lee closed her eyes. "We both loved her, Laura and I, but of course Laura loved her in only a spiritual way. Laura and Margaret shared a strong devotion to God, while

Margaret and I enjoyed long walks at sunset, poetry, rainy days, picnics...I took every opportunity to be with her, taking such joy in her...until one day Laura and Margaret were accused of...being too close. Laura denied it, of course, but no one would understand. They separated Laura and Margaret—Margaret and me..." Lee began to weep.

"Where is Margaret now?" I asked.

"She left the Order. We never saw her again." A sob escaped from her throat.

"And then Jackie came into your life?"

Lee nodded. "Yes, and so much like Margaret. I was happy to have her in my life, but careful not to risk anything like I had with Margaret. Then Laura became Mother Superior, and later, Beth joined our household." Anger crept into her voice. "At first I believed their friendship was innocent, but one morning I woke very early and found Beth in Jackie's bed! I confronted Jackie, warned her against allowing Beth to enter her bed. I tried to make her understand that what they were doing was a sin against God and the work of the devil! She promised she would never touch Beth again, and I believed her. Not long after, Beth took up with Anne Hollis." Laura cleared her throat, coughed.

The nurse moved back to her side, checking her vital signs, and giving her a bit more ice. When she moved away to write on Laura's chart, I asked, "How did you feel about Beth's relationship with Anne?"

"I was unhappy. Beth lied, saying she was spending time with her sister, Claudia, when all the while she was going to the bar owned by Anne Hollis. Before long she began spending weekends with that woman in Cobleskill."

"How did you know all this?"

There was hate and rage in her voice now. "You know how! I wanted to know what that Beth was up to, how far she had gone. She never caught on I was following her because I used Laura's nephew's car. At first I was glad about her being pals with that Hollis woman. Thought she would leave the convent, quit bothering Jackie. Move far away. But then I heard her pleading with Jackie, and I was scared that Jackie would leave with her."

"So you figured the only way to stop Beth was to kill her."

"No!" Lee looked me straight in the eyes. "I never planned on killing Beth and that's the truth. I just followed her that night to the bar, waited outside for hours till finally they came out and got into Anne's Jeep. I wanted to see the truth with my own eyes. I planned to follow them to Anne's house and watch them through the windows. I thought if they were sleeping together, if they were...you know...doing things to each other, then Beth wouldn't want Jackie anymore. She'd leave her alone."

"So you could have Jackie all to yourself."

Her voice was defiant. "I just wanted things to be back the way they were!"

"But they never made it to Anne's house...."

She closed her eyes. "No, they didn't. I don't know what happened. I was following behind at a safe distance, and I was thinking about Margaret." Her voice softened. "I think about Margaret a lot."

"You were thinking about losing her, and how much that hurt?"

"Yes."

"And suddenly it wasn't Margaret you were thinking about losing, but Jackie."

"I was afraid Laura and I were going to lose Jackie the same way. Beth was going to take Jackie away. Anne Hollis was pulling Beth into her way of life, and Beth was going to take Jackie along with her!"

"And that made you angry."

"Yes, sure it did."

"So angry that you pressed your foot on the accelerator and caught up with Anne's Jeep. You came up so close on her rear end that you forced her to drive faster..."

"...yes..."

"...until suddenly you came up alongside her and pushed her Jeep over the guard rails!"

"Yes!" Lee was breathing hard. "I wanted Beth to die! She was hurting Laura. She was hurting me!"

"You hated Anne Hollis too. You got out of your car and you watched her from the highway. You knew she was still alive."

" I didn't want her to get away with what she was trying to do to Laura. I reported her for reckless driving. I thought they'd put her away, but they didn't."

"So you planned to make sure she would pay for hurting Laura, didn't you?"

"I would have left her alone...but not after she was the one that took Jackie away from us."

"You blamed Anne Hollis for Jackie's death?" I asked, incredulously.

"Jackie killed herself because of the trouble that Anne brought to the Convent!"

"Wait a minute. Laura's the one who suggested Jackie was murdered—"

Lee sneered. "Laura never believed Jackie would kill herself, but that's because she didn't know what was really going on."

I stepped away and turned to Bill. "She doesn't know! Laura doesn't know!"

Lee's voice was weak. "What are you talking about?"

"Listen, Lee, Laura was right. Jackie didn't commit suicide. The police now have evidence that her stepfather, Dr. Loomis, murdered her for her inheritance."

My words took a moment to sink in, and when they did, Lee began to wail, "Oh, my Godddddd." Then she screamed, "Ohhhhhh Godddddddd!"

A nurse pushed me aside to tend to Laura. I lingered for another moment, observing the depth of the woman's grief. Then I sighed and turned away.

Before returning to the reception area, I stopped in the ladies' room, turned on the faucet and splashed some cold water on my face. I pulled out a paper towel and buried my face into it, pressing it against my eyes. My mind's eye held a vision of Sister Laura which I couldn't seem to shake. I sighed, and after a moment, stared at myself in the mirror above the sink. My eyes were bloodshot, my hair disheveled. I finger combed my hair, and wiped beneath my eyes with the coarse towel, trying in vain to erase the dark circles.

When I walked into the reception area I took one look at Anne and held my arms open to her. "God, Callie," she cried. "I still can't believe what's happened." A few minutes later Bill came over to where Anne and I were standing. My arm was still around her shoulder.

He extended his hand to Anne and said, "I don't know if you

remember me, Ms. Hollis. I'm Investigator Hughes."

"Of course I remember you," she said, gripping his hand. "You took a statement from me after the accident."

"I'm going to need to do that again," he said. "I'll need statements tonight from both of you." He turned to me. "Why don't you two take a little time to get pulled back together. Just make sure you get to the barracks tonight so we can close the Hollis file. Here comes Father Brannigan—I'll deal with him. You two, go on."

I smiled. "Thanks, Bill. We'll see you later." Then turning to Anne, my arm still around her shoulders as we walked out of the hospital, I said, "It's going to be a long night, Anne. I'll bet you can do with a hot shower and a change of clothes. Why don't I drive you back to Albany?"

"Yes, please."

More than an hour passed by the time I ushered Anne into my house. She flung herself on my sofa and clutched a throw pillow against her chest. "When I think of what might have happened..." She shivered. "What if you hadn't come?"

"Don't think about that, Anne," I said softly. "Try not to project what could have happened." I sat down and hugged her, feeling her body tremble. "Go in and take a warm shower. I'll find some clothes for you to wear."

When Anne finished showering she slipped into a pair of my jeans and a T-shirt from Cape Cod. I was glad to see the color had returned to her face and she appeared much more relaxed. I pulled her down next to me on the sofa and handed her a mug of hot chocolate. "I'm sorry I can't give you something stronger, like brandy...."

"Hot chocolate's fine," she said.

We talked for a long time about what had taken place, allowing ourselves some time to unwind, then we gathered our resolve and drove down to the police barracks to give our statements.

For the next three days Anne and I were together. I had convinced her to stay with me. I thought she needed some time away from her apartment and Hooper's but she insisted on working during the day while I was at my office.

On Tuesday afternoon we both planned to play hooky, deciding to drive down to Woodstock, poke around the shops, have dinner, but before I left, Bill called to update me on Sister Laura's condition. "Her doctors say she's going to pull through, but she's severely depressed and will need intensive treatment for a long time."

I felt sad for Laura who apparently had no memory of what happened and still had no clue about Lee. Maggie says that is common with multiple personalities, that Lee would know of Laura but Laura would probably not know about Lee. Unlike Laura, Lee accepted her lesbianism. She was in love with Jackie, protectively afraid that Anne and Beth would snatch her away from the convent. When Jackie was killed, Lee blamed Anne, wanted revenge against her and against me for trying to save her. "Too bad Lee didn't know that Jackie was murdered by her stepfather," I said to Bill. "That knowledge could have saved Laura from injury."

"Not necessarily, Callie," Bill cautioned. "Who knows what Lee might have done if she had known? Maybe something even worse. At least no one else has been killed and the police were able to arrest Loomis today. The medical examiner did find traces of ether in Jackie's lungs, and the police also found a witness to Loomis' silver Saab being near the convent the night Jackie died. No hard evidence yet to tie Loomis to the death of Rose Vanderslice, but they're working on it."

"That's great news, Bill."

"Yeah. By the way, how's Hollis doing?"

"Anne's doing fine under the circumstances. We're anticipating a dismissal of her case next week."

"Then what?"

"What do you mean?"

"What're you going to do for excitement?"

I laughed. "I'll think of something."

"I'm sure you will, Sinclair. Just make sure that next time it's out of my jurisdiction."

"Aw, Bill, I know you don't mean that."

After I hung up the phone, I realized that Bill's question had hit a raw nerve. What would I do for excitement? Aside from some scary moments, playing detective over the last couple of weeks had been, well, stimulating. Closing the Hollis file promised to put my job back where it was before: boring.

I mentioned my concerns to Anne when I arrived home that

afternoon. She jokingly promised to find plenty of ways to stimulate and excite me. We kidded back and forth, then she became pensive. I didn't want to intrude on her thoughts. I figured she'd talk again when she was ready.

"I was just thinking," she said after a few minutes. "Today is Tuesday, isn't it?"

"Yes," I replied.

"I know it's more than a week after the fact, but I don't think that matters, do you?"

"What matters?" I said, perplexed. "What are you talking about, Anne?"

She smiled and reached for my hand, holding it between both of hers. "You said lesbians meet on Tuesday, fall in love on Wednesday, and move in together by Saturday." She kissed my fingertips. "Do you think you and I will be living together by then?"

"Oh, Anne," I said, mystified, my mind spinning. Sure, Anne had been staying with me for a few days, but she was due to go home soon. I began to speculate...no, I began to project, about three years down the road. Of course, I had no easy answers, but love, like sobriety, should be taken one day at a time. Perhaps the near-death situation with Anne was a catalyst, finally bringing me to realize it was time for my fears about commitment to die.

She pressed. "Well, do you?"

"Oh, yes," I breathed, my heart quickening. "I want very much to live with you."